A PSYCHOPATH'S PAUSE

A CAPTAIN RUDY BEAUREGARD MYSTERY
POLICE PROCEDURAL

K. B. PELLEGRINO

Copyright © 2024 K. B. Pellegrino.

All rights reserved. No part of this book may be reproduced, stored, or transmitted by any means—whether auditory, graphic, mechanical, or electronic—without written permission of both publisher and author, except in the case of brief excerpts used in critical articles and reviews. Unauthorized reproduction of any part of this work is illegal and is punishable by law.

This is a work of fiction. All of the characters, names, incidents, organization and dialogue in this novel are either the products of the author's imagination or are used fictitiously.

ISBN: 979-8-89419-298-7 (sc)
ISBN: 979-8-89419-299-4 (hc)
ISBN: 979-8-89419-300-7 (e)

Because of the dynamic nature of the Internet, any web addresses or links contained in this book may have changed since publication and may no longer be valid. The views expressed in this work are solely those of the author and do not necessarily reflect the views of the publisher, and the publisher hereby disclaims any responsibility for them.

One Galleria Blvd., Suite 1900, Metairie, LA 70001
(504) 702-6708

"Let me state unequivocally that there is no such thing as the person who at age thirty-five suddenly changes from being perfectly normal and erupts into totally evil, disruptive, murderous behavior. The behaviors that are precursors to murder have been present and developing in that person's life for a long, long time – since childhood."

— ROBERT RESSLER,
'WHOEVER FIGHTS MONSTERS'

MAIN CHARACTERS

West Side Major Crimes Unit Detectives
Captain Rudy Beauregard
Lieutenant Mason Smith
Lieutenant Petra Aylewood-Locke
Lieutenant Ashton Lent
Sergeant Ted Torrington
Sergeant Lilly Tagliano
Sergeant Juan Flores
Sergeant Bill Border
Sergeant Bobby Barr

Other Recurring Characters
Chief Coyne
Attorney Norberto Cull
Sheri Cull
Mona Beauregard
Mayor Fischler
Jim Locke
Luis Vargas
Roland and Lizette Beauregard
Liam
Monique Smith
Charlotte Torrington
Martina McKay
Lavender James
Beryl Roisin Arabella Kent
Ian Nathan Connault
Oliver Kent

CONTENTS

Chapter 1   A Questionable Fall? 1
Chapter 2   Beryl 11
Chapter 3   A Visit 16
Chapter 4   Surprise 22
Chapter 5   The Captain's Ex-Wife 29
Chapter 6   A Quiet Bon Voyage 36
Chapter 7   Whales, A Castle, and Beach 43
Chapter 8   Murders 46
Chapter 9   A Visit from the FBI 52
Chapter 10   The North End of Boston 60
Chapter 11   A Day Full of Surprises 65
Chapter 12   Bird's - Eye Views 72
Chapter 13   Close to Home 80
Chapter 14   Beryl Visits a Convent 89
Chapter 15   Details 97
Chapter 16   A Rhode Island Murder 106
Chapter 17   None Solved 114
Chapter 18   The Past 121
Chapter 19   Movement 130
Chapter 20   Slow Developments 139
Chapter 21   What is True 149
Chapter 22   A Dark Past 161
Chapter 23   More of The Same 165
Chapter 24   A Sad Story 172
Chapter 25   The Feds Help 181

Chapter 26 Moving Faster 191
Chapter 27 Evidence, Evidence 200
Chapter 28 Happiness Despite a Cloud 210
Chapter 29 Difficult Closure 223
Chapter 30 A Mess in Crime Solving 233

A QUESTIONABLE FALL?

The West Side Food Pantry daily luncheon/dinner presented some problems today for those who cooked and served the food. Beryl Kent who chaired this month's program was now cursing to herself. Dinner/lunch would be served from eleven to two-thirty in the afternoon. Prep and serving required her to open the pantry for workers at seven in the morning. Beryl didn't expect a dead body to crowd the backdoor preventing her from opening. A tear dropped from her eye. He was a regular and a bit of a rogue but she liked him. She blessed him with a prayer thinking, *that's all I can do for him. I can't believe this. West Side has another murder. It's such a beautiful small city. Now we may as well live in California or New York or Chicago.*

Beryl called Captain Beauregard of West Side Major Crimes Unit rather than 911, because the man's neck and head were at an abnormal angle. Beauregard did not answer his cell, leaving her one option; calling one of his lieutenants. Beryl was often prescient and typical of her had collected from past experiences all the MCU detectives' cell phone numbers.

So early in the morning, she thought they'll answer shortly and Lieutenant Petra Aylewood-Locke did. And that was just the start of her day. Could she hang around as she would if she could and get the scoop? Nope, Beryl, the infamous buttinsky snoop literally had other fish to fry. She said she'd wait for police; she'd be inside cooking. Beryl could hear the Lieutenant laughing.

Two hours later Beryl faced post COVID-19 caused shortages of help. Most of the usual volunteers and a few paid employees came, but today, Laela Greer, a most efficient and reliable volunteer did not show up. Beryl thought, *unusual for Laela. And where the heck is Jane Aubergine? She lives two doors down from Laela. We named them the twins because they do everything together while not looking or behaving like twins. Jane has not been feeling well. I understand her not calling, but why wouldn't I hear from Laela. It's just not normal.*

After Beryl, her face flushed from the hot steam, moved the heavy spaghetti pot over near the sink to drain, her friend and co-worker Alice whispered, "Finish with that, Beryl. We have to talk."

Beryl didn't notice Alice's tears, and out of frustration, said, "Not now, Alice. We're so short of help. I've no time to chat."

"Stop, Beryl, you have time for this. Laela's husband is dead. Jane is there trying to comfort her. The police are there. Why would they be there?"

A stunned Beryl answered, "I don't understand. Barry is healthy. He's had no physical problems I know about and I would know. I can't believe he's dead. If he had an accident, the police would most likely be called along with the 911 for an ambulance. It's likely the fire department will also be there. They are first responders in this city. Where's Mona? She'll know."

Mona Beauregard's job working the dinner today was setting tables and keeping the homeless from accessing the beverages too soon. As the wife of the famous MCU Captain Rudy Beauregard, and a high school teacher and counselor, she was skilled using her firm but kind voice in crowd control. Alice approached Mona leaving Beryl without assistance to complete the massive work of presenting dinner including her now pouring ground beef sauce over the hot spaghetti. The fish fry would be next. By now, Alice, known as a bit of a drama queen, enlarged on information shared. She asked, "Mona, you must be in the know. What really happened to Laela's husband? Call Rudy. He'll give you the scoop."

Mona's pleasant face crinkled into a deep frown. "What are you talking about?"

"You mean you don't know?"

"Know what? Has he been arrested?"

"Well, Mona, you know all kinds of things connected to the police. Barry Greer is dead. The police are at his house. What happened to him? And why would you suggest Barry was arrested.? I thought he had his own business."

Mona answered, "Well you asked why the police were there. It's the first thing most folks would think. As to what happened to Barry, how would I know? I've been here since seven-thirty this morning. I wondered where Laela was. I'm so sorry. Barry was a nice man. Did he have a heart attack?"

"Laela, the police would not be there if he had a heart attack. There must be suspicious circumstances for the police to be there."

Mona said, "Don't jump to conclusions, Alice. The police are often called in on a death case. I will call Rudy and ask, but not now. There's too much to do. Forget this for now, Alice, Beryl needs help."

The luxurious 23 Splendor Drive Barry Greer home was almost hidden by police and fire including a fire truck. Captain Beauregard and Sergeant Border surveyed the scene. The Medical Examiner Gerard Simpson arrived before the Captain. He did not have Barry's body removed; instead he called and waited for Beauregard and his team. He addressed Rudy. "I'm glad you came quickly. This scene doesn't look quite right. It is most likely an accident, but something bothers me about it. What do you think?"

Rudy scowled. "It better be off, Doc, it's five o'clock in the morning."

He checked the position of the body and asked, "Fell backwards, Gerard?"

"Looks that way. There are twenty steps, steep steps, not to code, but this grand house is about seventy years old. Builder didn't have the same code restrictions as today. His head hit hard. Must have turned his head in the fall because he landed with his head turned to the right. The neck twisted. The right shoulder was impacted and he was dead on landing. The question is, why would he have his back to the stairwell? Was someone there speaking to him? The wife says she was sleeping."

"Who else was in the house at the time?"

"I don't know. Mrs. Greer did not wait around. She's in the kitchen crying with two others. She is one emotional wreck. When I arrived, I was met by a friend Laela called before she called us. She's a neighbor. Her name is Jane Aubergine. Go to it, Rudy. I need some time; here, the body's all yours. This is questionable, so I'm taking good care."

"Gerard, when haven't you? Thanks, I'll do the same. Before I go to the kitchen, this staircase has a weird design. You can't see the opening from down here. I have to go to the third stair to see the opening on the right side. The body probably did not go over the railing. There is no damage and he's a big man. If he fell from the right-side entrance, he would have fallen down only nine steps and landed against the wall. There's no damage to the wall and the fall wouldn't have killed him unless he broke his neck. The autopsy will tell, but this is strange."

Entering the huge industrial style kitchen appointed with every conceivable stainless-steel appliance, Rudy was introduced by first names to three people, two women and one man. He thought, *handsome women in their late fifties. Can't tell today with all the facial repairs being done. The guy's maybe eight to ten years younger. The brunette must be Mrs. Greer. She's a mess. The less emotional one, the blonde must be Jane Aubergine. Who's the guy? He's calm. They haven't even looked over at me.*

Rudy coughed and noticed suspicion registering on each face. He introduced himself and Sergeant Border. Jane Aubergine spoke first. "Captain Beauregard, I'm a friend of Mona's. Why are you here? Barry's death could not be more harmful to Laela without police creating stress asking questions."

"Mrs. Aubergine, the police are called in on all sudden deaths. In this case, Mr. Greer's doctor called it in. It is normal procedure. Now, I'd like to talk first to all those who were in the house last night or early this morning when Mr. Greer fell."

The widow mopped her tears and whispered, "Captain, just me and my sister Delilah were in the house."

"Where is Delilah?"

The man, Jad Morton, spoke. "Delilah has some problems, Captain. She's been staying with Barry and Laela for months now. When she heard about Barry's fall, she went into a screaming fit. We sent her upstairs to rest. Laela called a nurse friend in. She's upstairs with Delilah."

Beauregard directed newly-made Detective Shaughnessy, who had joined the police presence, to escort Mr. Morton into the study while he spoke with the widow and her friend.

The conversation with Laela was slow and arduous. She insisted she be called Laela saying she was never comfortable with the 'Mrs. Greer' moniker despite her years of marriage. She spoke at first in a flurry of unnecessary history of the house and her Barry. And tears flowed. Despite the waterworks and drama, however, Rudy caught glimpses of a sharp mind and great beauty. He worked patiently until he felt an opening for direct questions. Barry was the best husband, a bit of a workaholic, but loved vacationing in exotic places. They had no children. Barry had a daughter from his first marriage who joined a convent in Louisiana after her first year in college. Barry was desolate and felt he lost his first wife from cancer and his girl to the Church. Laela shared many details about their life together without a prompt from Rudy. Aware of his own dislike for non-relevant mindless chitchat and despite his attempt to be considerate of Laela's circumstances, Rudy could take no more. He asked, "Laela, where were you at the time of Barry's fall?"

"I was sleeping. Barry woke me up when he moved. He's a big guy, Captain, or was. The bed-clothes were thrown over me and I was already too warm. His movements woke me. I thought he was going to the bathroom. I fell back asleep."

"Do you know what time that was?"

"I'm guessing, Captain. He wakes up once a night. It's normally about three a.m."

"When did you know he had fallen?"

"The screaming woke me. We have a bathroom en-suite, but guests must use the large bathroom in the upstairs hallway. There is also one at the end of the hall for the last two bedrooms, but my sister Delilah uses the one closest to us. She was screaming."

Beauregard pursued the time of the screaming. Laela not only didn't know, but strangely did not look for help from her husband. Instead, she ran out to help. When questioned why she did not try to wake Barry, she said, "He's never been of any help in a crisis. Barry is a man geared for business and fun. The rest I handle. I didn't even think to ask for his help, especially when I knew it was Delilah's voice. So, I never looked for him on his side of the bed. Barry is so sick of Delilah. He thinks… thought she had overstayed her welcome."

Apparently, Laela thought her sister was overly dramatic in situations. When Delilah found Barry, the screaming began. Beauregard asked, "Well, Mrs. Greer, finding Barry falling down the staircase and dying would unnerve most people."

"You don't understand, Captain. It's always about her. Delilah turns events and makes them about her. Barry died. The pain is from Barry dying. It should not be about 'poor Delilah,' traumatized again. Barry was my husband. I feel the loss but you don't see me screaming and throwing a tantrum."

Beauregard asked her if Barry had a drinking problem, but was assured Barry was a most conservative drinker, never took drugs, and was not a womanizer. Laela laughed, assuring Rudy that Barry would rather play golf or mess around with war movies or his friends from the service with whom he stayed connected. The Captain wondered what that meant for their marital relationship. Beauregard peppered her with questions about whether he was a cautious man, his choice of footwear when getting up at night, did he need glasses, did he have a tendency for losing his balance, and did he have major health problems. There was a resounding negative to his questions.

Mrs. Greer appeared open in her answers. Barry was touted as a generous and outgoing guy loved by all, even his enemies. When asked what enemies, the answer was just business competitors. Rudy questioned Jane about the couple's relationship. The answer was the marriage was one of the best. It was Barry's second marriage, but he often said Laela was the answer to his dreams. The difficulty he had with Laela's sister was no more than what everyone who knew her experienced. Jane said, "I honestly think Delilah was jealous of Laela and loved creating problems. Barry saw through her and told Laela she was to be out by next week."

The Captain questioned, "Is this Delilah's first visit?"

The yes answer from Jane was a surprise. Rudy said, "First visit after twenty-five years of marriage? The sisters weren't close?"

"Well, Captain, Delilah was married several times and Laela said Delilah was too busy with marriages and divorces to visit before. I think she ran out of folks she could control and thought Laela would put up with her shenanigans. And she did for a while. A lot longer than I would have. Laela has staying power, but Barry had had enough. He asked Laela to tell her to go and when she didn't, he did. I guess there was a major argument. It must have been hellish because Laela wouldn't tell me what was said. Normally she would share everything."

Laela interrupted, "Barry had put up with so much during this visit to appease me. He thought Delilah was a troublemaker. She did make innuendoes and they were hurtful. I think she is lonely and envious of Barry and me and our relationship. She never had that kind of closeness in any of her marriages. To be fair to Barry, I saw her trying to come on to him. His reaction was brutal. He told her she was a vicious witch. Later he said he'd had enough and insisted she leave by next Friday. She threw a hissy fit. Told me I was letting him control me. I wasn't. Barry did what I wanted but was too chicken to do."

The Captain told the widow to sit tight in the comfortable chair. He explained he would question Mr. Morton in the study.

Beauregard entered the study and was wowed. He thought, *every chair and painting and the library of books appear to be from a movie. I love the desk. Mona dragged me to museum after museum. She is especially fond of French Louis the XIV style. This desk may be an original period piece.*

Jad Morton said, "Quite a testimony to French Baroque, don't you think?"

Knowing his limitations, but certain Mona had steered him right, he answered, "Louis XIV maybe, and original?"

"For sure, Barry would have nothing less. He had exquisite taste as does Laela, but he was more forceful in bidding."

Beauregard shook hands with Jad as they seated themselves across a gilt and wood table holding an antique silver coffee service. When questioned about Barry's death, Jad said he was called in by Jane after Laela had called her. Exploring this, Rudy asked, "Are you that close a friend to Laela and Jane?"

"Both, Captain. They are lovely ladies and neighbors. My wife died two years ago leaving me with too much time on my hands. I play some golf, have some business interests, and keep the house. I'm not interested in remarriage but love the company of women. These two fit the bill."

"What did you notice when you came on the scene?"

"Jane and I walked over together. These housing lots are big, so I guess it took us a full ten minutes to get here. By that time the police had arrived and Delilah was in a full drama fit. It took us and the police to stop her from screaming and pushing Laela. I sent her to her room. Actually, I threatened her. I did not look closely at Barry's body, but noticed he was in an odd position for a fall."

Rudy was about to ask how so when he was interrupted by a call on his cell. Sergeant Barr said, "Captain, you better get over to the feeding pantry. A homeless man has been murdered."

Charging Sergeant Border with finishing the interview, Rudy rushed to the murder site thinking, *damn it, Mona's there doing her usual social work, when she has a week off from school. Why can't she stay at home for once? When did being kind leave a murdered body at the base of feeding the* hungry? She's with Beryl today. Wouldn't you know? Murder has an affinity for Beryl, and now, I guess, for my Mona.

By the time Beauregard arrived at the pantry, the press there were ready to attack. Queries about the increase in homeless joining West Side's high social profile were hammered by each news source. Beauregard's answer was the usual, "Murder ignores social status."

Sergeant Barr waited inside the police barrier to fill in the details of the death. "Looks like a strongman twisted his neck. Learned this technique in my Special Forces Training. It's not a natural death, Captain, it's murder."

Rudy interviewed Beryl. She'd not touched anything, liked the dead man, did not know his name but once heard him called Charlie, and said, "He was always polite. His manners were far above most of the older men. He looked sad to me, Rudy. I never got his story. Mona may know more."

Rudy asked if Mona had viewed the body and was satisfied with Beryl's 'no' answer. The last thing he wanted was to list his wife on the witness list.

Gerard was busy with the Barry Greer's body, leaving his assistant Jill Healy at this site. Jill said, "Murder for sure, Captain. I'll check with Gerard about the how. I'm sure the perp must have military training or maybe is into some martial arts. I've heard of the 'neck break system training.' Gerard will measure and if anyone can, he'll tell you what happened. Just know this was done to this man."

Sergeant Barr already had an identification obtained easily from a military database. He said, "Meet retired U. S. Army Captain Mel Laurent. He has a stellar military record, was wounded. Apparently he retired after his recovery. It was a head wound. His record shows treatment for PTSD as well as a serious back fracture. He's local, Captain. His family owns Laurent Builders in southern Vermont. Good people. He's divorced with two grown children. I don't know why he would be called Charlie when his name is Mel."

"If he was in Vietnam, I may know why."

Barr said, "Gonna share it, Captain?"

"Some of our illustrious warriors had a thing about fraternizing with the Vietnamese. If you befriended children and women over there, they called you Charlie. It was not a welcome nickname."

BERYL

Nathan Connault's face showed his famous patient look normally used when folks didn't understand his messaging. It was surprising since he was sitting across from the love of his life Beryl Kent. He thought, *how could she not be happy? I've searched military archives, the internet, and reached out to old friends scavenging info on her second husband. How many times has she asked me if there was a trail leading to his death? She thinks because I've worked for the government in what she calls 'those shady agencies' that I can discover all that's ever happened to every person who's served in the military or as a military consultant. Now, I have a trail and she's weepy. Damnit, Beryl, don't douse me with tears. It unnerves me.*

"Nate, you're opening an old wound. I tried for two years to search for Joel. The kids and I were devastated. He was the most loving stepfather. For them it was a second loss, one that happened later in their lives and left some damage. The State Department tried to help but would never say he worked in government; just insisted he was a citizen in the wrong place at the wrong time. At first I was told he was missing with a claim he was in Turkey and just disappeared. So, we waited. I pushed. Next they said he was killed in a crash on a short air flight from Beijing to some remote Chinese province. They never found his body nor the bodies of the others. I don't believe any message from China's government. The State Department declared him dead. That's how I met Cliff. He was a liaison for a company where the State Department said Joel had worked. I grilled Cliff about the company. His story never changed. The company did work for the military. I told you its name. Cliff said it was a legit company, this Gulf Industries, Inc. I looked it up. It's a private not public company and was formed like so many others in Delaware. It's still in operation. I spoke with its president. He denied Joel was doing top secret clearance work. Insisted Joel's disappearance from Turkey was the truth. He said he knew nothing about a plane crash in China. Joel was not a liar but he lived a lie. He never told me where he worked. Instead he insisted he was doing secret government work. I thought he was in the CIA. I never got a federal pension. I received a great deal of money from a private insurance company. Naturally, I grilled them on the deposits. The report I received showed three deposits of very large sums and earnings which did not meet any standard rate of interest. I think the insurance company is a government entity."

"Beryl, you realize your story is bizarre, particularly the insurance payout. Could he have been CIA or working for some other government agency? Looks like it and it must have been important work. Don't ask what happened to him if you don't want to know. Are you afraid he's still alive?"

"No, I don't think that, Nate. I don't believe he just disappeared in Turkey. Something happened."

"Why, do you have any evidence?"

"I have no evidence, but I know Joel, or I thought I knew him. If he disappeared from his hotel in Turkey he was either taken or he was undercover for his home agency. Those are the only reasons he would not call me. Later, much later, I'm notified he died. I shook all the branches of the government's tree and what do they come up with? He's killed in a plane crash in China. That's not the real story. I believe he's dead, but I want to know the how, why, and who."

"I've leveraged every connection I have in the system, Beryl. I've met with military personnel who admit to knowing him. They knew him in Iraq. Does that make any sense?"

"He never mentioned Iraq; Turkey yes, Iraq no."

"I'm meeting with a contractor who worked with him, supposedly in Iraq. I will meet him in London next week. OK?"

Beryl nodded her head in the affirmative and changed the subject to dead bodies. Nate asked her what mess was his inquisitive little busybody into this time, and if her nosiness would put her in any danger. Her answer, "Nate, one of my volunteer's husband died suddenly and there may be questions about his death. Then I found a homeless man murdered outside the Open Food Pantry today. He was a nice man and a veteran. Why would anyone murder him It must have happened outside the pantry because he looked like he fell right after having his head twisted."

"Wait, Beryl, describe his positioning on the ground."

Beryl described it causing that focused look on Nate's face she knew so well. "You think there's a problem with the positioning. I know there is one."

He said, "Yeah, from your description, it's not an accident. As to your friend's husband, were you close to them?"

Beryl nodded saying, "They're good people. I can't imagine who would kill Barry, and certainly, it wouldn't be Laela. I'm frightened for her, Nate. I know the police are involved and I won't let them railroad her."

"Captain Beauregard won't railroad anyone. You know that. Why are you assuming Laela would be charged? You don't even know if Barry's death is suspicious. What about the homeless man? You said he was military and a nice man. I'll look into his death for you. I don't like the homeless being killed off. While I'm busy looking for Joel's history and the homeless man's murder, you stay out of trouble. Okay?"

The closing of the front door startled them as Beryl's son Oliver arrived. Beryl moved to hug him saying, "I thought you were to be away until the end of next week. What happened?"

"Big news is here, Mom, and without your push. I'm about to be engaged to be married."

"Who is she? Is it the B&B owner Leeann?"

"None other."

"But, Oliver, I've barely met her."

"Not to worry, Mom. You'll love her."

Nate saw the worried look on Beryl's face. He said, "Beryl, think about it, we married our way. I guess, Oliver can do the same."

Beryl grimaced. "Oliver, I am your mom. You could at least had have us meet for a longer period before you made your decision."

"You'll meet her tonight. Dinner at The Federal in Agawam. Don't worry, we'll wait a couple of months before the wedding. Her sister has responsibilities and can't get here until later. I'd get married tomorrow but that's the engineer in me. I have to learn to be socially astute now. You know marriage might cut into my investigating for you."

"I never asked you to investigate. And you don't think I have a busy calendar. You assume too much, Oliver. Where did you get the ring? I mean a ring is traditional. Does your sister know?"

"Not to worry, Jocelyn guessed when I took ten days off, and as to the ring, Leeann deserves the best. She gets the ring tonight in front of you and Nate. You're coming aren't you, Nate?"

"I wouldn't miss it for the world. You know it's five o'clock. What time are your reservations?"

Oliver said 6:30 leaving Beryl rushing to get out of her yoga pants. Nate's questioning was more fruitful. He learned Leeann's last name, Sessions, which he had not known and their plans.

The medical examiner Gerald Simpson welcomed the Captain and his detective saying, "Interesting stuff for you. Where shall I start?"

"What about the homeless man, Gerry? Not important in life, but important to me in death."

"Wrong, wrong, Rudy. He was important in life, just not recently. Meet Colonel Mel Laurent, winner of so many medals, you wonder if on every day he just did the extraordinary. He left the service five years ago."

"Gerry, he could end up like this after only five years? Must have had a drinking problem long before that. I'm thinking of the kind of quiet drinking problem."

"Nope, wrong again, Rudy. The guy was healthy. He was not an alcoholic. I'm jealous of his liver and his skin is perfect, also are his musculature and everything else. I don't know his history, but unless he had a severe mental condition, he is in perfect shape for a man of sixty-two years."

"Then what the hell was he doing dressed as a bum and visiting the food pantry weekly?"

"You're the famous detective, Rudy. You tell me."

"Speaks of being undercover. For whom and for what purpose? We'll get on it." Then he asked, "Do you have a report on Barry Greer?"

"I'm having a problem with that tune, Rudy. Just as you had."

"What have you found?"

"Blood alcohol level was at 0.04. He's a big man and it's hard to determine if he had two or more. I'll tell you what is interesting. He had heart problems including a valve problem and some arterial blockage. Talk to his doctor. I can't easily explain his injuries from falling down those steps, but it's possible."

Rudy said, "I've thought about it. If he fell or was pushed down the first set of nine stairs and found leaning with his back against the wall, how could he have fallen onto the landing ending up positioned there? What about his neck? It was twisted to the right."

"No question it was torqued, but the back of his head sustained a severe injury which caused a brain bleed. I don't know, Rudy. It's strange the back of his head hit that hard. Maybe it is an accident."

3

A VISIT

From the outside, the Greer house seemed the same. Beryl and Mona knocked on the front door. Laela did not open the door. Instead her friend Jad and her sister Delilah answered. Unknown to both visitors, Jad pushed Delilah aside and welcomed them. Introductions were made. Delilah had been a frequent subject for conversations in the past, and the in-person meeting did not match previous descriptions made by her sister Laela. Beryl thought, *she is quite charming, and does not appear to have the explosive temper of legend. Although one never knows about a person until you witness them under stress.*

Delilah welcomed them, saying, "I've heard so much about you ladies. Laela has so many good friends. She is fortunate with Jane and Jad at her beck and call. Jad is so devoted and he and Jane were the first people she called after we found Barry. You know I discovered his body. I'll never recover from the shock of it all. I'm not strong. I'm not Laela. I can't cope without losing my grip."

Mona soothed Delilah with words of kindness while Beryl wondered, *yup, it's all about her. The drama is starting. Just how does Mona go into the supportive neighbor role when I know she sees through Delilah's nonsense.*

While following Delilah into the kitchen, Beryl whispered to Mona, "How can you act like her big sister? You know from the past she's a phony."

"Easy, Beryl, I teach teenagers and the drama never stops. In this case, the drama is not a result of reckless hormones attacking the personality; in this case it's permanent. Pretend she's fifteen, you'll have better luck."

Beryl, whose past included dealing with a collection of difficult people thought, *I can learn from Mona. She is so more practical, and kinder than me.*

Beryl greeted Laela, saying, "Laela, you must feel such grief."

Delilah gasped for breath and while shaking said, "She lost a wonderful husband and she is trying to deal with that loss."

Laela Greer's blotched face twisted as she looked at her sister. A kind of sadness set in as she turned to Beryl who hugged her saying, "I am so sorry."

Laela's tears exploded as she moved to include Mona in the hug, bringing Jad also into her arms, saying, "I know you are my friends."

Beryl caught a glimpse of Delilah whose visage projected deep anger and more. She thought, *this is not good. This is not sisterly. She is jealous?*

Beryl said, "Delilah, come on. There are enough hugs here to go around."

The invitation did not go well. Instead an uncomfortable group of four made a fuss about water. Who wanted a glass and who didn't. Awkward was the word used by Mona on the retelling the situation to Rudy.

In a sorry attempt to recover some normalcy, Beryl asked Jad, "You and Jane were the first friends Laela called. Did you see where Barry fell?"

Delilah answered, not Jad. "Please, Beryl, be more sensitive. Barry has just died. Laela does not need to hear any more about it."

Beryl tried to apologize, when Laela interrupted. "No, ask away, Beryl. I don't know how Barry died in a fall down those stairs. I want to know more. He has been very tired recently. At my insistence, our doctor saw him just last week. I don't know if all the tests are back, but I would not be surprised if there were heart or blood clotting problems.

His mom died of a stroke and his dad died from a massive coronary attack. They were older than him at death though."

The doorbell rang. Jad opened the door. There, Captain Beauregard and Sergeant Flores entered and were directed to Barry's study. The questions were for Laela, and in respect Jad, Beryl, and Mona moved to the kitchen area. Beryl asked Mona, "Rudy barely spoke to you, Mona."

"Of course, Beryl, he's about business and no chitchat. That's what he calls conversation without direction."

"Doesn't Rudy know chit-chat is normally more fruitful than direct questioning?'"

"I'm certain he knows, but will he acknowledge it? This gives him an excuse to move things along."

Beryl listened at the closed kitchen door but found Laela's voice too soft to garner the direction Beauregard was going. It appeared to be about Barry's health.

Laela said before they could sit down, "What have you found out? How did Barry die?"

Question after question rained on the widow. She answered quickly: yes, he was not feeling well lately; yes, his balance was poor; no, he did not drink much; yes, he loved life; no, he would not be by the longer railing looking down. Barry was direct in all his actions. The last question posed annoyed Laela. "No, Captain, Barry would have no reason to leave our room, he wanted a middle of the night snack. He often did that and left crumbs on the counter. The doorway to our room is not quite opposite the opening for the stairs. He would have been entering the opening of the stairs and fell. He must have gotten dizzy and fell."

"Did the position of his body strike you as odd?"

Laela showed a puzzled look. "Perhaps, it was a bit odd. I do think if you fell you would not land with your back facing the stairwell wall.

He is a big man, so I can't see him tumbling over and landing that way. Unless he fell forward and his body was moved to sit up against the wall."

Sergeant Flores queried, "Mrs. Greer, did you see an object near the stairs? Maybe, you moved it?"

"Sergeant, it is Sergeant, right?"

She continued, "I did not see anything except Delilah screaming and my poor Barry lying quite crumpled up. I would know enough not to move anything."

Beauregard asked, "Did you see blood coming from the back of the head? It was visible when I got here."

"Yes, and I thought he cut it when he hit the wall, but I'm not sure now. There is nothing on the wall to make that cut. Ask Delilah what she saw. She was there first."

"Are you suggesting Barry's death was not accidental, Captain?"

"Not at all, Laela. I'm putting the puzzle pieces together. You moved when Barry rose. Do you think you would have heard an altercation right after he left the room before he fell to his death?"

"Yes, I think he could have. I wasn't quite awake but quickly fell back asleep. If it happened within five minutes of his rising, yeah, I would have heard the fall. Maybe he fell after he returned from going downstairs. I heard nothing until Delilah screamed."

"Did you hear him speaking to someone or talking to himself?"

"No, Captain, Barry would not be talking to himself. He was stingy with his words. Every sentence uttered had precise and timely meaning. To outsiders he was quite personable but still careful with his comments."

"Were you the last person in the kitchen, Laela?"

"Barry was the last one there. He went down to shut off all the lights. I'm known for leaving lights on. He always double checks."

Leeann Sessions excitedly viewed her face in the mirror thinking, *just enough makeup, can't look like a lightweight. Oliver has spoken so lovingly*

about his mom, granted with sarcasm, but I feel the love. I hope she likes me. She was lovely to me when we met, but it was such a short time together and she didn't know we would marry. He didn't even check with her before he invited me to dinner. Does that mean she'll just accept me and he knows that. I've waited so long for this and my meeting him was random. It took a murder of my neighbor for me to meet him. It took my buying this B&B with all its risks. It took a few heartbreaks.*

The doorbell rang and she heard her sister answer. *Addie must know Oliver is special. Her welcome is warm, warmer than she's welcomed any of my friends.*

Joining the two, Leeann reveled in their flurry of compliments about her dress. Oliver saying, "Mom will love your styling, Leeann. We'd best go over to the restaurant. Mom's involved in another case. It will be great fun pulling the facts from her. Her friend Colonel Nate is fun. Don't worry, Leeann, you'll have a good time."

"Let's not be late, Oliver. It's time for showdown."

"Honey, have you always anticipated events negatively?"

"Not always."

The short trip to Agawam taken, the two lovers entered to find Beryl and Nate already seated. Beryl stood and greeted them with hugs even before being introduced saying, "You're lovely, Leeann, more fashionably dressed than when I last met you. This is Nate. Nate, this is Oliver's lady, Leeann."

"I guessed. Hi, Leeann. Don't worry about the hugging stuff, you'll get used to it with Beryl."

Beryl thought later, *it was easy. She is for Oliver. I'll take credit for raising a son who despite being an engineer, has the insight to choose her. I can take some credit for this with my interest in crime investigation. He met her while checking out a murder site. Thank you, God. Oliver is staying close. Lucky me.*

Leeann prompted Beryl about her latest murder probes. A long discussion about Captain Beauregard and Beryl's partnership with the police ended two hours later in a collapse of laugher. Leeann left with Beryl for the restroom leaving Oliver asking Nate, "How do I do this. I want to give her the ring now. I thought it was a good idea. If she says yes, it's a good idea, but what if she says no."

Nate said with a laugh, "Well you'll never be able to face Beryl and me-ever, ever. Other than that, it'll be all right."

"Thanks, Nate, I needed a little bit of sarcasm to wake my spirit."

Oliver stood when the ladies returned, saying, "Please don't sit down, Leeann."

Before she could say 'why,' he took a ring box from his pocket. Not a word was spoken until Leeann said, "I want a proposal. This is a proposal, right!"

Abashed but persevering, Oliver said, "Please take this ring. I love you. Marry me."

"Finally, I get the words from an engineer. Yes. Yes. I can't wait to marry you."

The staff at The Federal had been informed of the special occasion and quickly presented a lovely dessert and a bottle of Prosecco with glasses for a toast. The other guests joined in the toast with cheers for the happy couple.

SURPRISE

Reading the report on the homeless man/colonel lying on Sergeant Flores' desk led Beauregard to curse, and quite loudly. Surprised, Juan asked, "What's up?" Which was repeated by several other voices.

The Captain said, "Listen to this. Captain Mel Laurent was never homeless. He has an apartment in the flats under the name of Bud Hover. The place looks like shit on the outside, but the report shows sophisticated computer equipment in a closet, security, and cameras everywhere. Other than that, at first glance, it looks two levels above a squat. The guy's undercover."

Juan asked, "How'd they find the apartment, Captain? Was it under his name, because we couldn't find it."

"Nope, you wouldn't. One of the blues at the scene recognized him. They monitor the homeless and where they go. This guy went to this dump regularly after eating at the pantry. The discovery result was just part of their Neighborhood Watch duties in that area. Good for us. Now get the equipment over to IT. If he's undercover, it's not for local or Massachusetts. More likely, it's the Feds, but check it out with the D. A. What value is he, as a homeless man in undercover?"

Lieutenant Smith, the department's resident IT man said, "If he's government, the guys will have trouble getting in. Let me have a go, Captain."

Realizing Mason's direction was to protect him, Beauregard responded correctly. "Go ahead, Lieutenant, but it's not likely he's government. He could be some social worker working for a cause. I can't touch government stuff. You know that."

"Right, Captain."

Sergeant Flores questioned, "Do you want prints? We didn't get them on the quick inspection."

"What do you think, Sergeant? It's a murder."

Mason, leaving, slapped hands with Petra as she entered the Bullpen. "Captain, you're not going to like this. Laurent's military record coincides with Beryl's boyfriend, Colonel Connault. I had Barry Greer's file open on my desk and his term also aligns with the other two."

"Lieutenant, what do you mean coincided? It's a big Army."

"They didn't enter on the same date but all went through Criminal Investigation (CID) Training at the same time. Barry Greer left the service a year or two after his first wife died. Captain Laurent retired later after he was wounded, spent a long time in rehab, and was spun out five years ago. Connault seeps into everything. Not much we can see in his records. We've been there before. They've been seriously doctored."

"Get Connault in here and see what he has to say. Could be he knows Mel Laurent."

"Barry too, Captain, or are we forgetting about him?"

"No, always get info from a source, but I think right now, there's not enough to actively pursue further investigation into Barry Greer's death. I'll leave it open."

Mason thought, *not like the Captain. Not his typical stance. He's not closing the case. He's just waiting, for what - only he knows.*

Beauregard took a call. As Mason moved away, the Captain signaled him, saying, "Don't make a call for a couple of hours, Lieutenant."

Beauregard got up from his chair and moved quickly out the door at a speed unknown for the slow moving fast thinking Captain.

The cell call from his wife Mona was disturbing. Laela Greer was in the hospital suffering from a fall on the same stairs where her husband Barry died. Mona inferred it felt abnormal to her. Laela was there with Beryl and the neighbor Jad. He thought, *I've only been gone for three hours. What the hell was Mona still doing there, or the others.*

Mona was waiting at the hospital entrance. At his scowl, she said, "Not a word, Rudy. I stayed to comfort Laela and give her a hand. There will be visitors coming, even Barry's daughter Patricia, the nun, now called Sister Patricia Marie, will be there. We ordered some food from a caterer Laela uses. He will come in each night. We estimated the numbers for her. She is in pieces. She held together for you, because you have that authoritative air about you. She went upstairs and ten minutes later she had a bad fall. She is still unconscious."

"Who was upstairs at the time?"

"Delila and Jad."

"Mona, what was Jad doing on the second floor?"

"Don't think he did anything. Laela sent him on the attack to get all Barry's old phone records, pictures and other papers to go through for the funeral. You know, all the videos and old pictures you see at wakes. Barry had a whole life before he married Laela. She has always been sensitive to his daughter and friends' feelings from the past."

Laela was sleeping when Rudy entered her hospital room. He looked at her severely bruised face noticing the temple area had a bandage covering it. To his eye, she did not look good. He wondered as he recalled her fall site just how she got so much damage thinking, *maybe the damage to Barry is just the result of a fall. I mean he was a really big guy.*

Rudy did not stay long. In the waiting room, he asked Nate if he could have five minutes alone with him. Beryl and Jad moved so Nate could get by them.

Rudy said, "Nate, why are you here?"

"Beryl asked me to come. She knew I knew Barry."

"You knew Barry Greer? When did you meet him?"

"Locally, I played golf with him. I have a problem with his death, Rudy. Look at this video: it'll help show my questions."

Nate pulled up a video on his phone of Laela's body lying halfway down the stairs with the left side of her head against the wood paneling on the side stairwell. The video caught Mona and Beryl below the body and Jad at the top of the stairs. Nate said, "She fell from the open stairwell pretty hard. I can only think she slipped or lost balance. Notice the five-inch heels. Why would she wear them at home, I don't know, but to me they invite falling."

"When did you take the video? Do you know who was first on the scene?"

Nate said he and Beryl rushed to the stairs when they heard the loud sound. Jad had been on the third floor about to carry two boxes down to the kitchen when he heard Laela cry out, "Oh no!" Jad found her. Mona and Beryl must have heard the fall because they arrived a second later and Jad got a glimpse of Delilah."

"Foul play or a true accident?"

"Unless she has some drug in her, Rudy, it's an accident. And if she could hit that hard from a fall, I think Barry could have done the same, maybe."

The two returned to the waiting room finding Mona missing. Beryl said, "She's in with Laela. The doctor said Laela's awake and we can go in one at a time for five minutes."

Rudy asked Beryl, "Does Laela always wear high heels around the house?"

Beryl said, "No. No one does, Rudy, Laela went upstairs to freshen up. Friends are coming in later. She must have changed her shoes. She did not have them on before she went up."

Mona entered the waiting room allowing Jad next to visit. Beryl asked Mona, "What shoes was Laela wearing today?"

Mona said, "Those '**ros hommerson**' flats. She loves them and talked me into buying a pair despite their being pricey."

Rudy showed Mona the video. Mona's eyes widened. "Rudy, she did not have those on before she went upstairs. I'd fall wearing those. She only wears heels when she's having a party."

Jad quickly returned to the waiting room saying, "You all don't need to stay. Laela is doing well and the nurse said she won't be really alert until tomorrow. They believe the injury is mainly to the side of her face with a fracture in place on the cheekbone."

Rudy agreed and quickly left the room with Nate following him. Nate said, "Rudy, when we were going through the old pictures in the attic, I realized I knew Barry Greer, but not with that name. I knew him as Bob Grayson. Same man, I'm sure. I met him in CID training. He kept a very low profile, nothing like how Laela described him. I never saw him after the training."

"How about a Captain Mel Laurent? Did you ever meet him?"

"I surely did and in CID training. He was the best of the best. I heard he spent his career in domestic undercover investigations. I haven't seen him in years. What does he have to do with Barry?"

Rudy said, "Probably nothing but coincidence, but I hate coincidences."

"Tell me what coincidence."

Beauregard explained Captain Laurent's dual persona and his cover as a homeless wino.

Nate said, "No way! The guy was to be looked up to, never drank much, certainly would not end up on the streets. I looked up to him. I ranked high in investigations, he was better at everything. Did he look like a drinker to you?"

"No, Nate. I'm trying to explain the dilemma. He regularly visited the food pantry. Beryl and Mona thought he was homeless. They said he was one of the happy ones. He was called 'Charlie' by some veterans there. They thought it was his name. His cover name was Bud Hover."

Nate laughed, saying, "Of course it is. Close enough, Bud Hover was in the CID class and he was the biggest kiss-up ever. This is Mel's way of getting even, by making him a homeless man. I guess he never lost his sense of humor. But why did he use that guise? What info can a homeless man in West Side effectively get? Drugs, maybe? He has to be with the Feds somehow. I didn't know Mel was from here."

"He wasn't originally. He was from Vermont, but being Army, he lived in a lot of places. The file says his ex-wife lives in Woodstock, Virginia. No extended file found on the divorce. Must have been amicable. Need to check up on his medical file. See when he was considered fit for duty. I say this because he didn't immediately leave the service. His retirement is weird. It was applied for and wasn't given for three years. The Army doesn't do that."

Nate contradicted him saying, "Oh, yeah, it does when there is a use for him. You said a head wound and now he's undercover as homeless. How did you get the retirement info, Rudy?"

"Mason was unable to get his retirement sheet, but was able to retrieve his request for retirement, and a note in his medical when he was no longer able to get services as active."

"And you don't think that's fishy? He was active and undercover. The Feds are going to interfere with this investigation, Rudy. Let me go see his ex-wife. She'll tell me what she knew. I'm an old friend. You'll get nothing out of her."

Rudy said, "I can't have you out there. If you go there as her old friend, I can't stop you. We haven't notified her. Mason will make the call tomorrow. Give you enough time to see her quickly before the call."

"Okay, will do. But, delay the call until later in the afternoon, Rudy. Two different former CID officers die on the same day, both with aliases and found in the same city. Don't like coincidences like that. Leaves me thinking there's a connection."

"No doubt, Nate, no doubt."

Laela left the hospital without permission while leaning on Jad's arm. She sputtered, "I am not going out this way. I may be a widow and sorrowful and looking like a battered wife, but I am resilient. I must get away from all those memories, Jad. It was such a good marriage.

We have no children together and Barry's daughter's head is in prayer. I can't lean on her. I'm so alone."

"Laela, stop it. You have many friends and I have loads of time. We enjoy each other's company. Nobody thinks we're an item so we can go wherever you want without causing gossip. You name it, I'll go. Maybe Beryl and Jane will take turns in joining us."

"No, Beryl won't. Oliver is getting married. That's big for her. Beryl has worried he would never leave home. He's in his thirties. He lived in Boston for years, but when that whole bleeding man business happened, he came home. As to Jane, you know better. She is so structured and attached to her routine. She never leaves West Side. And I can't leave until Barry's services are held. The police still have his body. I have to face his daughter and all his old friends. I want to hide, need to run away from my memories to calm myself. Barry and I were going to take a road tour around New England and New York state. We had it mapped out, Jad. We were going to see all the special places in little towns you'd never know about unless you live there. I want to do that, but I can't take a trip like that alone. Barry was always the navigator. I can drive but not all day every day. Would you come with me, I'll pay for your hotel stays and meals? I can't be alone. I'm afraid of what I could do."

Jad answered quickly, "Of course I'll go. I need a distraction. But I'll pay for my own room and meals. I will not be kept by a lady even for a short time."

Not for the first time Laela wondered why the ladies in town had not found a way to Jad's heart thinking, *he is handsome in a casual way. Men like him too. I think Barry was a little jealous of him. No need. Jad is years younger than me. If I were thinking about a man, I measure them not on looks, but interests like music. He probably doesn't like the same music. That's how you can tell if the relationship will endure, when the guy keeps changing the music station. It's one thing if it's for a football game, but music. Nope, music, my music is dear to my heart. Well, we'll see how long I can endure his company or he mine. I need to run away.*

5

THE CAPTAIN'S EX-WIFE

Colonel Connaughton arrived in Washington, D.C., late that day having used his connections to get a flight. He leased a car and headed over to Woodstock. On the following day late in the morning he pulled into Mrs. Laurent's neighborhood surrounded by eight homes widely spaced. Most were constructed of brick with two in wood siding, not vinyl. He thought they were probably all built over forty years before. Phyllis Laurent's home was a wood sided garrison with a two-car garage connected in the rear by a glass enclosed walkway. Nate thought, *nice house! Rudy said she'd not remarried. Captain's pay in divorce doesn't pay for this. The family business is construction. Maybe that's the answer. She's only been divorced for two years meaning Mel lived here with her. If he is Federal, why did he live so far from D.C.?*

The woman answering the door greeted Nate with a smile saying, "Thank you for your call, Nate. I feel as if I know you through Mel. Please come in."

Nate now felt uncomfortable. He was directed to a chair in the spacious living room. The home could be described as a ranch house, but he thought, *not typical. No, this ranch house was large with windows and glass doors everywhere. The room caught the noon sun bouncing off the walls. Warm but not too warm.*

Phyllis said, "Are you expecting Mel to meet here? You know he's on a trip. I'd hoped your call had meaning, that he was to meet you here."

There was a second of silence before Nate answered and because he saw a touch of fear in her eyes, he quickly said, "Mel is dead. I am here to ask about him. He was my friend and his death is not normal. I want to know who was involved."

Tears streamed down her eyes. She did not wipe them; just let them stream. He said nothing. He waited for what seemed to him to be a very long time, certainly not a normal period. Still he waited until she spoke.

"Nate, you're saying he was murdered. I knew this one was serious. He's been undercover for about two years with only an occasional visit. He's never been gone so long before. How did he die? He wasn't tortured, was he?"

"No, Phyllis, he died quickly. I know he wouldn't tell you what he was doing. Working for the Feds doesn't allow couples to discuss the work. You were divorced two years ago, but I see your interest in his work continues. Can you talk about your reasons for divorce?"

"We divorced because Mel worried about my safety. He said this work was risky and a divorce would mean he'd cut ties with his previous life. He'd be one more serviceman with PTSD who couldn't cope with life. He put all the assets in my name in case anything happened to him. I'm now a wealthy widow. I don't want to be a widow. I loved Mel."

"Did he call on your cell phone?"

"Yes, only three times in two years. He visited me three times in the middle of the night. I had to tell the kids and friends when he was here I was sick to keep them away. I supposedly have had Covid three times."

"Do you know if the calls were traceable?"

"I doubt it. I called back on each number many times when I was lonely and no one ever answered. I have the numbers. They're from different area codes. I have them."

"May I have them?"

"Of course. What will I tell the kids? They already think we gave up on a good marriage just because his work required traveling. They each live a couple of hours from me, although in different directions. They think we were constantly fighting. We weren't." And she cried again.

Nate said, "You'll be notified by the authorities soon. I will find his killer, but it's best if no one knows I contacted you."

"Where did he die? Wouldn't it be the police from there who would call? Do area police call the Feds on a murder?"

"No, they don't, but it's my guess and probably yours that Mel was doing the government's business."

Her phone rang. She took the call. The call was from Lieutenant Mason Smith. Nate watched her reaction. She was either a good actress or her loss was fresh enough for her to react normally over the repeated news. She grilled Mason which to Nate's mind was what one would do.

Nate called Rudy and explained what he'd learned asking, "Take these numbers. Mel made calls from three different numbers and three different area codes (413, 203, 860). Also, pass his photo around feeding stations for the homeless. I'm guessing Bridgeport and Hartford from the area codes. The full number may help more. He knew he was in trouble. The whole divorce thing was a cover-up. That's a lot of trouble to go through when he's been undercover for many years. This one lasted about two years. I'll shake the bushes to see what's going on."

The call triggered action from the normally slower acting Beauregard. He called Sergeant Bobby Barr and Lieutenant Petra Aylewood-Locke to his office. "Our homeless man was absolutely undercover. What for, I don't know, but the Feds will be involved, and once that happens, they will want us, at the best, to work as their information gophers. I need an edge on this murder to know what's up before the Feds step on our toes. Sergeant, you've been military. Follow his file for connections and use any connections you have to learn what major problem in our area would bring in the Feds. This Mel Laurent guy deserves our best efforts. Lieutenant, I want you to visit other homeless sites in the area and Connecticut. Take a photo of him. Follow every possible connection. Send Lieutenant Smith and Sergeant Flores in. They'll work the computers, the phones and any internet connections Captain Laurent ever had."

Laela's absence from the food pantry was filled by Beryl, Alice, and Jane. Jane commented, "I'm just tired, Beryl. I can't do this all month. Laela needs me and I've just gotten over being sick. I think you should get next month's team in and we'll cover their month. A swap is reasonable. Please do it. I can't bring Laela home from the hospital because I'm on call here."

"Jane, we get out at three-thirty. There's plenty of time to spring Laela from hotel hospital."

"Beryl, I have a husband and son at home. They need me. You're free. I just can't do it for the rest of the month. I know you'll say it's only one more week, but…."

"You go, Jane, and don't worry, Alice and I will get Mac to help. He knows the drill. We'll pay him for today until I find a filler."

Jane was gone before Alice commented, "Jane has been coming in late and leaving early. I don't think dishing food out to the great unwashed is her thing."

Beryl laughed. "It's work, I agree, but again the work energizes me. You're a regular, Alice, and never slow down."

Alice laughed saying, "I've almost been in these folks' shoes. Don't be surprised, Beryl. I was an unmarried mother at seventeen with no resources. One of the ladies at my food pantry saw something in me and gave me a job and helped me with my son. I met Chris on the job and I'm here living the good life. I do this because I identify with some of our diners and maybe I do it out of guilt as well."

Surprised at this personal tidbit since it was uncommon for Alice to share so freely, Beryl said, "Guilt is a positive in my mind. Healthy guilt, I mean, not that crazy stuff some people have. Did I ever tell you, I enjoy working with you? I know now it's the empathy I see in you."

"Well, my love of gossip keeps you interested as well, doesn't it? Thank you, Beryl, you are the best. I don't think you'll have Barry's death to investigate. It was an accident. Good thing I think so. Laela can't take a lot right now."

Beryl queried Alice on what she had heard, but to no avail. Alice copped out with the 'from the grapevine' excuse. Beryl thought, *on the one hand I am pleased, but the angle of his rested body looks off to me. On the other hand, I'm interested in the Captain who died outside the pantry. I thank the heavens the press didn't say the location of his death. The quotes stated '… in the flats.' We know he was murdered. Investigate that, I will.*

Later, Beryl, pushing an overfilled basket, met Mona in Paul's Gourmet Market. She questioned her about the surety of Barry Greer's death by accident. Mona laughed. "How did you hear that? I think Rudy just made the determination. If I tell him you already know he'll be grumpy all evening. You know I sometimes think the station is riddled with bullet holes letting gossip escape."

"Alice knew the decision early this morning. I am pleased for Laela, but I can't forget the scene. I thought it was questionable. Now, I have to put it out of my mind."

Mona responded, "As to Alice, she knows one of the cops assigned to the station. She tells me what's going on. You are not alone in disliking the accident scene. Rudy's letting it go for now, but he has not closed the case. If your eyes and ears pick up relevant info, let him know, but do not mention me."

"Of course," said Beryl, "I can't hold myself back. What are you sending for memory? I've sent a check to Tunnel-2-Towers in honor of Barry. The Obituary listed it. Other than supporting the florist and looking lovely, flowers can't help someone the day after the funeral. I suppose the memory of the beautiful blooms is enough."

"It's been the tradition for so long. Like you, I sent my check to St. Jude's to do good work. I'm late, Beryl. I'll see you at the funeral, which I heard won't be for another ten days. They're doing an autopsy right now."

The funeral at St. Peter's Episcopal Church was traditional. Father Kirk's eulogy was thoughtful and came close to bringing the essence of Barry Greer to the audience. Barry's daughter, a Catholic nun, appeared to appreciate his words. Her tears slowed silently while Laela, bruised face and all, appeared stoic. Not so her sister Delilah who coughed and choked as her tears gushed down her satin collar leaving water stains. Beryl thought, *you'd think she was the widow or daughter. She puts on quite a show. She opted not to sit in the pew where the family was seated. Why? Seems strange to me.*

Refreshments were to be served in the church hall after the service. Unlike most church hall celebrations this would be a feast catered by the best caterer in town. Alas, 'no cocktails' would be the missing item pointed out by Delilah who while sitting in front of Beryl said, "At least Catholics have these sad affairs at a place with a bar. This will be a dry party and boring."

Laela heard Delilah's remarks and tried to stifle her, but failed. Laela's stepdaughter Sister Patricia Marie walked smoothly to the pulpit and said, "I wish to thank my wonderful stepmother Laela whose kindness and support has eased my life. My Dad, Barry Greer was a military man whose attention to duty was paramount. My entering a convent of another religion was such a shock to him. It meant no grandchildren for this loving man. I suppose to many I wasn't a dutiful daughter. But he accepted my decision and was generous to my chosen religion saying, 'it could have been worse. You could have married a bum.'"

Patricia continued after the laughter and shared a loving portrait of this man. She also included praise for Laela and her own biological family. Beryl wondered, *how would Jocelyn and Oliver view me? I imagine the eulogy would include references to my nosiness and three husbands. I hope they'll not be too sarcastic. I'm certain of their love and loyalty, but their words may not be interpreted that way.*

Delilah was wrong. White wine practically flowed. And with wine came words. Jane Aubergine asked Mona and Beryl, "Did you know Laela is leaving town right after the funeral?"

Mona answered, "I hope it's for a cruise. Anything to take her mind off Barry's death until her psyche is ready to deal with the loss. Beryl, you've suffered loss. How did you handle it?"

"One doesn't handle loss, Mona; one lives through it one day at a time until the pain dissipates a bit, making life tolerable again. Later, the pain still exists but takes up a smaller place in your heart."

A QUIET BON VOYAGE

"She's gone already Mona. Left me a listing of where she'll visit. Can you believe she didn't call. I've tried calling her, but she doesn't answer."

"You mean Laela. Slow down, Jane. She told you she was leaving after the funeral. Why does that upset you?"

"She left the same day, not even two hours later. She and Jad drove Barry's daughter, the nun, to the airport and just left. I don't think it's wise to go off right after a loss such as this. I worry your husband Rudy will think there's something going on between Jad and Laela. There isn't, but it looks strange. I'm not crazy, Mona. It's what many people would think. And remember how Barry's body looked against that wall. Even I thought he should not be facing that way. I know Rudy must be questioning the normalcy of it.

Mona said, "I understand it's not normal to die falling down your own steps you've traveled daily for years. It must have been checked out in the autopsy, but right now it is an accident and causes no hindrance to Laela's ability to travel to forget. And the police let her bury him."

"Here is a listing of their travel destinations and you can bet I'll be calling her. She'll be in Nantucket tonight. If she doesn't answer, well, I'll worry. What does worrying do for me? Nothing, but I still worry."

Mona left Jane to jump to Costco for the $100 off sale on an air purifier. At the display she found Beryl Kent taking advantage of the offering. Both were happy to get one of the limited supplies. At the exit they could not rest in the sitting area and eat forbidden hot dogs with mustard, relish and onions. Costco did away with that during the pandemic. They instead made their way over to the White Hut. On downing one of the juicy rolls, Beryl remarked, "Sodium, sodium – will be my downfall. Not sugar."

Mona disagreed. "Sugar and salt, like in ice cream are mine. On another note, Jane Aubergine told me Laela left for her trip with Jad."

"Already? With Jad? When?"

"Yesterday."

"I thought Sister Patricia Marie was to stay at her home for two days."

"Change in plans, Beryl, and it was abrupt and certainly unlike Laela who is a good hostess. Could it be Patricia couldn't bear to stay in the home where her father died?"

"Mona, it is unusual. Where are they going?"

"Take a look at this. They are going to visit five destinations in the Northeast that have area celebrations in this season. Barry and Laela were to take this trip of places they wish they'd visited. Now Laela and Jad are on their way. I know Laela wanted to get away from the grief and sadness, but I could not go with another man if Rudy died. I just couldn't and people will talk. Laela thinks because Jad is younger and she has no interest in him that way, that folks will not make remarks. I'm certain she's wrong."

"Well, I think Jad is the only person available for travel now. I would have gone, especially now that I see the travel plan. I've always wanted to go to Maine's Blueberry Festival and maybe to some of these other places I've never known existed. But, Oliver's wedding makes me happy. Nothing else compares. If Laela had been willing to wait a bit, I'd have gone with her. Could be this trip is perfect for recovery; not that she'll get over the loss of Barry, but it will give her a diversion while the loss sets in and having a friend who will listen ."

Mona said, "Look at one of the first destinations, the Portsmouth New Hampshire Chowder Fest. Laela and Barry went there a couple of years ago with friends. Why would she now want to visit there? She said they wanted to travel to different places. This is not new to her."

"For the chowder," Beryl said. "She does love chowder. Or maybe she wants to feel close to Barry, to remind herself of their past. She's not had time to grieve and this could be the start of that process."

"Looking at the travel route, she's been to two others I know, the Providence Food Fest and the St. Anthony's Feast in Boston. She must be returning to happy memories. Jane is worried about her mental state and said she will call tonight. We'll know more tomorrow. I'll call you, Beryl. Don't think I'm crazy but when people suffer a traumatic loss, I worry about their decision making."

Beryl dressed carefully, thinking, *first time as mother of the groom. I never thought he would leave the nest and now not in two months as promised but two weeks. I asked, Why the hurry. When Oliver lived in Boston and I visited, he lived in the neatest apartment but it had no sense of hominess. And he had no pictures of ladies nor garments in the closet left by ladies. I pushed him into two relationships. They didn't work. I thought for certain Mathea and Oliver would survive as a couple. Wrong, wrong! He would not live where she lived and the same for her. I suppose her love of music and the whole music scene would have been difficult for Oliver and the relationship just seemed to lose air like a popped balloon. Just how do I feel about Leeann? I barely know her. She is intelligent. She works hard and does look good. I just don't know her. Nate has taken a shine to her and told me my reservations are those of a mama cat trying to hold on to her kittens. I'd never do that. I won't do that.*

With a quick look in the mirror she shook her hair, checked her cocktail suit for lint, and left her bedroom. Downstairs, Nate and Oliver waited. Nate kissed her and whispered, "You look stunning."

Beryl asked, "Where's your sister Jocelyn, Oliver?"

Oliver said, "The ladies are waiting at the church with Addie, her husband Ted and the kids. Small wedding, Mom, and the way I like it." "You said it would be a big wedding, Oliver, and went back on your word."

"Nope. You should have listened more closely, Mom. I never said big, I did say church. I can't help you think church means big wedding."

"I suppose I do. Let's go and have a wonderful time."

Addie and Oliver, Father McInerny, Addie's sister Leeann, and Jocelyn were the wedding party at the altar accompanied by an audience of forty. The couple had chosen their siblings as witnesses. Father McInerny gave the most wonderful homily which included selected references from the couple's personal experiences and goals. Beryl read a choice selection from "Captain Corelli's Mandolin" by Louis De Bernierse: "Love is a temporary madness, it erupts like volcanoes and subsides. And when it subsides, you have to make a decision. You have to work out whether your roots have so entwined together it is inconceivable that you should ever part. Because this is what love is. Love is not breathlessness, it is not excitement, it is not the promulgation of promises of eternal passion, it is not the desire to mate every second minute of the day, it is not lying awake at night imagining he is kissing every cranny of your body. No, don't blush, I am telling you some truths. That is just being "in love" which any fool can do. Love itself is what is left over when being in love has burned away, and this is both an art and a fortunate accident."

All joined in a reception line outside the small Catholic church named for Our Lady while Jocelyn arranged an array of rose petals to be thrown on the line up. Slowly the party left for the lovely gardens of the West Side Museum dressed in rose, blue, and yellow flowers. Ten tables of six were circled around the large fountain and pond. At this point, Beryl said, "I guess it's goodbye now to decorum. The champagne and drinks are being served. I can't wait for Jocelyn's toast. Nate, you are assured it will be a roast."

And a funny roast it was. Beryl was seated with Nate, the Beauregard's, and the Locke's. The violins and bass with piano sent the wedding march to the heavens and Mona Beauregard expressed what all were thinking, "This is so beautiful with the sunny sky, gorgeous flowers, and this music. I'm in heaven. Beryl, I can't thank you enough for the invite. How did you arrange it so quickly?"

Surprising the table guests, Beryl said, "I didn't do much. Jocelyn, our artist, came to town two weeks ago and voila. She has connections to great vendors. There was only one caveat and that was to let her fly solo. And we all got out of the way including my new daughter-in-law, Leeann."

Nate repressing a laugh said, "Imagine Beryl letting Jocelyn control. Leeann may be the bride but she clearly doesn't care about running this show."

Rudy joined with, "How do I keep Beryl out of my business? I'll have to learn some tactics from Jocelyn. That's my mission for the day."

Beryl's answer was quick. "You don't, Rudy. And while we're having this discussion, what more news do you have about this Bud Hoover?"

Petra asked, "Why does everyone keep using his undercover name?'

Nate's answer that they all loved the joke Mel used in renaming himself did not satisfy her. She rallied with, "He was honorably discharged and his name is Laurent. I don't want to forget his personal importance."

The cold strawberry soup with a side of ceviche was served and broke the momentary stress. Beryl asked the waiter, "I've never see these two items served together."

He laughed. "What the bride wants, the bride gets. Seems it was common when she was living in the dorm at college."

Nate responded, "Beryl, you are a tad questioning today. Can't let your baby go? Don't worry, I'll fill in for his maintenance efforts now that he has a full-time job pleasing another woman."

Rudy thought, *for such a cool dude, that remark was dumb. Maybe I'll change the subject back to murder. Remove the stress at this table.*

"Beryl, I never forget the victim. You should know that, and he was military and now was undercover. He was undercover much longer than average, which is about one year. One of the most dangerous actions attempted is when an undercover attempts an arrest. Why then, because the criminals believed in him. They won't think undercover officer; instead they'll believe he's trying to take hold of the operation. Any action taken by the officer may be perceived as drug violence resulting in a fatal violence response. Jack Garcia is regarded as the most successful undercover agent in the history of the FBI. He lasted about twenty-four years. Mel or Bud had been out there a long time but not that long."

Beryl answered, "Do you think he tried an arrest?"

"Don't know now. But he was killed in a nonconventional way for drug dealers, unless one was into martial arts."

Petra asked, "Twenty-four years of living a lie must have been psychologically costly. Jim, have you ever counseled an undercover cop?"

Petra's husband the charming, brilliant, and psychologist former cop took time before responding. Not happy with being put on the spot, he sighed saying, "It takes a special personality to go undercover for a long period and live an alternative lifestyle. My experience is officers who love risk and the adrenaline rush seek it, but are often ruled out for the same reason. Still, any officer who chooses to do this kind of work has to have a highly developed memory, ability to lie well, not show any nervousness, be a planner and be decisive. I believe it has a negative effect on any officer who's been out their awhile. How can you live a whole different way on the edge of society without some psychic confusion? Alcoholism and drugging are two of the ways used for coping with the stress. I'm amazed when an officer comes back in and shows little behavioral changes and I'm talking about a year or two not twenty-four years out in the cold."

Beryl said, "The fact he was murdered may mean he was spotted by someone in his past life. I mean his disguise, well, he never dropped it. I was never for a minute suspicious of him. And the weapon sounds to me like a military exercise. What does Gerard think?"

Rudy laughed, saying, "Enough, this is an open investigation, Beryl. You know the rules."

Mona changed the conversation to the two travelers. "I spoke with Jane. She says the traveling is working out quite well. Apparently, Jad doesn't mind going in any tourist trap Laela wants to visit. He likes the same foods and laughs at the same silly posters. After eating dinner, Laela goes to bed and she says Jad must be out on the town because she hears him unlocking the door; pretty late, like two in the morning. She says she's afraid she'll gain weight because their dinners are at the best places. They go easy on breakfast and lunch."

Rudy asked to Mona's chagrin, "Always trying to give nutrition news, Mona, but is it your business? What I don't know is how they've spent three or four or five days going from Portsmouth, Maine to Boston."

"Rudy, unlike you, Jad is willing to be a tourist. They probably hit Gloucester on the way to Portsmouth and maybe doubled back to Rye, New Hampshire. That town is so attractive for shopping and dining. I envy this trip when 'King Curmudgeon' is not sitting in the driver's seat saying 'no.'"

Jim entered the debate. "I don't know if I could do tripping to cute little shops every day. One day on and one day off would work for me."

Nate now waded into the gender war. "I'd be exhausted after two days. A day sprawling in the sand would give me some energy to shop the next day. Us racing horses need rest and feed."

Their attention was directed to the bridal waltz. Beryl watched thinking, *those dancing classes I gave Oliver when he was eleven were costly. I hope they were effective. Oh, he looks so in love. I never expected him to be happy like this. He always carried the façade of a non-emotional engineer. He's tearing up.*

7

WHALES, A CASTLE, AND BEACH

Jad and Laela were lying on a huge Mexican striped blanket on a jutting rock on Wingaersheek Beach trying to recover from the morning's whale watch. The couple noshed on small bites purchased from a food truck along with downing some tapas. Laela acting comfortably satisfied, said, "This is heaven, Jad, and I feel so guilty enjoying myself without Barry. He was such a good man. Probably it's why his daughter is a nun. He was generous with his money and gave to so many charitable causes. I told him many times he gave too much and his answer was always 'never too much.' You never went out with us together. I don't remember if you ever even met Barry. Did you?"

"Yes, I met him. Not long enough to talk about. Tell me more."

Laela spoke about how she met Barry. He'd been in a slight depression for a long time over the loss of his wife and his daughter Patricia's vocation to God. Barry often regretted raising a girl with strong moral feelings saying, "Why Catholic? We were Episcopalians and rarely attended church. That's all changed now. I let her go to St. Jerome's Catholic High School only because of its programming strength in math and science. She bloomed when she went there. She had more boyfriends and she loved to party. After her first year in college she announced the news. I never saw it coming. And my wife had just died."

Laela assured him, "When God calls, it doesn't quite matter what man thinks."

He regretted the no grandchildren factor as did Laela. He calmly said, "I didn't know the future. We thought one child was enough. How could we have known she'd become a nun, and worse yet, be so happy as a nun? Now I go to her church just to be close to her in spirit. Funny things we do to adapt."

Laela added, "Barry may have been drawn to me because I am Catholic, but I never cared. Whatever works, works."

Jad assured her Barry must have loved her dearly because in Jad's mind Laela was just a wonderful woman. This remark made Laela shift uncomfortably. He said, "Did I say something wrong, Laela?"

Tears dropped in a landfall and Laela started to shake her head. "No, it's just Barry would always say those exact words, Jad; that I was a wonderful woman. I miss him and I feel guilty about enjoying this beautiful beach. This rock is indented by weather and although hard it fits our sitting perfectly. Everything is perfect and I go between wonder and grief."

Laela again cried which forced Jad to recall their wonderful lunch. "A girl has to eat, even one who is grieving. Don't tell me another piece of calamari, or croquetas or tortilla Espanola or the last sip of this lovely Spanish sparkling wine will interfere with bringing your mind back to the realities of everyday living. You have to live, Laela. You also have to grieve. This trip is to cover both. Think about the whale watch. We were fortunate to see three and when one came near the boat, I saw real fear in your face. I can tell, you don't want to die yet."

Laela nodded. Crunching on a croquetas, she said, "No, I don't. I feel guilty I don't want to join him yet, I don't."

"Okay, decision time is here. What about going to the Cape Ann Harbor Shuttles. It's Thursday and they have a culture tour from four to seven today. Don't know what the hell it is, but it's new. Forget about a big dinner, I'm tired. The harbor tour is all I can manage. We have a few days to stay here before going to Boston for Saint Anthony's Feast. A go?"

"I am tired but this sounds good. I will need some food later."

"Not to worry, Laela, there will be lots of opportunities for food. I'm thinking big desserts."

Laela laughed thinking, *he is really a nice man and so decent to take this trip. He understands I like to rise early and am in bed by ten.*

"Did you enjoy the castle, Laela. It was quite dark and medieval, don't you think?"

"But beautiful and he, Mr. Hammond, was brilliant and creative. Who could believe one could build that castle in what is nearly the modern era. It's not even one hundred years old yet. There is so much to see."

"I had to see the dudgeon. Must be left over from all those horror movies I saw as a kid."

Laela laughed at the childhood memory and said, "Let's follow your plan and learn culture. Patricia used to say, "Let's get some couth."

MURDERS

Lieutenant Mason Smith, the only Black detective in Major Crimes, stirred his espresso with too many sugars and asked Rudy, "Captain, do you think this is a thankless job? I mean, remember the case of all those dead children on Sunnyside Road. All the task forces working it got nothing. We did and felt good about it, although you did do some off the books kind of work to close the case. And the murderer gets such a limited sentence. Should be out soon. What I think is a psychopath will be walking amongst us again soon."

"Lieutenant, I'm a realist. I'm pragmatic. I'm a worker bee. You know that and you know my answer. We do our best. We navigate the system we operate in. The courts do their thing. Families and society do their things. We have freedom to make judgments on the street and sometimes on the charging if the District Attorney's Office isn't uptight about some political issue of the Mayor or the Congressman or a connected State Senator or Representative. We're a center of psychological and sociological services and sometimes God sits right with us. That's enough for me. I'm good with it."

"Yeah, I'm not always, Captain. Look at this Barry Greer's death. I can't accept the accidental fall. My gut and my brain agree and they rarely agree on anything. My gut wants a third bagel and my brain says no. You know I'll go with my gut and regret it later. This time they agree. And the dead homeless guy who's not who he portrayed himself to be bothers me even more. We haven't heard from the Feds and this has to be one of their adventures. Two different guys and they both look like planned murders despite one looking like it was really well planned. I think I'm just hungry."

And the phone rang. The Captain answered to a call from a good friend, Gary in Exeter, New Hampshire, asking if they'd heard about the murder of a forty-year-old woman last night. Her body was found raped and cut up in the waste gulley on Route 101, going west. The lady was generous with her charms and could get really loud when she was drinking. Ronnie inferred that Exeter, although a charming historic area, has one of the highest crime rates amongst the neighboring towns. He said, "Look, Rudy, I know Jaycee. She's the victim. She probably had a few drinks and took a ride from someone. I heard she left the bar walking and was found eight miles away not in the right direction. She couldn't walk eight miles in the heels she always wore. They're looking at everyone in town. It's scary. I have her mother in the other room. She doesn't think our police are up to solving this. I told her you were famous for solving murders and I'd call you. You don't have to do anything, Rudy, just tell me and I'll know what I need to do to get our guys are up to par."

Rudy squinted. *What the hell do I know about the police in Exeter. I've been there, I think. I'll have to ask Mona. She remembers every detail of every trip. Only one thing to do.*

"Gary, hold on a minute. I can't interfere in a non-West Side inquiry. A murder in Exeter, New Hampshire, investigation is a process with many parts. It doesn't work if stray inquiries, not part of the plan, interfere. I don't know your town. I don't know your people. Do they think this murder is connected to other murders? If so, more police both local and state will be involved. Look, let's talk in a week and see how it's going. I'll reach out to the Chief and offer help. He won't take it but he won't be annoyed I called."

A few nicey-niceys ended the call.

Sergeant Juan Flores listened to one side of the call and questioned, "Captain, who was murdered? I've been to Exeter. It's a nice little town. Must be a domestic. Can't think of any big-time operators there."

The Captain said, "Apparently there is more crime there than in the neighboring towns. The dead lady was last seen late at night barely walking home from a bar in high heels. They'll get the guy."

"Where was the body found?"

"On Route 101."

"Captain, the killer took a chance. It is a well-traveled road. Crime of passion with no planning is my guess."

"You think every murder is a crime of passion, Sergeant. And maybe so, given greed, hate, love, sex and jealousy all involve passion. Now, anything on our homeless guy?"

"Hmmm. Yes and no, Captain. I had a long talk with the FBI profiler we used in the Sunnyside Road case. He says there's talk about an undercover placement having been exposed but no name has been mentioned, and the gossip is low-keyed. He doesn't think it's drugs. He'd know. Those guys on drug task forces can't shut their mouths. It may be guns, or international smuggling of people or goods. He thinks the silence means it's really serious; probably an important Confidential Informant. If so, why haven't they been all over us?"

"If it's an important loss, they'll come in quietly, they'll be here. We need to do more first. They must have been at the wife's house. Mason called there. Have him make another call. Ask her if anyone has called her. They may have asked her questions. She wouldn't necessarily have thought the questions were unusual."

The newlyweds were exhausted. Their honeymoon was to be in Bermuda, an old and tried destination for lovers. And what happens to them but a 24-hour cancellation of their flight. Not to waste time, they spent the day celebrating, first strolling through two museums, next an amazing lunch in Boston's Italian section, only to walk out to one of the North End's Italian Feasts, St. Anthony. The parade of the Blessed Saint was almost over, but the action wasn't. His statute was still there with money attached everywhere. Music and food and kids sitting on the curb inviting tourists to bet on which hand covered the marble, along with a clown and mimes; all were part of the entertainment. Oliver, who had been to these street festivals before had never seen mimes. He thought, *they may have moved over from Quincy Market. I lived in Boston for years, but you can't see it all.*

The loving couple strolled through the small and darker narrow streets taking in the history of the old North End. The sights were new to Leeann and some were also a revelation to Oliver. He remarked, "I thought I knew this area end to end, but I've not seen it all. You know it used to be home to the Mafia. Now it's one of the safest areas to live in Boston. Probably because there are walkers all times of the day and night visiting the markets and restaurants. Love this area."

Leeann dragged Oliver off Endicott Street to Endicott Court and the lovers under the shadow of a building stopped to kiss. There was a green garbage bag near Leeann's foot and when she moved, she stepped on the bag. One look down and she leaned on Oliver saying, "I feel an arm under my shoe and see the shape. Will you look? I can't."

He laughed but thought, *you've been around my mom and now you're feeling bodies under your feet.*

Oliver kicked the bag and although still closed tightly, it felt like a body. He opened the knot with great difficulty and saw a woman's head. Holding Leeann away from seeing the face, he called 911, but only after taking a picture of the scene. He included a photo of the head sticking out of the bag.

The speedy police response was impressive. The police moved them away from the body to wait for a detective's interview. The time allowed Oliver to call his mom. He lied to the detective who didn't want him to make calls before the interview. His excuse was his mom was waiting for them at their hotel to go for dinner.

Beryl was alarmed. "Say nothing but the facts to the police. Only say what you've seen. Immediately write down what you've said. You'll be called back as a witness and there can be no discrepancy between any of your statements. Do you need me?"

Oliver said, "Mom, don't you know me better? I'm an engineer. I only say what I know. I always need you but not for this."

Oliver turned to Leeann, who whispered, "She has expensive earrings. She's a redhead. What a shame."

"I told you not to look, Leeann. This is not a good honeymoon memory."

"You are such a big teddy bear, Oliver. I don't need that kind of protection. I just need love. I think your mom is awesome in the way she sees what has to be done when evil strikes. What happened to this woman is just plain evil."

Boston Detective Greg Brown directed the honeymooners to a quiet area and took notes. His particular interest appeared to be whether the two saw any other person walking the short street before they discovered the body. They said they had seen a man and a couple on the street as they turned into the Court. They could not identify them, but thought they looked quite normal. Detective Brown said, "It's Festival day and you say you only saw three people on this street before you found the body?"

Oliver said, "Yes."

"Why do you suppose that could be?"

Oliver said, "I don't know why, just that we only saw three walkers. I'm certain you don't want me guessing. You'd do guessing better because you've been here before. I haven't nor has Leeann."

Brown asked, "How could you find the garbage bag? It was leaning against the building. Walkers don't walk so close to buildings and certainly don't open garbage bags."

Before Oliver could answer, Leeann said, "Detective, we're on our honeymoon and looked for a protective spot to kiss. This was it. We leaned against the building but we never looked down. My foot hit the bag. I have sandals on. I felt the shape of an arm. I knew immediately the shape."

And tears flowed causing Oliver to finish the story.

Detective Brown cautioned them about leaving town until he was told their honeymoon plans. "Look, I don't want to have to search you two out. Leave contact numbers. Now get out of here."

Oliver grumbled as they headed towards the Parker House for dinner. He said, "Well, this is a honeymoon story we can tell our grandchildren. There will be grandchildren, Leeann, won't there?"

"Of course there will. We must bring good people into the world to fight evil and our kids will be good people."

9

A VISIT FROM THE FBI

Captain Beauregard showed no surprise when Special Agent Robert Alcore entered his office at the same time as Rudy's phone rang to announce Alcore as a visitor. The Desk Sergeant said, "He walked right by me, Captain. I tried to stop him. Those guys are arrogant as hell."

The Captain welcomed Alcore with, "Not protocol, Bob, to bypass my Desk Sergeant. You hurt his feelings."

Alcore ignored the remark and said, "Look, Army CID will be here next and you won't enjoy that visit as much as you should be happy I'm here."

"Wrong! Army CID is always polite and always works within the system."

"You are so full of BS, Rudy. Let's get down to the purpose of my visit. You have a Barry Greer death down as accidental. I want to see the autopsy report. I must be certain it's an accident. I'd like to do this on the QT. No notoriety, do you hear? I'm hoping it's accidental. In fact, I'm pretty certain we won't have an interest here, but I must check."

"I'll be happy to accommodate you, Bob, but I must have a reason stated for sharing and of course that reason belongs to the history of the case. You are not as of now a prosecutor. And what makes you think Greer's death is not accidental?"

"Rudy, I heard you haven't closed the case. That's enough for me. You must have some concerns. I want to know what they are."

"What grapevine were you listening to? Who is Greer to you? He's just an ordinary citizen who's lived in our city for quite a while. What importance to you can Barry Greer be? You'll have to share, Bob. Information sharing is not one-way around here."

Bob grumbled before offering, "What do you know about this Greer, Rudy?"

"I know his daughter is a nun and he goes to church every Sunday. I know he and Laela had a good marriage. I know he's retired and plays a wicked game of golf."

"Do you know why he changed his name to Barry Greer?"

"Maybe! I figure you could enlighten me. The fact you're here in West Side and know his name is not Barry Greer tells me he was operating out here. What the deal is may be known to you, Bob, but not known to us. Also hints at the possibility his death may be murder and not accidental."

"You're telling me you don't know. Come on, Rudy, I wasn't born yesterday."

"Nope, Bob, I didn't know. So, what is it, drugs, guns, major financial cons? I can't help unless you give me the scoop. It stays here."

"Rudy, I'll tell you it would be a divine coincidence if Greer or Grayson's death was an accident."

Silence dominated the room fueled by the stalemate between the two. The field agent squirmed first and said, "Rudy, we're following the trail of a serial murderer. He, we believe it's a he, floats around the East Coast and kills loose women. Notice, I say loose women, only in the most generous manner. Some are professionally loose and some are careless when under drugs or alcohol. They have a type. They are good looking and dress showing their wares. Some are just murdered by a twist of the neck. Others raped before being murdered. It's about fifty-fifty. Our profilers don't like the difference. The bodies are all found in heavy duty, forty-two-gallon, green garbage bags dumped in opportune places without any effort to be hidden. But, and this is important, every dumping is in the nook of a roadside or a building. We believe the killer has been to each site before. The body bags used typically are purchased for the construction industry. That's what we have. That is all."

"How many bodies, Bob?"

"We don't know for certain, but thirty-nine would be a conservative count."

"How does Barry Greer alias Grayson fit? You think he was in on the murders? Doesn't fit from his history. And it also doesn't fit he would have an alias. Explain that one."

"We suspect, Rudy, the killer has been in the area for a while. Seven of the bodies have been within fifty miles of Springfield. The killer is a traveling man."

"No way! I'd know if that many bodies have been found. I solved a case of about seven good looking women murders a couple of years ago. They were murdered by a local well-to-do guy who felt overlooked by the ladies. I would know about murders here. What time frame? Seven bodies within fifty miles? Name them."

"We guess from the trail of dead women, the killer moved to this area about two or three years ago. That's when the first body was found, but there were two other areas due south where twelve bodies were found. It looks like two target areas. The team believes the dude moves to new areas to confuse us. The very first murder group with a close match was in Florida and only in the winter. Think about it, Rudy. Must be a Northerner vacationing. Next area was around Atlanta, followed by southern Connecticut and New York and then Massachusetts and southern Vermont. As to names, I have some files for you."

"Do that, Bob, and while you're at it, tell me why Army CID is involved."

"I've a problem there. They don't want it out. Seems like the deaths by strangling were done precisely using a commonly taught technique called a rear naked chokehold. Taught to recruits, Rudy. Army wants no publicity until the killer is caught and it knows all the facts. Can't blame them. Getting new Army recruits has been difficult since COVID. No need to give another reason not to join up."

"I could use some help here. Will they give it when we have a person of interest?"

"General Alburton has suggested they use a Colonel you already know. It won't be odd if he's at conferences at this station since you already have worked with him."

It took the Captain a few seconds before he realized Bob was speaking about Colonel Nate Connault. Instead of readily agreeing, he said, "How'd you know about him?"

"The Colonel moves around, Rudy. He moves around in circles that affect the military. The General wants all requests to go through Nate. He also inferred Nate would be tougher to deal with than you. I don't agree but it's what he thinks. Is it a go for you?"

"Sure, it's a go. I expected nothing and got more. You were set up for this, weren't you? The General's been involved a long time before this. And why Barry Greer alias Grayson? You still haven't answered that question."

"Barry Greer's first wife was a victim. She was one of those who was raped and murdered in Florida. Barry changed his name because of the publicity. Grouping her in with the other lady victims' profile was too much for him. His daughter joined the convent shortly afterward. He blamed the publicity for her becoming a nun. He thought she wanted to hide. I've known Grayson for a long time. I've known his daughter too. She was a deep thinker and religious at an early age. The loss didn't change her, but Grayson went on a week bender. He came back guaranteeing he'd find the killer. Later he met Laela on a cruise and the guy changed overnight. Said he was looking forward not back and God would take care of things. He slowed down on the searching and bugging us. Recently he renewed his nagging. He insisted he could help. He had an inkling about someone and his gut told him to follow through. I told him to give us the information. He said we'd screw it up. That the guy he was looking at was sharp and he'd have to find him in the act. We argued, but it was no go, Rudy. The one thing about Barry/Bob is he was smart and stubborn as a mule. That's where we left it. So,

I'd look close by for his killer, for someone who had access to the house, for someone who knew Barry was on to him?"

"It would have helped if you'd informed me earlier about these murders in the area."

"Need to know requirement. You didn't need to know. Sleepy little city like West Side and you head of MCU. What can you do? Rudy, I'm kidding. We all recognize you are the sneakiest of serial murder solvers. They don't want you to get the credit but I was sent here to involve you both by my firm and the Army."

"Involve me, hell, I'm involving you. Sit your ass down with those files, the ones in my area."

Agent Alcore left to bring the files in from his car. Actually, he left to tell his partner in the car they were stuck doing work with Rudy. His partner, Agent Al Corella, groaned, "I thought this was a drop and run. You promised a nice lunch out here. It's kind of a hokey place. Looks like convenience store robbery would be big stuff."

"Wrong, Al. Beauregard may look like a slow walking dude but he has the best closure in murder cases in the country. He's like a dog with a bone. He never gives up. And as to a sleepy little town, West Side is anything but sleepy. Meanwhile, when we get up there, keep nothing from him. He'll discover any of your secrets. I want him as a friend. It's like if I were a physicist, I'd want Einstein as my buddy. We're going to work with him now. Got it?"

"Yeah. Got to meet this Rudy Beauregard. See how he guesses about psychopaths and I hope he can come up with a better idea of the perp than our profilers."

"Al, don't knock the profilers."

The Captain announced to the detective squad the FBI was present. Further he said they would be working with them for the afternoon and maybe longer. Deep sighs from all made Beauregard roll his eyes in disappointment.

Work divvying up the files by area was met with interest. Particularly, the murder files from West Side's surrounding area were gobbled up.

Sergeant Flores was the first to say, "I knew this lady. How come we didn't know she died? Says right in here she went to Central High School. Must be her married name. Look, she lived in Brooklyn, New York. Still, don't hometown papers list murders when the victim is from the hometown?"

Lieutenant Smith said, "Probably not important enough to bother sending facts to the hometown. A murder near NYC of a shady lady, particularly if she is a minority, does not necessarily call out the whole murder squad with all its investigative tools. What's the lady's name?"

"Rivera but her married name is Colon."

Lieutenant Aylewood-Locke said, "It's not always about race, Mason. It's mostly about carelessness or laziness or a dropped message. I think we may find another lady we know of who is not a minority, and whose death is unknown to us."

Sergeant Tagliano answered, "Juan thinks he should know what happens to every Latina from the area. I think Juan should follow up on this one. Was she strangled or raped and knifed?"

Sergeant Flores answered, "Strangled, Lilly."

And suddenly the team appeared to have an appetite for their work. Sergeant Torrington, who had an aptitude for organization typed up a tool for listing all salient facts about each murder. Actually, he listed two formats; one for strangled victims and the other for those who were raped and knifed. He sent them to each detective's computer saying, "Let's not waste time. We'll capture the twenty-five closest murders' important facts as a starter."

Agent Alcore said, "I'll take my lunch now and come back later. It will take you a bit of time to do this. We'll talk later."

The Captain said, "I'll go with you. Bob. and we'll come back in an hour and a half. Probably won't take my detectives that long. And I don't want to lose your expertise."

"You mean you don't want me to escape?"

Two hours later, the lunch-goers returned bringing bags of salads and desserts from the Hope Deli. Hope Deli was new in town and not one detective had yet to dive into its offerings. Midst loud munching, discussions began. The Captain started, "Okay, Mason, how many can you put up at a time?"

Mason said, "Go look at your screen for each one. Scroll down for each victim's sheet or if you'd like it better, find a sheet with each item and all twenty-five victim's answer to that item. Whatever works for you, but we already have some ideas."

Sergeant Torrington said, "Big difference in victims might explain why some were killed by strangling. Those victims were ladies who drank too much one night but were not easy with their wares. They did leave their kids alone when drinking and they all had intact marriages. Their families were all desolate with the news. The victims who were stabbed and raped were ladies of easy virtues and only a few were currently married at the time of death. If the perp is the same for both kinds of murder, he wants the bad girls to suffer. Worse yet he is sexually attracted to the bad girls."

The Captain said, "Interesting conclusion but too early for that."

Sergeant Bobby Barr commented, "I'm going by the victims' pictures. Good photos are missing in five of the cases. But of those we have, the strangled women are uptown girls while the others look and dress like typical ladies of the night. The ages are between 27 and 42. The victims are mostly blonde but not all naturally light. They all had good bodies and would easily have been picked up."

Sergeant Flores agreed. "Their education almost matches Bobby's description. The strangled women almost always were graduates of college. Only a few of the others had just some college backgrounds. If we have the same perp, he has two motives for his damage."

Petra focused on locations of bodies, saying, "Two motives work for me. The strangled ladies knew the perp. I know many of the places they were dumped. There were eleven of the twenty-five who were strangled and they were dumped in places a prostitute would not go to with a first-nighter john. The perp had to have been there before. The locations are strange and often in the city or town. I don't know why we can't find cameras. It says there was some footage but I think we have to go through all of it again and also look if other footage was missing."

Rudy asked Bob, "We can count on your help there to get what we need?"

A nod reassured the Captain who questioned Petra, "What about the other dumping sites?"

"All by highways in more rural roads, Captain. Again, there must be some camera footage. I think he is a risk taker. Dumping a big trash bag on a highway at fourteen sites must have caught notice even if dumped at three in the morning."

Bobby Barr said, "The weapons of choice reinforce the concept of Army training. Every strangling was done in precise Army methodology. The knife slashes have left a trail downward from a right-handed man about six feet tall who killed with vengeance. It has a seven-inch blade. I think it may be the Army Ka Bar knife. Fits with the perp's profile. I'm telling you the perp is in good shape. It's a good knife if you know how to use it, but you have to do major damage with the first stick to keep the victim in place for the second stick. I found nothing about the site for the rape and murder. They looked into the victims' homes and there was no site of blood. That's where the investigation left it. Surprises me."

10

THE NORTH END OF BOSTON

Laela and Jad spent three days in Boston, the first day visiting Newbury Street shops and the Copley Plaza Mall. The second and current day at the Saint Anthony's Festival. Yesterday, Laela was in her element. Tiffany, Balenciaga, and Fendi shopping was a treat and she treated herself. She appeared to feel some joy again. She thought, *I must admit Jad is most helpful. Unlike Barry, Jad has real opinions on women's clothes and understands the differences in designer products better than any of my friends. He must have been a wonderful husband. The only fault I've seen is his occasional need to be alone. Yesterday, he took off for a couple of hours. He said he had some business to take care of and did not explain. He tells me everything about his personal life but never shares his business dealings. But he came back with a Miss Dior bottle of perfume for me for which I was most thankful. I wonder if I should accept a gift of over two-hundred-dollars. He knows this trip is one of companionship for us. It will never include romance. I've told him over and over I miss my Barry. He is about eight years younger than me. He knows not to push the envelope. What a joke. My thinking is off. Why would such a catch look at me? The ladies at the country club have all made passes at him. He just buys a drink or two and goes home. I miss the security of my Barry. I hate the thought of living alone.*

Jad poked Laela's arm saying, "Thinking about Barry, Laela? It's okay. From what you've said, he was a wonderful man."

"Actually, I was thinking about this trip and how helpful you've been in joining me. I did want to discuss something with you and I don't want you to be hurt."

"What's that, Laela? You can tell me anything. You know that."

"When you came back from your business meeting, you brought me an expensive bottle of Miss Dior. It was so thoughtful. You even chose my favorite scent. I don't know how you knew. Your sixth sense is on target. But, Jad, it's too expensive. Gifts like that are given within a special relationship and we are just friends."

Jad's face took on a severe look of disappointment. He said, 'Laela, the gift was meant in friendship. I left you for a couple of hours. I felt a little guilty. Think of it as assuaging my guilt. I like to see you happy. I don't want you to feel anything but joy. I'll take the gift back, but I don't want to. Who would I give it to? Right now, I have no one in my life. Maybe someday I will, but I still haven't recovered from Shelley's death. Grief has many stages. You're in stage one, Laela. You have a way to go. I hope you will enjoy the perfume. We done on this subject?"

Her eyes dropped a tear as she nodded yes. Laela asked, "How did your business meeting go yesterday? I never asked you. I've never asked about your business before. I'm so selfish, I talk about myself and have not been a friend sharing your concerns. You can count on me to keep anything you say private."

Jad smiled. "Look, Laela, I'm in finance and do some day trading. Money is simply not important to me. I have enough for a small gift."

"Barry did some day trading. I was his good luck. He'd give me three stocks to pick from. He said my choices were perfect. I made money for him. I'll help you if you want."

"No, I'm old-fashioned that way. I'll make my own money."

Laela thought she heard some stiffness in his voice. In response she redirected them to enter Saint Leonard's Church. Jad excused himself saying, "I have to find a restroom. Take your time. I'll meet you out here."

"Don't you want to come in, Jad. I'll wait for you."

"No, church isn't my thing. Too many funerals in my life. That's all I can think of when I'm in there."

"I'll pick up a St. Anthony's medal in the store for you; to protect you."

Jad said, "Please do not do that, Laela."

Jad's statement had such finality in his voice, it stopped Laela in her tracks thinking, *he really has a thing about church. I'll leave it alone but he would do better if he had some faith.*

Laela sat in the rather simple church and prayed. She felt at home. She noticed some disruptions at the altar. Ladies were adding baskets of flowers. She looked around and only saw tourists. Would the church allow a wedding during the feast? *I don't think so. I don't know about funerals. It's definitely for a wedding, but a small wedding. I'll phone Jad and ask him to give me a couple of hours. I want to see this wedding. I need to see a happy occasion.*

When the guests arrived, all forty of them, they were dressed to the nines. Laela thought, *I've never seen so many floral arrangements for such a small wedding. And the bride is in a three-thousand-dollar dress. She is gorgeous. They look so happy. I remember marrying Barry. It was the best day of my life. He was a bit overprotective.* He never spoke of his first wife's death of cancer, just their marriage was wonderful. *Sister Patricia Marie also didn't. It must have been so painful. Patricia practically shrunk from the question when I asked about Marie, her mother. I felt I'd inflicted pain by just asking. I never did again.*

Laela witnessed the whole service and found tears dropping at the lovely blessing. She walked out into the sunlight to see Jad patiently waiting. "Was the wedding beautiful? The bride certainly was. It was a small wedding given the extraordinary wedding dress."

"Jad, I'm certain they'll have a wonderful life. They looked so pleased with each other."

"Don't be so sure. The bride could be a closet alcoholic or a sex fiend who will cheat next week. You never know."

"Such a cynic! I can't believe you'd be thinking that. They're a lovely couple. Your marriage worked out. I know the sad ending, Jad, but you told me you were happy and you could never find another woman equal to Shelley."

"Laela, Shelley was perfect in every way. Then there was the very imperfect ending to our lives."

"Stop that kind of thinking. Cancer is a horrible disease and has nothing to do with love."

"You're right, Laela. The ending had nothing to do with love."

They stopped at several street stalls feasting on arancini, quahogs, calamari and finishing up with pistachio and chocolate gelato. Laela said, "I feel like a complete hog. It's all so good. Did you see the bride at the gelato stand? Why isn't she at the reception?"

"Laela, you missed her at the calamari vendor. I saw her and her wedding party hand tickets over to the vendor. This is her reception."

"No way, how can she cut the cake or have a bride's dance or throw the bouquet?"

"She had her bride's dance. When they were playing the theme from 'The Godfather.' You know, 'Speak Softly Love.' They were dancing to it and dancing beautifully. Maybe they won't divorce given they waltz with the stars."

"Jad, I am so happy. You are a romantic at heart, perhaps a bit cynical but you saw them dancing and were moved. You are not a lost cause. How come I missed the wedding dance?"

"You were watching the police cut through the crowd. They must have been after some thieves because they were not polite."

"I did see them, Jad. Are Boston Police always so rude during a festival?"

A man overheard them and said, "Nah. Must be big trouble over there. The police have orders to be respectful at the Fest. It's a big tourist spot and likely you're one of them. Read the papers tomorrow. The crime will be reported then."

Laela practically grabbed his arm. "The bride's over there. Look."

Jad noticed the glamorous couple cutting the cake to music with the crowd yelling, "The bride cuts the cake, the bride cuts the cake…".

He thought, *the bride or her parents are brilliant. They don't have to pay for music or photography and the couple's picture will be all over the news. Wouldn't be surprised if someone offers them a paid for honeymoon.*

Laela was now focused on the cake cutting song and while she was immersed in the moment, Jad's eyes followed the coroner removing a body. The officers directed the move using the shade of the buildings. He could see the van around the corner. The bride and groom kept most of the crowd looking in their direction with only those close to the buildings aware a body was being moved. Jad mused, *people must be thinking there is a guy who died of a heart attack from the heat. It is hot. But there are a lot of police for one body.*

11

A DAY FULL OF SURPRISES

Rudy was sitting at his favorite café drinking a double espresso with cream all the while fighting his wife's mental messages about his abysmal diet. He knew he wouldn't even acknowledge the addition of the lovely lemon cake on the espresso connected plate when discussing his day with Mona later. No need to feel much guilt. He thought, *I'm guilty over my diet and another guy's out there murdering ladies. It's strange. Two victim profiles with one murderer. What does the perp of each have in common to make us so certain it's one perp? Well, the victims are between the age range. The bodies are all committed in the same areas. Just what is the timeline for all the bodies? The FBI's analysis is probably on target. They have the wherewithal to have been thorough. Still, I need to see all the cases. I need to know all the victims. I need to know dates, especially considering the idea some victims may have been snowbirds in Florida or North Carolina. Where did those snowbirds go for the rest of the year? The clean strangling execution style means he has made a decision to kill but the victim doesn't bring out great anger, therefor these killings are in the category as a need to kill. Could these killing just be necessary? Don't think all. Remember using words like all, every, none can cloud the vision. Take those words out.*

Attorney Norbie Cull placed his hand on Rudy's shoulder. "Giving into yourself with that luscious dessert, Rudy. What would Mona say?

What's going on in your murder world? I heard about the situation with the homeless man. Big question for you, why is the FBI snooping around? What would the homeless man be involved in: drugs, child pornography, ladies of the night, or guns? He must be important. We know he was undercover."

Rudy practically sputtered, "That damn station house leaks like a sieve. Keep it to yourself whatever you hear. I don't want to hear it. And just now you figure he was not who he said he was, homeless. Brilliant, Norbie. Even for a lawyer, it's brilliant."

"Come on, Rudy, cut the sarcasm. We've played golf together. You can trust me. Remember, I let you win once."

"Murder is not a joke, Norbie, and I won more than one golf game, I think. As to the homeless man, his death is not a joke."

"Homeless man killed at the food pantry is at the very least interesting. Even the uncaring wealthy thought it was shameful. Of course, it's important. My mind couldn't compute a Mel Laurent using the name Bud Hover. Then, I ran into Special Agent Bob Alcore and he spilled the beans."

"Just like that? What the hell do you take me for, Norbie?"

"Playing golf and having dinner together does loosen the tongue, Rudy. I don't deny that. But I wouldn't have known about Greer and the homeless man as significant if my wife Sheri hadn't informed me Beryl discovered the body at the Food Pantry. I went to Barry Greer's wake because I already knew him from the Army."

"You knew Barry was Army? Remarkable!"

"No, actually, I knew Bob Grayson from the Army. I ran into him a couple of years ago and he had changed his name looking for a new life. Sad, what happened to him."

"What happened?"

"His first wife was murdered in Florida by a serial murderer. He was devastated. He told me he changed his name because he couldn't take the publicity. I wondered about it. No one up here knew the victims, and his daughter went into the convent. Seemed a lot of work to make a name change, but I got used to it. Now, I wonder."

"Wonder about what? You seem to have all the answers, Norbie."

Norbie, aware of Rudy's annoyance said, "Well, you do know Greer was Army all the way and your homeless guy was also Army and that I knew them both."

"And you also know Nate Connault. Sounds like you're a person of interest, Norbie."

"Cut the BS, Rudy. Is there a connection to the two deaths? FBI, Army, and two former CID officers dead do make me wonder. If I didn't know Bob Grayson so well, I'd say it was a drug investigation, but not Bob. He was white hat all the way and the dirty drug world was not for him. I heard the other guy has been connected to the Army or some other federal agency for a long time. At least that's what I've been told."

"Told by whom?"

"I can't help it if Special Agent Alcore talks a lot and believed I already knew everything. Remember, unlike you, Rudy, I don't ask questions. I just go along as if I have an inside on every investigation you've ever had. He wanted to believe that."

Rudy suppressed a symptom of dyspepsia and growled, "I came here for a coffee and to think about this case, not to be riled up. Get out of here."

"I'm not the only one who's going to be disturbing your gastrointestinal functions, Rudy."

"What, the Army's here all ready? I've not gotten a call."

"Not yet but Beryl is interested in this case. She'll be in to see you. After all, she is a witness in one case and Mona is a witness to the other. They both know everything. If you think Beryl, now that Oliver is married, will just go away and not disturb you, you're dreaming."

Rudy grunted with a dissatisfied look on his face. "You think you and Beryl are an extension of the West Side Police Department. Wrong! Norbie, I can't have that woman interfering. Before I know it she'll be tracking the two victims' backgrounds. And there's Nate's connection in all this. Let's get off this, who knows what for now. How would you play this, Norbie? What would you look for?"

Norbie took his time before responding. "First, don't be so defensive about getting information from outside sources. Second, Laela doesn't know about Barry's previous name. I find it strange since she had to sign the marriage application. Did Barry tell her about his formal change in his name?"

"You know he didn't, Norbie. She's up front with info. She said his wife suffered from cancer and died; not killed by a serial killer."

"So, Rudy, I'd be all over Sister Patricia Marie. She must know the whole story and why Barry changed his name."

"I'm on it, but she's been basically out of his life for a long time. She will know about her mother's murder."

"Have you background checked Laela, Jane Aubergine, and Jad Morton?"

"Why do you think they're involved in the murders, Norbie? Have you heard something I haven't?"

"No, but we don't know about them. For instance, does Jad have a military history? How did Barry meet Laela and who is Jane? Seems like necessary gumshoe work. You have to see the whole picture. I'm not as interested in the homeless population; only those Mel spent some time with. I really don't think they have anything to do with the murders. The homeless being fed were probably a source of information or gossip on murdered ladies. Mel would use any source, plus don't you think a homeless man is the best disguise there is?"

"I do, Norbie, I do. We're all over backgrounds and interviews. The split murder weapons used does cast doubt on motives. I'd feel better if there had only been one weapon used connected to one motive."

Norbie asked, "What about the knife? Is it commonly used in the military?"

"The coroner believes it's standard Army issue seven-inch blade ka bar knife and used as taught in the military."

"That helps, Rudy, the perp has history of training in the Army and is a male who is how tall? Can you tell by the angle of the knife?"

"Maybe. If he was standing facing the victim on level ground we guess he's over six-feet in height. But he could have been shorter and standing on a stair or something else. We've never found the sites of the murders and assume there are many sites since we think the perp has lived in several areas based on the congregation of murders peppered around a center. The FBI has honed around each central spot but has no other detail. There so far have been no witnesses to any suspicious person near the murder sites or in the center of the vortex of murders. We've no evidence of a car being used. No DNA evidence despite the rapes. We assume rapes because the vaginal area was a mess. It's forcible rape. Think about it, some of the ladies were prostitutes and yet they fought him. No tissue was found under the nails. He washed their feet, hands, nails, hair and some of the body. He sprayed alcohol all over the body. Nada."

"Rudy, the FBI must have road camera footage of the drop sites. How many cars went by before and after the drop? There has to be more."

Rudy said, "The files are not complete with every detail. Road camera footage wasn't included because they found nothing."

Norbie replied sarcastically, "So we wait for another murder? Getting additional information from the FBI beyond what they've given you will be like pulling teeth. Not good, Rudy."

Rudy appeared to have a thought. He lightly pounded the table and sputtered, "What is the matter with me? I'm sitting on another string in the murders and haven't thought about it. Norbie, who do you know in Exeter, New Hampshire?"

And details of Rudy's earlier call from Gary were shared. Norbie listened with great interest saying, "Rudy, is he Gary Albrecht?"

"Yes, he's a Captain in the force and a really stand-up guy. I met him when he was on the force in East Longmeadow. He married a gal from New Hampshire and they settled up there. How do you know him, Norbie?"

"From the service and later from his East Longmeadow policing. Now you think this is another case in the serial murders? Problem for you is the perp must have moved again. Exeter is not quite the center of area covering New Hampshire, Connecticut and Massachusetts. I think you should look at timelines for each group of murders. Might be important to figure out what role moving could have. Could be a new job if he's employed or if he's a transient, how can he move so easily and pay for it? Will you warn Gary?"

"I'm thinking I must, mostly because he has new information. To me, it's connected to the others, but I could be wrong. My gut says it is connected."

"You mean the famous Captain Beauregard's gut being fed by fast food and sweets. Difficult to trust any brain fueled by that stuff."

"Norbie, you could do me a favor. See if Beryl and or Nate know more about Barry and Mel than they've shared. Small details often give hints as to where to investigate. Mel as a homeless vet was at the food pantry many times. I can't imagine Beryl didn't pick up on his actions. He was not there for the fun of it. He must have thought the pantry was a source. Did he think the perp visited the pantry? Why could he unless he too was hiding his identity for some reason. What could be the reason?"

"Rudy, ask Mona. She's at the pantry as much as is Beryl. She also knows Laela quite well."

"You forget, Norbie. I don't want to deal with Mona as a witness. Some defense attorney will think she's making up stories to make me look good. You know better."

"I forgot. You are right. Anyway, I have to run. I will speak with Beryl and Nate separately."

Leaving the restaurant, Rudy headed towards the station and received a call from Sergeant Lilly Tagliano. "Captain, you coming in soon? I need a word."

Beauregard explained he was headed there and asked for an update. She declined to discuss it over the wire and would wait for him. He thought, *Lilly must have another personal problem. One of the best street cops I've ever had, but when her personal life gets in the way, we lose her for a bit.*

Beauregard was in his office in twelve minutes, which he figured was a new record for him. Lilly entered without knocking and sat directly in front of him. "Captain, I was at the Italian Festival in the North End with Juan and my family. It's an annual do for my dad. Well,

I saw police crowding the group and I followed them to Endicott Street but could go no further. Endicott Court, which is a little street, is off the larger Endicott Street. I thought I saw a large green lawn bag with a head of a woman sticking out of it. I showed my badge to a uniform and said I was a detective on this detail. He let me pass the tape. I made progress and got a good look at the scene. I was thrown out when a detective present asked for my badge and saw West Side on it. You'll be getting a call on me. But I need to tell you that when I read the story in the Boston papers, well it sounded related to our inquiry into the homeless man's murder with what the FBI was saying. You know, the killing of all the ladies from Florida to here."

"Sergeant, I want you to write down everything you saw. I want a layout of the body and what else was around, including weird bystanders. I expect complete details, but no assumptions. Understand?"

"I'll do it. But the festival is quite a crowd and many of the visitors looked weird. I'll try. What about my pushing myself in without authorization?"

"All in a good day's work, Sergeant. You're police even when you're not on duty."

12

BIRD'S - EYE VIEWS

The two women, busy with washing pans, were interrupted by Patti the Complainer. The Open Pantry brought in such a diversity of human nature that both Beryl and Mona, as all the other staff, often named their clients. Most names were related to normal everyday things such as 'Red' for Sally who had sprayed her hair fuchsia. Mostly the relationships with client and volunteer staff were respectful and friendly. Patti always created stress in her connection to staff. Beryl thought as Patti entered the room, *she thinks this is a hotel, always looking for a condiment we don't have or a second piece of everything or twenty napkins to take home or and the list goes on. Her food isn't hot or cold enough. She's often here before we start following us around. We've never had a locked door policy when we are in the building, but it's probably time. And she stays around until we leave. And never is a thank you given. I know she must have had a difficult life. However, she exhausts us all.*

Mona said, "Patti, it's time for you to leave. Once everybody finishes lunch, the staff has to clean and be finished by three. It helps if the building is empty with the exception of staff."

Patti answered with her forceful gruff voice, "I have important questions to ask and I'm staying until I get answers."

Beryl let out a loud sigh but said, "Go ahead, Patti. I'll try to respond."

"Where's Charlie? He has not been here for three weeks. Is he sick?"

Beryl quietly said, "He's passed away, Patti."

Beryl and Mona were not prepared for the sudden screaming and crying and moaning. The attempts to calm her increased her loud cries until she practically fell into the chair near her. So, they waited it out, fifteen minutes of waiting. Until Patti the Complainer said, "Now we'll never know."

Mona asked, "Know what, Patti?"

"Know who was doing it? I can't tell. It's a secret. How can I do my job now? Charlie paid good."

Beryl thinking Patti would be out a little money for doing some running around for Charlie said, "What did Charlie pay you to do? Perhaps we can help."

"I can't tell. He said never to tell, but who will do it if I don't. I'll have to but I need Uber money. I don't have any."

Mona, who unlike Beryl, was used to a world of negotiation what with her husband Rudy and three sons said, "I'll tell you what, Patti, you tell me what your job is and I'll pay for the Uber. I can't pay for the Uber unless what you're doing is legal. You know, what with my husband being with the police, I have to be very careful."

Patti looked at Mona with interest, saying, "Police are like priests, huh? They won't tell the bad guy, will they?"

Mona answered, "Neither will I tell the bad guys. Tell me your job."

"I'm ashamed. I never talk about my past. Charlie just knew about it. He saw me one night watching. I was lonely."

Beryl asked, "What did Charlie see?"

"I was just standing there watching over on Underlook Way. Watching the ladies being picked up by johns. He was there too. He asked if I was lonely and thinking about when I was in the trade. There is a balcony on the bridge and you can see the ladies lined up under the bridge waiting for a pick. The police only go by at eight in the evening and two in the morning unless there's a call. It's safe for a john and they know it. COVID didn't make a dent in business."

Patti started crying again at the reference to Charlie. Beryl persevered in her question. "What did Charlie ask you to do? Did he ask you to look for a woman?"

"Not really. He asked me to take notes on the johns. At first I thought he was undercover as a policeman. He said no. He was looking for a guy who harmed some ladies he knew. I think it was his wife, because he was kinda on a mission. He knew a lot about the life and said he knew right away that I was a street worker. He already knew I walked the streets when he first met me. I told no one. I've never been arrested. I asked him how he knew. He said he took psychology classes."

"Did you take notes?"

"Yeah, I had to. He wanted builds on the ladies and the johns' descriptions and if a car was being used, the plate numbers. I sometimes had to follow them two blocks to the john's car to get the plate. I couldn't get all the numbers from a few plates. He still paid me."

Beryl, trying to hold her excitement, said, "Could I see your notes? Do you have them with you?"

Patti said, "I need to get paid. The notes I have are all that's worth anything. I can sell them to the police. $200.00 is my price. Take it or leave it."

Acting as if this were a normal bargaining sale, Beryl said, "I won't give you any money until I see your notes."

Beryl and Mona noted the glint in Patti's eyes when she said, "The notes are too long. Don't think you can memorize them at a glance and not pay me."

Patti handed the notes to Beryl. True to Patti's warning, there were twenty pages of notes neatly written down. They included the dates for each sighting. There were ten pages dated after Charlie's death. When questioned, Patti claimed she had not seen Charlie for one night before his date of death. In fact, he had said he wouldn't be there that night. He had a meeting.

"He said I was responsible for the meeting but wouldn't say why. I thought I'd done something wrong but he told me it was all good. I want my $200.00 or my notes."

Beryl dug in her bag and produced the money in hundreds. Patti complained no store would accept bills that large causing Mona to grab the cash and make change from the pantry till.

As she was leaving, Patti said, "You never said how Charlie died. He looked healthy and cleaner than the other homeless."

Without giving it a thought Mona said, "He was murdered."

Patti shoved the ladies aside saying, "I want nothing to do with this. You never talked to me. This is why Charlie said never to tell. I should have listened."

She ran as fast as she could struggling with the heavy exit door. Beryl and Mona finished their kitchen duties in record time and headed for the West Side Police station. They were on a mission to tell Rudy. Mona drove while Beryl scanned the last ten pages. An idea sparked and she said, "First, let's hit Staples. We need a copy."

Mona said, "I didn't hear that. You said you need copy paper. Okay?"

Twenty minutes later the ladies entered the station house with only one copy of the notes to give to Rudy.

It is an understatement to say the Captain appeared slightly apoplectic at the sight of his wife accompanied by Beryl Kent. He thought, *I know they are interfering in my murder cases. It's one thing to be stuck with Beryl, but I do not want Mona a witness. I can't tell her to stay away from Beryl. I wish I could. If I did try, it'd only make matters worse.*

Instead of reacting, Rudy said as he kissed Mona on the cheek, "You make my day, ladies. What can I do for you?"

Beryl told the tale of Patti the Complainer. Naturally, she went to great extent to relay every word and nuance. Captain Beauregard's dislike for any kind of loquaciousness was known by the ladies, but Beryl ignored his discomfort in order to give a complete report. Rudy said, "She didn't say more about his pursuit of the johns?"

He quickly took the notes, saying, "I can see at a glance the same plate number duplicated three times. Does that mean the john picked up a woman three times or was seen trolling?"

Beryl laughed. "Rudy, see the last column. I think 't' means trolling and 's' means success. I don't know that. I've just assumed it. Patti was quite thorough. Notice some trolls never are successful. It means in my mind their conscience, or their fear of being caught by police, or their dissatisfaction with the group of ladies streetwalking that night got to them. Still, I think every plate number of those who did not pick up a lady should be investigated."

"And I think all, Beryl. This is only one location where Mel got someone to watch. How many more locations had watchers? We've had no murders in this area. Chances are the perp has not been here or if he had been, he didn't choose a lady these nights. Why would the perp be looking for hookers? Maybe looking for one type, the look of a woman who he wasn't to rape. Thank you for getting these notes. I may need to speak with Patti. Who do you think would be the best person?"

Mona said, "No one right now. She's petrified, thinks someone will be after her. I'd wait, Rudy. You don't even know if this is relevant yet."

Rudy agreed, thinking, *Mona is right. Not evidential yet.*

The detectives took two hours before approaching the Captain. They had watched his body language when his wife and Beryl arrived and knew enough to stay clear for a while. Not surprisingly, Lieutenant Aylewood-Locke took the initiative and approached the Captain. "Beryl in again on one of our cases, Captain?"

He knew they were fishing for info. He answered, "Okay, Beryl is involved. She got hold of some notes that may have a connection to Mel's undercover work."

The Captain went on to a discussion on the notes. He asked Lieutenant Mason Smith to put them up on the detectives' computers. Sergeant Tagliano, who had history as a sex sting undercover officer worker, said, "Let me see the notes. I have a phenomenal memory of car plate numbers. I'll know some of the regulars."

She was jeered by the Sergeant. "Remembering those romantic nights when you wore five-inch heels and a see-thru dress, Sergeant?"

Ignoring the barb, Lilly scanned the list, saying, "I can get rid of fifty per cent of these plates. Unless the perp is a perpetual sharer of the ladies' gifts, this should help lower the load."

The Captain thanked her and left them to their work. He called his wife Mona saying, "Please stay out of this investigation."

Mona did not try to deny it, but instead forcibly said she would follow any information she thought important. Nothing more was said.

At Beryl's home the work took the ladies several hours. They did not have the luxury of a source of phone numbers and their billed names and addresses. They did what they could with a reverse number directory on plates given Beryl by a close friend. They made calls offering free Geek services for the owners' computers. Mostly they were looking for an address. Success evaded them on sixty percent of the numbers. The others they saved thinking they could drive by the addresses and maybe rule some out. Beryl said, "This is probably a waste of time. A serial murderer's home doesn't have a sign saying 'I live here.'"

Mona agreed but pointed out there were three numbers whose addresses were in Laela's neighborhood and one in Beryl's. "Wealthy addresses have johns because they can afford it."

"Mona, you may be right. The ladies' cost is about $300 on average for a trick. Most middle-class men can't afford that. I suppose once a month maybe, like a cigarette habit."

Their surveillance of these houses mostly demonstrating children playing in the driveway would not assure a daddy who stayed at home for sex. Beryl thought, *this is just too personal. I don't want to know this much about my neighbors. I'm certain if I meet these folks at a party and learn their address, I'll remember this connection. I wish now I could forget.*

One address was not of a house, but of a barn tucked into heavy foliage. It looked deserted to the ladies and they determined it was time to go back home. Beryl dropped Mona off at the Open Pantry to pick up her car and she headed home.

Nate was waiting for Beryl saying, "Did you forget, we're having an early dinner. I've been trying to call you."

She had forgotten, but instead of apologizing, she shared her afternoon's experiences with him. He asked to see the notes which Beryl had kept. Mona did not want Rudy to know they had made a copy. Although fascinated, he said he'd look at it more seriously later and that he'd wait for her to change leading to Beryl saying, "I'm not dressed up to par for you, Colonel."

"Not that, Beryl Kent, but you smell like fried sausages. It's not a perfume you normally wear."

Later at one of their favorite spots, Punjabi Tadka's Indian Restaurant in Springfield, they discussed the notes. Beryl was quite hungry not having eaten since an early breakfast. She said, "Love the Northern Indian cuisine here."

Nate said he knew and that she said the same thing every time they visited here. She ate with vigor while Nate talked about why Mel would be looking at street walkers in order to out a serial killer. He posed the question, "Does it appear Barry gave him this info?"

Perplexed for a moment, Beryl paused and questionably said, "You mean because the Open Pantry is near his home? You think Barry put Mel onto something? You think it's why Barry was murdered?"

"Hold on, Beryl. We could not understand why Mel was undercover as Bud Hover a homeless man. He hooks up with Patti after seeing her at the best and most known location for streetwalkers. He hires her to watch the johns every night. He had a source or some evidence to think the perp is looking at these women as a source for his more violent kills. Is there a pattern that some of the violent kills are sourced from the homeless shelter? Did Mona tell you that?"

"Mona doesn't know anything more than what I'm telling you. Rudy does not want Mona as a witness and so he tells her nothing. She is smart and listens carefully when he does talk, but he does not want her as a witness in court.

"Why would he source from either the homeless or the streetwalkers? Why not just pick up any woman he saw soliciting?"

"I don't know. Think about it, Beryl, he wants to kill prostitutes when he is angry. In today's world, girls are often dressed as hookers but don't sell their bodies. How would he know who did and who didn't?"

"How does he know which feeding station to visit for the homeless and find a woman who watches streetwalkers? Farfetched even for you, Nate."

"That is the gist of it. The FBI must have a history on his going after the homeless for info or Mel wouldn't be undercover as homeless. Patti gave you a gift. She practically told you he sources from the streetwalkers. The question is why this pantry and why this location for streetwalkers is still out there. And then we have Barry's death. The Captain sees a coincidence in the victims' Army background. I do too. Why would Barry have to die? If the perp recently knew about Barry's interest in the murders or if he knew Mel and Barry had connected on the murders, Barry would become dangerous. But how did he know? Can you speak with Jane Aubergine about Barry's comings and goings? She lives near him."

13

CLOSE TO HOME

"I feel silly, Jad, staying in a fancy hotel in New Haven to go to the taco festival. I mean we could have gone home and come back here just as easily."

"Laela, going home now will bring back memories too soon. New England is pretty small. We could have done day trips for all of it, but think about what we would have missed. We've mostly taken older roads and seen so much more than traveling highways to a destination. You picked this fest because you like tacos and let's enjoy it."

The Guilford Fairground hosted a slew of food trucks mixed in with stages, mariachi bands, wrestling called lucha libre, and dancing. Children were everywhere. "Oh, the color, primary colors are everywhere, Jad. I'm a little girl again. I feel young. I want a taco and fried ice cream. Let's watch the dancers."

"Read the program, Laela, the dancers are on in an hour. We can watch lucha libre if you'd like."

Laela looked around and said, "I don't think that's on yet, Jad, just some crazy fighting and what a crowd."

"That is lucha libre."

"Such a pretty name for wrestling. I don't want any violence. To think a homeless man died where I would have been if Barry hadn't died the same day."

"I wanted to ask you about his death. If it doesn't bother you."

"He was a nice man liked by everyone. Charlie put out fights and calmed our hysterical clients. Who would kill him outside the pantry? Why was he there so early in the morning? Doesn't make sense to me."

Sounding as if he'd thought long and hard before speaking, Jad said, "Violence does make sense in some cases. Evil was inflicted on a person and payback is violence. Sometimes violence prevents a bigger evil. I'm not judgmental."

Before she could completely grasp his statement, Laela saw a family handing out a pamphlet. She wondered if the group, and it certainly looked like a family to her, was an evangelistic group. Since Laela always read any handout, she took one. "Jad, their daughter is missing. She's married with children. She was to meet some friends and go to this fest last night but didn't come home. They look like such nice people. I do hope she's okay."

"Me too, but you never know. Why wasn't she there with her hubby? Women are acting outrageously, even married women, much more often than years ago."

"You are such a chauvinist, Jad. Married women go out with their friends for a night out just as men do. Guys play golf and some women go to dinner without their spouses. You were married. You're telling me your wife never went out with her girlfriends for a few drinks?"

"You are so right, Laela, she did."

Laela reacted to his words with a shiver thinking, *I should get off this subject. Maybe his wife before she got sick was out flitting around. He never talks about her except in the context of her premature death. He hasn't told me much about her illness.*

The flyer for the missing woman said her name was Virginia Blouvin. Laela heard one woman saying she knew Virginia and she was a lovely and fun-loving gal. Shaking her head Laela said, "Let's go over there to the kids face painting. That guy is really artistic. Do you notice the fathers are much more interested in the kids' faces painted than the moms?"

Jad's answer rankled her when he said, "I'm not surprised. I've noticed lately dads are more involved with their kids. I think it's because the mothers who so wanted to be mothers got bored with the job and want to run around and be a kid again."

To quell her disquiet, Laela headed for the margarita stand and ordered a salt rimmed giant peach drink. She greedily sipped and her discomfort over his remarks went away. Now she was ready to party. Cutting in front of her were two men and a uniformed police officer who were headed toward the man and woman handing out flyers. The conversation caused the woman to drop to her knees and scream, "No, no, no. Not my baby. Not my baby."

The man, probably her husband just said, "No, Virginia, no."

Laela gulped her drink down and said, "Let's go back to the hotel. I can't take this. Their loss burns like my Barry's loss. It's all too much."

Jad said, "It's not your problem. Why make it your problem? This Virginia was most likely pretty loose. She's not worth sympathy. The parents do feel pain. I understand your empathy for them."

Slightly not her best self from the drink, Laela stumbled as she walked only to be caught by Jad. He said, "You need me right now. Don't think about others' losses. Just enjoy yourself. You don't understand women who carry on behind their husbands' backs. Don't waste your tears, Laela."

Laela excused herself at the hotel and went to her room to take a nap. She was restless but sleep came easily. She slept for forty-five minutes. When she woke, she thought, *that's what alcohol does to the body. It puts you to sleep and wakes you. I am picking at everything Jad says. It happens when you spend too much time with another person. I'll cancel dinner with him, get room service, and call Jane Aubergine to catch up.*

Jad was quite unhappy to lose a dinner companion. He was unable to change Laela's mind. He thought, *damn family with the flyers. Didn't think enough of her to watch her behavior before she went missing.*

He ordered his dinner at the bar and watched the women being picked up. There was only one conclusion to be made. Despite its high rates, the hotel had some ladies working it.

Jane was excited to hear from Laela. Her first words were, "How are you dealing with your travel companion? Has he made a pass yet?"

"Jane, I've just lost Barry. He wouldn't do that no matter how he felt. He is quite proper. I do enjoy his company. He's been great, but I realized today he's a bit of a chauvinist. Surprises me a man his age doesn't approve of a married woman going out with her girlfriends. There was a family with flyers searching for a woman named Virginia. I forget the last name. Later, the police came through the crowd and gave them sad news. It so upset me. The fest was no fun after that."

"Where are you?"

"At the taco festival in New Haven. It's the third annual taco festival and really it was so colorful and fun. And the music and dancing and food was worth coming to, but the sad news on the missing woman was just too much for me, Jane."

"Laela, was the woman's name Virginia Blouvin?"

"Yes, that's the name. How do you know her?"

"It's on the news. Her body was found on the edge of Route 5 outside of New Haven. She was strangled. One reporter said it was the latest in some unsolved strangling murder cases. Don't let it get you down, Laela. It has nothing to do with you. You don't need any more negativity."

"I left Jad alone for dinner and took a nap. I am hungry now and don't want to eat alone after all."

"Go down to the lobby. He's probably grabbing a bite at the bar. All men do that when they're alone. That way they can talk to others. It's better for you not to be alone feeling as you do. I have to go now. Love."

After Jane rang off, Laela spiffed up a bit and headed for the hotel bar which she had noticed earlier had a great menu. Exiting the elevator, she spotted Jad leaving by the main door. She rushed and caught up with him, saying, "You have plans? I won't bother you."

Jad looked startled and for the first time in her experience being around him, she caught a look of confusion in his eyes causing her to say, "It's okay. Don't worry about me. If you have a date with a lady, go and enjoy. I'll see you in the morning."

Laela was thinking, *I'm so stupid. Of course, he'd want to break up this trip with some fun and a lady more his age.*

Laela turned to leave, only to have Jad grab her arm. He said, "I was so hoping you'd change your mind. I hate eating alone, and I don't have a date although a gal approached me in the bar. She'd had a few and was flirting. I'm telling you, Laela, not all women are like you. Let's go."

They headed for the main hotel restaurant with Laela wondering, *if I were a man would I feel the same as he does just because a woman flirts. We all flirt. My mother actually taught me to flirt. I hope men I've met in the past don't think my behavior was anything more than just light fun. I guess everything said is open to interpretation.*

Jane Aubergine could not contain herself. Inspired by the phone call from Laela she immediately made one to Mona Beauregard. Jane relayed every detail of her call from Laela saying, "Mona, she sounded so desperate as if the body of this Virginia lady had something to do with her. Really, Barry's death has upset her mental apple cart."

With some drama Jane tried to get Mona to see Laela was in a sorry state. Mona meanwhile was focused on only one sentence in Jane's comments. "Are you sure this lady was strangled and left on the side of the road in a rubbish bag? And the road was Route 5?"

"Yes. Those facts are what I heard. Is that what you heard?"

"The article did not go into detail. The police chief is giving an interview at six tonight. I'm watching for it."

"Mona, that's not my concern. The poor dear is dead and I'm sorry. Right now, I'm worried about our Laela."

Mona made nice-nice with Jane to get her to cut off the conversation. She thought about calling Rudy, but negated it thinking, *he'll already have heard. He told me to stay out of solving murders. Do I want to listen to his nagging. Nope. I'll call Beryl.*

Beryl was in the Specialty market getting double grounded veal, pork, and beef for her famous meatballs along with specially pounded veal for her cutlets. At first quibbling in her mind over the higher prices, she absolved her guilt over the extra expense. She welcomed Mona's call and moved over to a quieter aisle to talk. Mona was characteristically methodical in her retelling of Jane's tale. She had caught the news about a body found in New Haven but was distracted over her dinner menu for the evening. Oliver and Leeann were having their first post nuptial dinner with her and Nate. Jocelyn was to join them without her live-in boyfriend who was to attend another occasion. Beryl was all ears. Mona, it's connected don't you think? And this one was strangled, not stabbed and raped. Me thinks the perp doesn't want to get dirty. Rape and knifing leaves trails of blood. Do you think, part of his divided motive has to do with opportunity. If he's not near enough to his killing site but has the desire to kill, he chooses strangling?

Mona replied, "Part of the equation is opportunity but the passion is in the knifing. The strangling is logical. These women deserve to die because they have been the cause of great disappointment for him."

"You're right, Mona. Have you called Rudy to tell him?"

"I'm certain he knows and he won't want to hear it from me. Why don't you call Nate or Norbie Cull. Rudy will take the info from them better than from me."

"I'll tell Nate tonight. He'll still see your connection, Mona. Oh wait, there's Norbie and Sheri. That's my chance."

Grateful, Beryl closed her cell to speak loudly to Sheri and Norbie who were just entering the market. As they grabbed a basket she motioned them over. Sheri gave her a hug while Norbie said, "Such a greeting, Beryl, and for some reason I think it has nothing to do with your excitement about seeing us at our local market."

"Sarcastic are you, Attorney Cull. Did you see that woman who came into the store before you? She had a tee shirt, Sheri should buy for you. It said, 'Sarcasm is my equivalent for a hug.'"

"What gives, Beryl?"

"Sheri, you'll be bored by this. It's about murder."

"Not at all. I love all this stuff but Norbie can't tell me anything having to do with his clients. I have to discover it all from the news or my friends. Go ahead, we're all ears."

And Beryl told the story including stating her desire to leave Mona out of the equation. Norbie said, "I'll go see Rudy. This is important, Beryl. Further, I have some good connections with the New Haven police. To think, West Side's little police department is the center of these murder inquiries. The perp picked the wrong MCU Captain. Imagine parking by Rudy's back door. Sheri, I'm off. Grocery shopping doesn't have the same appeal as murder."

Kissing his wife on the cheek, Norbie left the two ladies who spent the next half hour over coffee in the attached cafe discussing murder.

Attorney Cull tried to bypass the desk sergeant but was caught and told to wait until he was announced. He had a problem with that. First, Rudy could be too busy, although he thought he'd want to see him. Second, the desk sergeant was getting into it with a citizen and would forget about him. Taking advantage of the situation he forgot about the desk sergeant and quietly moved to the stairway quickly disappearing from sight. Rudy welcomed him as Norbie complained about lack of open access being blocked by the desk sergeant. Rudy laughed. "You defense attorneys just can't take 'no,' can you? Sit down. Mason has brought in lunch and made fresh coffee. These grinders from Calabrese's Market are sixteen inches long."

Norbie replied, "And you can't eat a whole one. Getting old, Rudy, murder has made you picky."

The two men enjoyed each other while they scoffed down the salty deli meats. One was thinking he wouldn't tell his wife and the other was thinking this stuff still is preferable to the gourmet dishes Sheri serves. Norbie, still sipping his second cup of coffee asked, "Remember our conversation about the murder in Exeter, New Hampshire, the other day? As a follow-up, the news reported finding a woman in a garbage bag by the side of the road in New Haven. She was strangled. I have friends in the New Haven police department. The similarities are too many to ignore. She was of similar age, went out on the town, ends up strangled on the side of Route 5. It's another one, Rudy."

Rudy grimaced, a habit that transformed his face from kind to a bit threatening. "I've news for you, Norbie. Lilly was at the saint's festival in Boston's North End, and there's another one there. That's three in ten days. What's causing the perp to speed up?"

"Rudy, did the FBI give a list of dates for the murders. I mean just the ones that were left strangled?"

"No. We've a copy of the files, their profiling, and a list of important details on each file. We'd have to do that work ourselves. They don't give up their investigative tools easily. It won't take long to do the local ones, but I think only fourteen in this search area were strangled. I've included New Hampshire in with Connecticut, parts of New York and Massachusetts."

Norbie agreed to wait for results which took about fifteen minutes. Surprisingly, the results of the time matching showed approximately three to four weeks between murders until after Barry and Mel's deaths. Then the murders were only separated by less than five days. Rudy said, "Norbie, he's in a rush now. Why?"

"I imagine something in his life has changed. I'm not a psychiatrist but changing habits, particularly if we find when we list all the murders and the pattern is consistent has to have a meaning. For instance, you may find a complete time pattern change when he changes locations. Means he's been busy moving."

Rudy questioned, "Not enough. Must mean more than that. There's a need to kill more frequently and these murders do not include the raped and knifed ones. The perp is filling this need more frequently. Could be someone in his life reminds him of the woman who caused his need to squash her. Why not kill the new woman in his life. I'm betting he can't because he'd be caught or the new woman is making him reassess his feelings. If that were true, he'd be in a frenzy to keep his world order; in fact, he would need to kill more frequently."

Norbie replied, "Great! More murders, more frequency. That's what you're thinking. More murders, more frequency leaves a greater chance of error in the details. Maybe this is the opportunity to catch the guy."

"Wish I had a perfect circle. Exeter, New Hampshire, New Haven, Connecticut, and Boston's North End, Massachusetts, as a list is a triangle. Could be we need a full circle to plot the center. Something in Vermont, Maine, and Rhode Island would include all the New England states. West Side would then be the center of the murder clusters, thus keeping in with his patterns."

Norbie answered with a touch of cynicism. "So, you wait for more murders! He has to have had a problem in Boston. A two-lane highway wasn't available nearby, so he dumps the body on a side street in the middle of a festival. There have to be one or more witnesses."

14

BERYL VISITS A CONVENT

Beryl was making croissants using her father's family recipe thinking, *cooking does relax me when I'm uptight. Why would Sister Patricia Marie never tell Laela about her mother's murder. More than that why would she allow a cancer story to be told and retold. Nuns don't lie like that. I bet no one ever directed the question to her; thus, allowing her to not answer with a lie. It doesn't make sense. There must be relatives who knew and attended Barry and Laela's wedding and the lie was never exposed. I can't believe there was no talk. Maybe Barry and Laela had a small wedding. Why be ashamed to talk if your mother were a victim of violence.*

The dough was ready for the oven, making it timely, as the doorbell's chimes echoed out to the kitchen. Her visitor was none other than Alice. Surprised at this first and only visit, she invited her to join her with a cup of coffee. Alice walked around the enormous kitchen saying, "We need this at the food pantry. It is truly beautiful, Beryl. How can you work in our cramped quarters after having this at home?"

"I didn't always have these luxuries, Alice. I can work in any kitchen. So why the sudden visit? Is something wrong at the pantry?"

"I don't know. One of the homeless talked to me about Bud Hover, the man who died. He used to see me talking with Bud. Bud was very nice. We'd talk about classical music. He was even more knowledgeable than my husband. This man, Sam the Difficult, you know him, right?"

"Yes, I know Sam."

"Sam used to visit the bridge. In case you don't know what that is, it's a sight that streetwalkers use to pick up their johns. Bud frequented the place. Sam told him he was Army and knew he was undercover. Sam knew I knew Laela's husband. Barry came to pick Laela up one day and recognized me. I was shocked to be remembered. Sam asked Bud what 'undercover with the homeless' could possibly do for him. He said Patti was helping him. I know Patti. She's on the fringe. I mean she was back and forth with AA not always staying with the program. I mention this, because yesterday Sam said she was to give Bud a number that was important to his work, but he hadn't seen her for two days. He was worried she'd gone on a bender. That was two days before his death. I would have spoken to Sam about the number, because if it was important to Bud. It was about his work. Bud shouldn't have died that way, Beryl. Now I can't help him because he's dead and I don't know if it's about this number."

Beryl looked confused, saying, "You mean Bud, Patti, and Sam, and you all knew Bud was undercover?"

"Well, Bud told them not me. They told me. They know I have a past and am sympathetic to them. They tell me things. I think this one may be important, but I can't go to the police. I have history I don't want to discuss. Even as a witness they would grill me and I don't need to put my family through my past."

"The police will want to know how I know. I can't lie."

"I trust you, Beryl. Can't you figure a way to give them information without involving me? Promise you won't give me up."

"I can't promise for sure, but if there's a problem I'll call you."

Alice was not happy but kept saying to herself she knew Beryl would not let her down. The oven bell rang and Beryl invited Alice to sample her fresh croissants. Along with coffee the two ladies alleviated their frustration with bites of buttery pastry. Alice left soon after, leaving Beryl with her problem.

BERYL VISITS A CONVENT

Two days later, Beryl greeted the homeless guests at the door. She had swapped jobs this morning. Mona cooked. Alice set the tables. The patrons often came in small groups, leaving Beryl hoping her marks, Patti and Sam, would arrive separately. Generally, the homeless came early. Today was not an exception. About seventy percent of her diners were almost finished before Sam arrived. Mona asked if they could talk for a minute. He growled, "Lunch first. And why do you want to have a conversation? I've done nothing."

Beryl asked him to get his lunch and join her in the back-storage kitchen telling him there was a table there. Grinning with pleasure Sam said, "Grab a coffee and dessert. I don't like eating alone."

Beryl had never seen a grinning with pleasure Sam and had high hopes he would be in a positive mood. He returned quickly with a plate filled with two Reuben sandwiches, two large brownies, one soup, chips, coffee, and a candy bar. She said, "How'd you get two sandwiches, Sam. Do you have an in with Alice?"

"Alice is one of us. Can't you tell? You can trust her. I stay away from Mona. She's married to a police detective. You have to watch anyone who's close with the police. She's nice, but..."

"And me. Can you trust me do you think?"

"You're a victim. I remember the article about the falling man landing on you. He almost killed you. But I don't deny you're tight with the police."

"Friendly would be a better word. I have to have a good relationship with the police to help manage the pantry kitchen. You know that. I've avoided many conflicts between our patrons because the police visit regularly. I do know you had inside knowledge about Bud Hover and his secrets. What did Patti tell you about the numbers?"

"Patti was all excited about some numbers she got at the bridge. I didn't see any numbers when I went there. She said she's concerned a murderer would know she talked to Bud. She thought Bud and she were in trouble and she was going to hide out for a while. In Patti's case that means a bender and then have the police take her to rehab. Smart plan, 'cause nobody can get you there."

"Did she give you the numbers?"

"Did I say she did? No, I didn't say that. Bud's dead and she's missing. I don't want nothin' to do with this. Your being so nice to me don't change nothin. I was only worried about Patti. If she's missing nobody gonna worry about her or me."

"Why do you think I'm talking to you, Sam, because I'm worried about Patti and now I'm worried about you. We're too late to help Bud."

"Funny about that, Bud was the important guy and he's dead. Beryl, we're not that important. If nobody knows about me, I'm safe. Maybe Patti isn't but I am."

Beryl did not want to throw Sam under the bus but said, "I think if the bad guy saw anyone from the pantry who was also at the bridge often, he'd be suspicious. You'd be better if you throw your allegiance with the police."

"You're scaring me, Beryl. How'd the police be able to protect me?"

"They'll put a uniform on you. You'll be safe."

"No, I don't want that. It'd just make me feel unsafe for sure. Look I don't know the numbers. I really don't. I do know the license plate of a car that would come and not pick any lady up. Since it happened by me on five occasions, I think it's important. Patti can tell you more if you can find her. Now I'm getting out of here."

"The number, Sam, maybe it's important, maybe not."

Sam pulled out a wrinkled paper with a plate number and handed it to Beryl as he walked out. Beryl took the paper, waited a few minutes until she was alone and called Attorney Norbie Cull. "Can you do a reverse phone number look-up?"

His answer was yes when she explained the situation. Beryl stayed on the line and Norbie said, "It's a business number listed to CT Investment Group (CIG). Probably not our guy but I'll have Sheila, my admin call, and get details. There's my friend who's a drug and alcohol counselor. I'll ask for his help in finding Patti. I'll call tomorrow. If I have a problem, I'll have to call Rudy."

"And I'll look around for Patti. Thanks, Norbie. Sometimes it's difficult to assist Rudy. There are so many rules and regulations and people to protect."

And Beryl did make some efforts to locate Patti starting with the address she'd given at the pantry except it was no longer her address. The current tenant had no info on Patti. Slightly frustrated, Beryl headed for home. She'd promised Nate a candlelit dinner by the kitchen fire. The thought warmed her heart. She thought, *Nate and my dog 'Amico,' what more could I ask for. Oliver and Leeann are happy and my darling daughter Jocelyn has stayed in love with one man for over two years. Soon, I think they'll have news. It's been a bumpy road, my life, but the rewards have been worth the ride.*

Nestled in two leather chairs by the fireplace, Beryl and Nate were each enjoying their espresso, when Beryl told the story of her day. Nate listened to her intently and when she finished he asked why she contacted Norbie and not him. She answered, "Nate, I was trying to protect Sam and thought Rudy would know if you spoke to him that I was involved and he'd go right after Sam. Norbie does lots of pro bono work with the homeless and he has a large criminal law practice. It wouldn't be odd for him to know a homeless man. Rudy would accept that. I'm wondering if you would drive over to the bridge tonight with me. Maybe Patti would be there. Would you?"

"Why don't I go alone? It would attract less notice. I may not know Patti but your description of her if she is an onlooker gives me a perfect picture. I will know her."

"Nate, that's bogus. What about couples who want a threesome. I'm pretty certain they drive through there all the time. I'm coming with you."

Ten minutes of discussion wore the Colonel down, but he insisted on conditions if Beryl joined him. She agreed they would go on the following Friday night which Beryl had been told was a busy trade night.

Beryl had made contact with Sister Patricia Marie through the principal of St. George's Primary School in Roanoke, Virginia. She arranged for a meeting at the school at four in the afternoon. The trip required a two hour stop in Charlotte, North Carolina, and the Uber to St. George's. Beryl barely made the appointed time. Sister Patricia Maria greeted her with a hug and an elated look. "It's wonderful to see you again, Beryl. We did not get enough time together after the funeral. How is my mother Laela doing? This has been very difficult for her losing my dad. They clearly loved each other."

The two women chatted about Laela, her trip with Jad, and about her dad's sudden death when Beryl asked, "Why did your father change his name, Patricia, and not tell Laela?"

From the look on Sister Patricia's face, Beryl reacted with, "I know this must be difficult for you, but I didn't fly down here just to be inquisitive. Your father was murdered. It was not an accident. I'm certain the police will be calling you."

A startled Patricia, said, "Do they know who did it?"

The conversation continued while Beryl explained why Barry's body indicated evidence of murder. Patricia appeared to accept the news until Beryl asked, "Why did your dad change his name when your mother was murdered?"

"You knew? I thought no one knew. My dad did not want Laela to know. He thought some of his actions would put her at risk. He kept trying to find Mom's murderer. He was in an awful state for several years. He'd disappear at night looking in places around us for the murderer. He'd sit in bars until late offering to walk ladies to their car. I'd say he was almost irrational at first. When the FBI informed him Mom was killed by a serial killer, he blamed himself for not protecting her. The press at that time would not give up asking questions. There was no mercy. Changing his name gave him a new life. I was all for it. Although I thought Laela should know the truth. He was adamant. It could put her in danger. So, we built a life on a lie. I truly felt prayers were needed for us and society. I feel that way, but suffer some guilt for leaving him. He met Laela. They loved each other. I believed it was enough."

Tears welled in the Sister's eyes. Beryl waited in silence. Then, "Sister, can you tell me the circumstances of your mother's death? Every detail is important. Where did she go that night? Why would she get in someone's car?"

"Beryl, I only know what was told to me by the police, the FBI and her girlfriend Molly. Mom was out on the town with Molly and a

BERYL VISITS A CONVENT

third lady who never spoke to me after Mom's death. Mom was at The Rafters, a bar and grill frequented by the over thirty crowd. It was not a kids' bar. She'd go there on girls' night, normally scheduled every two weeks on a Thursday. That was karaoke night. The police and the FBI said she left alone at ten. The other ladies stayed till closing. Supposedly, it was a jumping night."

Sister stopped talking until Beryl said, "What did Molly say? Was it different?"

"Molly said my dad told Mom to be home at ten. He didn't trust the other ladies. He thought they drank too much. Mom was not a big drinker. Molly later told me a couple of guys tried to hit on Mom. She flirted but turned them down. The police did not take that seriously because they flirted at eight o'clock two hours before she left the bar. When she left the bar, her car was across the street. She never got in her car. Across the street were residential housings with no cameras on that side. My dad looked at the footage on Rafters but no one exited at that time. Molly thought one of those guys was out waiting for her. My dad did too. Dad also said he wished he never asked her to come home at ten. It never occurred to him the ladies would let her go home alone early. He blamed himself."

And she cried, softly, leading Beryl to hug her. "I so miss her, Beryl. Thank God I'd decided to enter the convent before Mom's death or I would have thought my decision was because of her murder. It wasn't. The sisters have saved my sanity. Dad didn't understand that. He thought I needed him, instead, he needed me and I wasn't there."

"No one's to blame for a psychopath's terror. Maybe there was horror in the murderer's childhood or he is just evil. You do believe in evil, Sister, don't you?"

"Oh, I do and not from just my mother's murder or now my dad's, I've seen it in the homes where I do social work. Evil is my invitation to pray more."

"Did the police ever do a mock up drawing of the two men who flirted with her?"

"No, they ruled them out. Molly drew pictures of them both. I have them. I don't know how accurate they are. I've kept them with me hoping I'd get a glimpse of the murderer. I know it's hopeless and I'm just dreaming."

Sister spread out two drawings. Beryl thought they were rather good. Molly had also listed approximate height and weight, color hair and wardrobe worn. She thought Molly must be an artist to draw a likeness from just one view of each man. She asked if she could take them. Sister laughed and said, "I made copies. No one wanted them until this visit. Thank you. I don't know if they can help. Maybe if you find, what do they call it on television, a person of interest, this likeness can help. I think the man on the left is more likely to be him. Molly didn't like him that night and she is a good judge of character."

Beryl was invited to leave by a sister who she guessed was in charge. Sister Patricia said, "Oops, it's time for prayers. You understand I would spend the evening with you. This life places some limits on my time. Thank you, Beryl, for coming all this way. I will be in West Side for Christmas to be with Laela. I've been released to go."

DETAILS

Beauregard was at the Regional High School giving a lecture to the senior class on criminal investigation. His wife Mona roped him into this work every year. It wasn't that he didn't enjoy the kids. He did, but he had so much work on his plate at the station. He would have rescheduled but he did not want to disappoint her. So here he was. He'd been asked what is the most important skill needed to be a good investigative detective. He thought, *this kid asks the question in the right way. He doesn't just assume a detective is good because he's a detective. He even extends it to a good investigative detective. And I have a truthful answer for him.*

"I see your nametag says Joe. Well, Joe, I like your question and my answer includes the terminology in your question. A good investigative detective is willing to review details over and over. Murders not solved within forty-eight hours normally are without immediate suspects. If a family member, friend, or B and E known felon is not being looked at, the possible suspects are too numerous to close the case quickly. Details of the crime often point to motive or opportunity noting a person with access to the murder weapon. Details in the victim's life must be carefully examined. That means interviewing their family and friends and enemies for motive, opportunity, and connection to murder weapon. Details on the location of crime can bring in photo footage nearby, witness reviews, neighborhood interviewing, and unusual events nearby may bring information not normally considered. For instance, in one of our more difficult cases, the movement of a helicopter in the area of the crime narrowed the list of suspects. In another my detectives ran through the woods with a timer in an attempt to invalidate an alibi. Drones can give information for time and place. Details, details, details. A good investigative detective is willing to look for details, review details multiple times, and appreciate every nuance in an interview or a movement or a picture."

Joe said, "I watch detective shows all the time and it looks like hard work to me. There's no answer key and every murderer had a different motive. Some are smart and good liars. What happens if you can't catch the murderer? Does it get you down?"

The Captain said, "Yup, it gets me down. I never forget. For me it's a cold case. I review cold cases regularly. I have an almost one hundred percent closure on cold cases. You may ask why detectives can solve a cold case when it couldn't be originally solved. This occurs for three reasons: new information, perp confesses after being incarcerated for another crime, or another detective goes over details again and a light bulb goes off. Remember, we all can't be brilliant in the moment. Reviewing details later often eliminates bias and narrow thinking."

The bell rang and the Captain was out of there heading for his office thinking, *that kid Joe is going to be a detective. I feel it. He'll be interested in details. At his age he's already looking at details.*

And to the agony of his detectives, the Captain discussed details in the afternoon meeting. Sergeant Barr asked, "I don't believe a perp could commit all these murders without making a mistake, what you call a telling detail showing up. Captain, we still don't have a fact sheet showing difference or variation in the murders. We've only gone over the ones in New York, Connecticut, Mass, and New Hampshire. I agree about details being important. There's got to be one detail in these cases that will hang the bastard."

And the work began. The files were heavy. Lieutenant Smith, a big man, said, "If these are only a portion of what they investigated, how do we know we got the important stuff? The FBI has digital on the important stuff. All they've sent on digital are summaries. They must be offering extra support to the postal service. We'll be here forever."

His complaints were ignored while some other complaints were heard loud and clear, "What's this story. It's four pages and it's a waste of time" or "They didn't follow up on this piece of evidence, a shoe print, because they thought they had the guy. They didn't but didn't go back. Idiots."

And the rumbling and grumbling continued. Late in the day the detectives finished. Beauregard was pleased and thanked them given there were the usual calls coming in on other cases. On the plus side, there were no new major criminal activities called in. He scheduled a meeting for ten the next morning to review and comment on the spreadsheets.

Sergeant Flores complained loudly, "I'm ready, now, Captain. I'll forget my thoughts overnight."

The response from his colleagues was to take some notes.

The Rockland Lobster Festival offered days of fish sampling, lobster dinners, boat cruises, and fun for family and friends. The fresh sea air and smell of fish hovered over the crowd gathered for the annual gastronomical delight of pure food with no preservatives. The sun shone off and on as potential rain clouds gathering held fast to their vapors. Laela was bright as the sun today, gushing, "I've never been here, Jad. This is a sensual delight. Everywhere I look are familiar sea and food smells and such fun. I needed this. Three museums in one day yesterday I thought would wear me out, but I'm energized. I love our little inn. Can we go on a cruise tomorrow? The whole marine stuff on this big harbor enthralls me."

"It's your vacation. I'm just happy to get that missing girl behind us. You overreacted, Laela. You must contain your emotions. I get down at negativity."

"I wasn't negative, Jad. I was horrified. That murdered girl and my husband's death was too much all together. Let's try and forget it for now. What do you think? Is it time for our lobster lunch."

"The parade with Neptune wasn't big enough for you? Now you have to eat. Come on, I've been checking out the best of the best in lobster with a sea view."

Laela thought, *I'll put away all those negative thoughts. Jad is oh so right. Beryl if she learned about the dead lady would react but she'd go on with her life. She'd be trying to solve the mystery and she's lost three husbands. And Alice would not react this way. I have to get hold of myself. I don't know what I'd do without Jad. Barry's death has been such a shock.*

Sitting on the edge of a section of sea wall, Laela oozed contentment. "Jad, I've never had such culinary delight in my whole damn life. I'm as content as any woman ever could be. Thank you for coming with me. You must have had a wonderful life before you moved to West Side. I have often wondered why you'd settle into such a suburban area. Clearly, you're a big city guy."

"Are you looking for information Laela, just ask. I'll tell you anything. Big cities bring crime. Big cities bring fear. Not for me anymore. My wife suffered before she died. It gave me a lot of time to think about what's important. Time is important to me. Being with good people is very important to me. Good people make me feel balanced. Like you, Laela, you are good people. It's an honor to be here with you in your recovery."

Laela actually blushed. "You are truly a special man. I thank Alice for bringing me into your life."

The two shopped in the charming alcoves of specialized goods in town. Laela was quite satisfied to see seamen globes with fishing and lobster traps complete with a Christmas tree in a ten-inch diameter size. She appeared almost gloriously happy with her find causing Jad to give a puzzled look. "Are you sure Beryl and Alice will want one? And you're buying one for Sister Patricia Marie, and Oliver and Leeann, and Jocelyn and whatever the hunk's name is. I don't know. Seems kind of tchotchke to me."

"Oh, you're just like Barry. If it isn't a signed original, it's not good enough. He'd rather give an expensive wine. I think he was always afraid of being criticized."

"Laela, I'm not like Barry. If you think they will like these gifts, I bow to your insight."

She gave him a brilliant smile as she checked out her purchases suggesting, "We'd better get these to the car. They are much too heavy to continuously carry."

"You can't carry these. Let's settle you down over there at the ice cream shop. There are some tables. I'll order. You sit. Before you know it I'll be back."

And orders for a large chocolate sugar cone and a small frozen pudding in a dish were handed over lickety-split. Jad, balancing the cone and the purchases headed for the car. Laela watched as he struggled with his load thinking, *he is so good to me. Barry would have made me help him, telling me the walk would add to my steps for the day. Why when I'm so desolate at losing Barry do I now find fault with him? Barry was right. He knew I could easily slow down. I do think Jad is one of a kind with his thoughtfulness and kindness.*

Jad joined her and they headed for the harborside. There was to be a special tour for them. Earlier, Jad had noticed a guy holding a sign offering historic tours. He'd bought two tickets and was told there would only be six on the walking tour. He assured Jad with such a small group, they would miss nothing worth discovering. Two hours later the bedraggled couple, much smarter from their adventure, sat on a bench struggling for energy enough to return to their hotel. They passed the young tour guide and attempted to wave at him. He was involved in a discussion with a woman holding a child. The words got louder. They heard, "I don't want you to go out with her tonight. I'm tired and need help putting Jessica to bed. Look, you've gone out with your friends more than twice a week for a month. How does that look. I'll bet you haven't told your mom."

The wind changed and the words were now unintelligible. The woman walked away . She looked angry while the young man looked resigned to keeping Jessica. Jad said, "How old are they? I mean the couple. I think in the late twenties. See what I said, Laela, these women are looking for trouble, traipsing out with their friends."

"They're older than that, Jad. I think middle thirties and you don't know the circumstances. She may have been home alone with the little girl for days and needs an outlet. She can't go out with him. There's probably no money for a sitter."

"I don't agree, Laela. She's sick of her life and she's not thinking about him or the kid."

Laela mused, *I'll never forget the look on that woman's face. She looked trapped and although talking very loudly, she did not say anything to show the husband or boyfriend was anything but a decent guy. She looked corralled. She has to now live the life of responsibility. No longer is the bar scene available.*

Later after they took a short nap and a bath, Jad and Laela headed for The Landing restaurant which had been touted by their guide. The two-story structure on the water offered seating on any level both inside and outside. They looked at the gathering storm clouds and chose inside; a decision they did not regret later when a short rain cloud broke almost directly over their heads. The food and service, despite the crowd, was what Laela stated as impeccable. They finished dinner by nine and practically rushed to their rooms. Laela thought as she turned the key, *I will certainly sleep the sleep of the just tonight.*

Not true, Laela tossed and turned and did not sleep well. She rose and stepped out onto the small balcony to have a look at the harbor which she was able to see from the corner of the landing. It took her breath away. Stars twinkled. She could see boats swaying and heard people noise in the distance. Breathing the wonderful air, she caught sight of a man walking near her hotel. She thought he looked like Jad and waved but, of course, he could not see her. She checked her watch. It was four in the morning. Why would Jad be walking? *Of course it isn't him. The man's not wearing the same shirt. It's hanging out of his pants. Jad is always neatly tucked away. He is built like Jad. Ah, go back to bed.*

Breakfast on the hotel patio refreshed Laela more than her fitful sleep from the night before. Between a mouthful of eggs benedict and a sip of dark roast coffee she asked Jad, "Did you go out walking last night?"

He choked on his bite into a buttered croissant before answering, "Sorry, Laela, that bit went down the wrong way. I didn't go out last night. I don't know about you but I had the very best sleep. I needed it. Did you see someone who looked like me or wore similar clothing? And where did you see him? Were you in the lobby?"

"Although I've never been as tired as I was yesterday, I had trouble sleeping. At four a.m., I went out on my patio for some fresh air. The view was exquisite. Then I looked down at the long walkway and I could have sworn it was you. He even walked like you but he wasn't dressed like you. His shirt was hanging outside of his trousers and he looked a bit disheveled."

"Not me, Laela, I can't stand that look. It's for guys trying to hide their beer gut."

"Jad, are we going to stay another night? What are your plans? You are the driver, but I think it's beautiful here."

"I'm sorry, Laela, we have to head up to Taste of New England in Vermont or we'll miss it. After that it's time to go home unless we do a detour."

"Too bad. You've been wonderful taking care of the details of this trip other than when we had to rush from New Haven to Providence for its Food Festival. I love we were able to spend a few days there. Although your day business trip forced me to do a tour of the Zoo and eat dinner alone at Hemenway's, one of the city's nicer restaurants. That was a lonely evening although the food and service were wonderful."

"I apologize for that lonely evening." He laughed and said, "I do have other responsibilities, other than you."

"I'm so embarrassed. I didn't mean anything. You've been wonderful. It's just all this attention and realizing what a night alone means, forces me to see what my future will be like."

Jad smiled saying, "Laela, you have me, Jane, Beryl, your golfing ladies and more. You will not be alone."

They left for the trip to Vermont. Jad explained he wanted to be there for the first day dinner and the second day tasting. "Laela, this is truly going to be a sensory delight. I love perfection. And we will find perfection. We were lucky to get reservations at the Lodge at Buck Hill. That's the name of the area in I think Arlington, Vermont. We'll find out soon. Have you decided if you're ready to go home after Buck Hill?"

"I don't know if I'm ready to go home. I may be ready to stop touring. What have you arranged for yourself for next week? Me, I have nothing."

"Don't worry about me. I have a farmhouse near Lee in Massachusetts. We could stay there for a couple of days; kind of a step down in luxury travel. I am a good cook. The place is lovely. You may find it a bit remote but the view of the mountains is glorious. How does that sound?"

Laela sighed in relief. She didn't want to return on the third month anniversary of Barry's death. Her calls to Jane worried her. Jane said the police continued to visit her home. She heard them asking questions about her marriage. They were to interview Sister Patricia Marie at her convent. She thought, *what questions could they possibly have. Delilah said they think he was murdered. Nonsense. If anyone were to murder Barry, it would be Delilah. And look she's still at my house. When I go home, I'll have war with her. She is leaving, no matter what she says. Off with the witch. I don't doubt she pushed me down the stairs but I didn't tell the police. Could she have pushed Barry because he told her to leave? I have to stop these imaginings.*

Meanwhile in West Side, a disturbed Jane Aubergine was on a long telephone conversation with Beryl, who was impatient with what she thought were Jane's baseless assumptions. Jane was insistent. "I just don't like the whole shtick. Her husband is murdered and she's on a jaunt with a single man."

"Wait a minute, Jane. How does Laela know Barry was murdered? Did you tell her?"

"I couldn't keep the murder a secret any longer. She's going to extend her vacation and join Jad at his second home. Besides, she already knew. Delilah told her. Delilah's still at the house."

"When is she coming home?"

"Laela says Jad thinks the second week in September."

"Jane, what was the last festival they visited? I mean what are the dates for that festival?"

"The last one was Festival of New England in Spruce Peak, Vermont, on the 24th to the 27th. I think."

"Jad wants another two or more weeks alone in his house. Where's this house?"

"She didn't know. He said it was near Lee, Massachusetts."

"That's right near us. This is crazy. She may as well come home. What do we know about Jad? He's had one marriage. His wife died of cancer. He used to live in Connecticut. He says he won't marry again. He lives pretty large for a single guy. What did he do for a living, Jane? You must know. You live next door to him."

"I don't think he goes into work because he often goes out walking to the local for breakfast and leaves his car in the drive. I see his computer light on in his study all day and he's in there a lot. He does go out at about nine o'clock a couple of evenings each week and gets back late. I asked him about it once and he laughed it off saying it's a good ole boys group he meets with."

"Do you like him, Jane? I mean do you think he's pretty decent? Laela may not be thinking clearly now. I hate to think she's being conned by a scammer."

"Don't those guys need money? Jad clearly does not. I do like him. If I were single I'd love to be with him. He's a bit young for Laela and me. What are you going to do, investigate his past?"

"No, he sounds perfectly harmless. But he does look too good to be true."

16

A RHODE ISLAND MURDER

The trash bag lay on the side of the road in East Greenwich, Rhode Island, for approximately two days before discovery by local walkers. They'd cut out from a wooded area to cross the road. The bag was shoved on a pavement indentation. The smell was pungent enough for Jake Connelly, an undertaker's assistant, to take notice saying, "That's a rotting carcass, Honey. Don't go near it. I'll check it and call the city."

Janet aka Honey was horrified and quickly moved away. She said, "Would a hunter dare shoot an animal in the city limits, Jake? It's a big one."

Jake noticed the string tie left a two-inch opening at the top. He pulled it open and noticed blowflies already developed. The body was a woman who had knife slashes all over her torso. He could not see her face and didn't want to. Dialing 911, he saw his hands shaking. He'd seen many dead bodies but never like this.

Detective Louis Strong appeared to Jake to be the lead detective. He asked them questions on what he called the find. He appeared to be inured to the horror of the discovery, acting as if this was an everyday occurrence. Jake thought, *even police detectives don't see this every day. He's putting on a show.*

Janet was sobbing and saying her rosary. Jake had forgotten death brought out prayer in his wife. He went over and hugged her while watching the cynicism displayed by the apparently in control police and coroner. He also noticed the traffic jam on this two-lane highway caused by the discovery of the body. Detective Strong could be heard by Jake speaking on his cell, saying, "We've been hit by that serial killer. This woman was raped and stabbed multiple times. Get the FBI in here. They're already on these cases as linked together. I had lunch with Bob Alcore who's an old friend yesterday. He's the FBI agent in charge of these cases. Bob gave me a summary of a whole lot of murders, each one claiming one of two suspected motives. This one reeks of the more violent motive. Didn't expect to see his words in action so soon. I need Connelly from the state's team. He's the best on crime scene details. I don't want to be on TV someday as the detective who missed something important."

A fellow detective approached him. "Lieutenant Strong, we think she's Nora Daly. She's pretty popular for her kindness in sharing her body. They say she was a looker. I can't tell from all these slashes."

"Are you certain it's her, Sergeant? There hasn't been time for a return of the fingerprints. Oops, here they are and you are right on the button. How'd you find out?"

"Her boyfriend is right over there. He's been looking for her since he phoned in a missing person. He described her."

"Bring him on over. Someone has to do this."

The boyfriend, Chet Mazeriewski, had tears in his eyes. His story was Nora left home at eight in the evening three nights before and never came home. When asked where she was going Chet said he didn't know; to work he thought. Strong appeared nonplussed before asking, "Where did Nora work?"

"I don't know. She said she'd been hassled by an old boyfriend once and decided she would not share her work and travel with any future boyfriend. She'd leave for work three nights in a row on Thursday through Saturday and come home around four in the morning. Occasionally she'd get home later. She got paid under the table."

Strong questioned, "Was your relationship with Nora a serious one? I mean you don't seem upset you didn't even know where she was working."

"You'd have to know Nora. She was beautiful and easygoing with just a few rules. She was smart, really mechanical, and could fix anything. We talked about marriage. She found it difficult to trust. You know, a pretty lady like Nora met a lot of bums along the way."

The Lieutenant thought, *I've met some dumb ones along the way but Chet takes the cake. He's in for a surprise.*

Strong said, "What clothes was she wearing when she left for work?"

"Nora's younger than me and her dressing mimics the gals on television revealing more than any woman I knew growing up. But she's not flirty. It's just her style. She had jeans with holes in the thighs and frayed in the back so you could almost but not quite see her behind and a short top baring her midriff and a short silky coat. She looked good."

"What type of work do you think she was doing?"

"She was good at computers, really, really good. I think she may have been on a night shift for some company doing repairs. She could lay line and all that stuff I don't know about."

"Chet, did she go to college?"

"Yes, but dropped out after three years. She meant to go back. Not going to happen now."

And Chet cried leaving the stone-hearted Lieutenant awash with shame thinking, *who am I to tell this guy his girlfriend was a hooker? Do I even know for sure? He'll find out tomorrow when the news comes out. I can't stop it. Women. My ex plays around but she's not a hooker or at least I never thought of her that way. I wonder if there's a difference or is it just money transactions that make us think it's a sin.*

Jake and Janet Halloway were allowed to leave after giving their particulars to a detective. They decided to head home to West Side. They couldn't wait to tell their friends about this terrible murder.

Lieutenant Strong did not take Chet in for a formal interrogation. He said, "Chet, come down the station later. I need a signed witness statement. Could you bring a photo of Nora and a list of her close friends with phone numbers and addresses?"

The Coroner, Bennie Case, said, "What happened to you. You're supposed to be amongst the meanest of detectives. You let a significant other who says he doesn't know what, where, or how his girlfriend works go. You need a brain scan."

"Probably do. This guy's a sucker for sure. You and I know this matches those serial murders and believe me Chet is not a serial killer. I know it looks like an up close passionate domestic kind of thing. Chet hasn't that in him. No anger, no misleading is in him."

It wasn't Janet who first exploded with her finding a dead body news. Jake was the first to show up at work the next day. His main job was as a social worker working with the homeless. He'd hit the feeding for homeless sites and invited patrons to come in out of the streets. That often meant getting them to the drying out sites first. The long-term housing site for the homeless stipulated no person who was drunk or disorderly could be on the campus. Other diners at the pantries were sober and waiting for him to connect. He thought at times it was grueling work. Today he had other more important things on his mind. He had been taken back at the sight of the mutilated body they had discovered the previous day. He'd told Janet it was one thing to know bad things happen, it was quite another to witness the damage done. He thought, *the women at the pantry trust me. I'll try to tell them what I've witnessed. Tell them to be extra careful. It's why I work so hard to get clients into homeless shelters or at the least into a sobering up clinic. I think they'll listen to me. I can visit four pantries today and three more tomorrow. I don't know what more I can do.*

And he made himself very busy. Busy enough for Beryl, who was on duty this day, to notice. She moved herself to be close enough to hear some of the conversation. Enough for her to hear about the murdered woman. She asked Jake, "You and Janet discovered a murdered woman; where, when?"

Beryl reacted after hearing three pertinent phrases, industrial garbage bag, side of two-lane highway and stabbed multiple times. She motioned for Jake to join her and as gently as she could in spite of her excitement drilled him on the specifics of his discovery. Since he was already aware this killing may be the work of a serial murderer, he was not surprised she had heard of another such case.

Meanwhile, Janet Halloway was at work at the high school. At the first break she held court in the teacher's room. Mona was late for a coffee because a young student was in crisis over a disappointing grade. As she entered the breakroom she was thinking, *the most difficult job here is to give an A student a B. Even good students have a bad day. Try telling the student there are some difficult questions that require logic not just studying and remembering facts.* Then Mona's attention was diverted to, "And the body was disgusting with dark blood wounds from a knife, I think. Imagine stuffed in a garbage bag by the road..."

"What are you talking about? What body? Knifed? I heard nothing about it."

Janet answered, "Mona, it will be on television soon. It happened in East Greenwich, Rhode Island. Jake and I were hiking in the woods near a highway and found a body. There's a serial killer out there. He hasn't hit West Side yet but maybe we're next."

Janet went on to describe every aspect of the scene. The other teachers were not surprised. Janet taught English and vividly describing any event in detail and remembering those details was her particular expertise. Mona actually took notes. Impressed, Janet said, "Maybe Rudy would want to know about this."

Mona quickly answered, "I'm certain he's received notice of this, but I'll tell him you are a witness. He may want to know more from a witness, but it's not West Side, Janet."

The two, Mona and Beryl, arrived simultaneously at the West Side Police Station. Beryl asked, "Mona, did you hear what I heard about the murder in Rhode Island? It's just now on the news. Jake and Janet found the body yesterday. Why did it take so long for the press to release it?"

"Yes, I'm here to give Rudy notes on Janet's finding the body. It's related to the one in Boston's North End. At least, I think so. Have you called Oliver and Leeann yet? They'll know specifics."

"Not yet. I was shocked to learn they found the body and on their honeymoon. Nate and I met them for dinner when their flight to Bermuda was cancelled. I know it's important for Rudy to know. Laela told Jane Aubergine about a body found in New Haven with some matching details. Smacks as serial killing to me."

Captain Beauregard greeted his wife and Beryl with some hesitation asking, "What do you ladies have for me today. Don't ask for donations to the library of the food pantry or the church, that's Mona's domain. She only comes to me out of guilt when she wants to donate too much. Is that why you're here today, Mona?"

Mona caused Rudy to stop wisecracking by saying one word – murder. She went through every word Janet Halloway had said; both Beauregard and Beryl were impressed with her memory. Detailed notes may have helped her, but here there was no denying her skilled recital. Beauregard called Lieutenant Smith asking about incoming murder reports for the day. Several minutes later, Mason brought in a murder sheet from Rhode Island saying, "Looks like another one, Captain. I know the lead detective if you need more info. We went to camp together, me from the inner city on special scholarship and him from a famous Rhodie family. His mom had an interest in that jewelry family business. They made class rings. Don't even know if they have that business now. He's a good kid although he was always a perfectionist."

"Get the file from Alcore. We'll use your relationship later if we have the need."

Turning to the ladies, Beauregard thanked him using what Mona would call his distant professional voice. Annoyed, Mona chastised him. "A little more of your true self could show your appreciation, rather than this cold thank you which means get out of my office; we detectives have important work to do."

Rudy's face had the grace to redden as he profusely apologized again. Noted with some slight satisfaction on her face, Mona moved to leave. Beryl did not. She said, "I'm not wedded to you, Rudy, and I have no guilt about wanting to know more. My son and his wife are witnesses to the murder in Boston. I discovered the homeless body and knew Barry. I'm involved and intend to stay involved. Further, Laela saw the family looking for their daughter in the Connnecticut murder and was unnerved. We absolutely have a vested interest in a solution."

Rudy sighed. "I see your point, but this is a police investigation, not a citizen nor a witness investigation. One-way street here as you know, Beryl. You give me information. It's not the other way around. I can't tell you anything yet as I know nothing. Now please get out of here."

The ladies left only to have a discussion outside the station. Mona said, "We did good. He may be upset with me but he now has a lead in Janet and Jake's witness statements. What else can we do?"

Beryl's reply was, "I don't know but will figure something out. I'll let you know."

Driving away, Beryl remembered the strangulation weapon used on the women and its similarity to what was used on her homeless man. "It just can't be a coincidence," she said aloud.

She thought, *Barry's death was from a fall and maybe a blow to the head. That method of killing doesn't compute as a match. Then again, it may be a crime of necessity. Who could have murdered him? Somebody had access to the house. Delilah and Laela were already there. No, it can't be them. Certainly not Laela. Jane Aubergine and Jad Morton came later to the parade. Everyone agrees they came later, but did one of them come earlier and didn't tell. That's farfetched even for me. They'd have to have keys. I can find out. Could Laela kill her husband? I need to know more about their relationship. I bet Delilah would deliver her sister to hell. Meanwhile, I must know more about her. Is she always daft or just about Laela?*

Beryl met Nate for dinner at a small restaurant in Holyoke called Amadeo's. Noted for its homey feel and Italian cuisine, and despite it being a family restaurant, it was quiet enough to allow for two hours of talking. Nate did not try to fluff her off. His interest encouraged her to tell him all her concerns. Like her, he did not think Laela and Jane were involved in Barry's death but said, "Never should we ignore possibilities. It wouldn't hurt to check their backgrounds although I can't see either as a murderer. Neither could have lifted the bodies, put them in a sack, and placed them on the side of the road. We can check the murder dates. Laela is tied up with Jad and it would be pretty damn difficult near to impossible for her to be implicated in the serial murders."

"What was I thinking? Not guilty in serial murdering, but maybe guilty of killing Barry."

"Beryl, you don't really think Laela killed her husband. You are just afraid. On another note, I'm flying to London tomorrow to meet a man who says he knew your husband Joel. Maybe we'll have closure soon."

"Oh, Nate, I'm afraid to know."

17

NONE SOLVED

Laela and Jad drove quietly in the lovely Litchfield County through small towns. Laela thought she loved Greenwich with its mansions but this county offered sites and waterfalls and New England woods that would feed her heart for many years. They stopped at a great earthy crunchy restaurant near Suffield Academy. Laela enjoyed Jad's conversation and the lunch. He told her stories about the military. She expressed surprise. "Jad, I was an Army Brat. Somehow I didn't detect military vibes from you. I always know. That fact alone, knowing it, somehow softens your perfection as the perfect gentleman. I feel more in touch with you."

"Military does give experience, Laela, but it's not all good. I've met some nasty guys there. Generally, as you know, I don't talk about my history in the Army."

"Wrong again, I'm wrong again. I would have taken you for Navy with all its swanky uniforms."

"No, Army all the way from West Point to Intelligence Specialist. I stayed for many years. I decided enough was enough. Left for a good position in IT and left that to join a friend in our own military consulting business. Still do some of that."

"I'm fascinated, Jad, tell me more."

"Nope, I don't talk about my business. Let's talk about you. Are you ready to go to my place in Richmond?"

"Richmond, I thought you said Lee?"

"It's only about 18 miles from Lee, but it's a much wealthier town topping 105th wealthiest zip codes in the country. Shocking since nobody's heard about the town."

"Really! How'd you find the house? I mean who'd look for a house there. I'd look in Lee or Stockbridge."

"That's a long story. I bought it from an older man who was dying. Someone I'd known for years. I had to make an instant decision. He didn't want his only son who lived in California to have it. Family problems made for a quick sale."

"I can't wait to see it."

"You'll love it. It's on top of a ridge looking over ten acres of farmland. It has two barns, one small and a larger one. The view is spectacular."

Laela was now excited. She drifted the conversation over to a review of their trip. Forgotten was her hesitancy over his judgements about women. Laela regaled the sights they saw, the hotels stayed in, and particularly both the familiar but better fast food, gourmet entrees, and ice cream. She oozed appreciation for him. And he appeared to love her accolades. Quieting down, she thought, *he is so easygoing. We've gone everywhere I've wanted and done practically everything I wanted to do. Barry would never have put up with all of this. It has been the best trip in my life and I'm not sick of anything. He even sneaked out and did my laundry four times. The woman who gets him is one lucky lady. I haven't thought about Barry in two days. What kind of a woman am I? I bury my husband who was a good man and now I've forgotten him. I know Jane wondered how I could go off like this. I must be the most selfish woman on the planet. Oh, I pray not to be alone again.*

They stopped at a grocery store in Lee to stock up for a few days. She noticed he chose only the best of everything. Laela attempted to pay for the groceries and when he said no she tried to pay for half. It was a no-go. Confused her offer was misunderstood she changed the subject and said, "I don't see you leave West Side, and yet everyone knows you. You must get here often."

Jad said, "It's only a little over an hour away from West Side and at night it takes less time. I can breathe up here. There's no pressure. I drive up here often."

"Why don't you move permanently here?"

His answer was, "So many questions from you, my pretty lady. I would not have met you if I didn't live in West Side."

Laela could feel herself blush. She checked her phone and pulled up a map locating Richmond, Massachusetts. She exclaimed, "I've been to some of these places and didn't know I was about five miles away from Richmond. Look, Jad, Hancock Shaker Village. I spent a whole day there. Tanglewood, I have season's tickets. Norman Rockwell Museum, Barry and I went to an auction there. I bought one of Rockwell's artist's proof prints. And the Yoga Center. Oh my, you're in the middle of the best of art and entertainment."

"Of course, Laela, I wouldn't just live anywhere. West Side also has some great attributes. It's near many colleges and universities. The Springfield Museum of Arts is a showstopper as well at Sturbridge Village, let's not forget the casino, Irish culture at the Elms College and the Irish Cultural Center, Springfield's Italian and now its Puerto Rican and Black communities are profiling their arts. I haven't mentioned their history in athletics as home of basketball. People don't appreciate what's around them. They denigrate their own environments and always seeing the 'grass is greener over there.'"

"But why, Jad, do you have two homes within an hour of each other?"

Jad answered with a smile, "I guess, Laela, there are two sides of my personality. This way I can satisfy all my cravings."

Beauregard's review of about fifty files on periphery of the serial murders locations created just a little anxiety in his detectives. As they worked the phones on current inquiries, he sat glued to a chair in the squad room glancing at times to the list of commonalities on the murder board. His eyes darted between an open file and the board. Lazily, he dragged his body to change a fact on the board. They read the correction. Rarely would a fact be corrected because facts are facts. But this revision clicked in their minds. "Why did I not see that?" Typical of the Captain to see what should be seen but often was overlooked. The change was on location. It was not enough to see the areas where the crimes took place. He saw a connection to events. Lieutenant Aylewood-Locke asked, "How'd you find the events, Captain?"

He smiled. "When I saw three of the murders took place in New England, I spot checked Florida and other Southern state murders. I could easily find seven near events, another eight near Disney, Busch Gardens, Lego Park, and more. Enough to convince me it is not coincidental."

Lieutenant Smith said, "So he's a nut that likes theme parts. Doesn't narrow the suspect list down, Captain. That's half of the U.S."

"Lieutenant, once we get a suspect list, what do theme parks have that will help us?"

Sergeant Flores jumped in. "Cameras are everywhere, and they keep track of everyone who enters. Given a time of the murders, we can backtrack to the park admission. Can AI help us on this one?"

The Captain answered, "Don't know, ask and get help."

Sergeant Tagliano, always the Doubting Thomas double checking, said, "The Captain's right. I just found all six recent murders in New England occurred near events, but they were yearly events, not theme parks. These are much more difficult to know about. We'd have to google to prove our premise."

Sergeant Flores said, "No need, Lilly. We make an audit assumption. You know, test a few and assign to all. Right, Captain?"

The Captain harrumphed in agreement. He continued to work on each file thinking, *what do theme parks or amusement parks mean to this joker. The ones murdered in New England were mostly just strangled with the exception of the one in Rhode Island. Why was she raped and mutilated and the other five just strangled? Need to check on her background.*

Rudy charged Sergeant Torrington, "I want the victim in the Rhode Island murder background checked giving details of every moment before her murder. His decision to rape her is based on some fact that influenced his decision shortly before her murder."

He turned to the other detectives present in the room and said, "What do we know about our West Side victims? You've chased down Barry Greer and the homeless man, but I'm thinking of the other victims of Barry's murder such as Laela, her sister Delilah, the neighbors Jane and Jad. What do we really know about them? We've been remiss on these inquiries. Get on it."

Sergeants Bill Barr and Bobby Border each grabbed a folder. Bill took Delilah because he didn't like her and Bobby took Laela because he did like her. Juan tussled with Petra and they agreed to work Jad's investigation together, while Lilly agreed to talk with Jane Aubergine. The phone calls began as appointments for the following day brightened the listing next to the murder board.

Lieutenant Mason Smith decided to play footsie with an old Army buddy, Joe Hodge. Joe had retired from the service over ten years ago as a non-com, but his Army life had been spent doing what Joe was best at doing; he was and is a natural at self-marketing. His habit of discovering who was the best 'go-to person' for any question was legendary both when he was in and out of the service. Mason knew his old buddy and also was aware that getting information would take almost the whole day. Hodge was a talker raised in the good-ole boy South. Difference was, he is black and better at the laid-back give and take of negotiations. Mason thought, *it's a test for me, but I'll prevail. I'll buy lunch, but may have to also buy supper. The guy is noted for stalling just to get a cup of coffee. He'll know I need him.*

Mason called his friend Lionel, the Locator. He knew where most folks in the hood may be sitting at this time of the day. Lionel would never tell anyone who he located. An hour later assisted by Lionel's directions, Mason stopped at a dive on Boston Road in East Springfield. He ordered a sweet tea which was fabulous and waited while reading a book called "The Black Experience in America."

"Ain't the same as you experienced Brother. Black police officers who make lieutenant ain't got much in common with us in the hood."

"Hi there Hodge. What're you doing here. It's out of your area."

"The Hood is expanding, pal. It's now in Longmeadow and Wilbraham, granted with smaller roots, but they all remember."

And as Mason thought later, *the bullshit continued for an hour over sweet tea.*

When Mason thought the time was ripe, he suggested lunch offering Joe his choice. Since Hodge was noted both by his girth and his tastes for eating only at the best restaurants his choices were limited. Unfortunately, his favorite gastronomical sites did not open for lunch. He settled for Maxx's Tavern. Mason groaned thinking, *$46 for the really good sirloin steak. I better get reimbursed for this.*

The ambience of the restaurant with its crowd and masculine steak house feel settled Joe Hodge into a cloud of memories of the old days in different cities. Mason let him talk and their food was served giving Joe another use for his mouth other than speaking. Left with a welcome silence, Mason filled it with questions mainly directed to Joe's current connections with access to file information on former military personnel. Joe's eating slowed. He wiped his chin and looked up saying, "What's this, Bro? You know there are proper police channels to ask for this stuff?"

"Yes, I do, but they won't work on this case. I've no person of interest and requests for fishing are either too slow or will be denied."

"Tell me your story. I'll decide."

Left with no alternative and a big luncheon bill, Mason asked him how difficult it would be to search military records on retirees. There were at least three and maybe five of interest. Hodge asked, "What do you need: name, personal history, where stationed, work, evaluation on separation, dates on all, etc.?"

Mason nodded and was told to give him a list of names. Hodge glanced at the names and said, "I know two of these guys. They're big and the files will be out of my league. I have a friend who can get those. Gonna cost you another dinner, big guy."

They finished their lunch, shook hands and agreed to meet on the following Monday.

18

THE PAST

Nate negotiated with Atelier on the location for dinner in Munich. The menu offered from Atelier's selection of restaurants ran the gamut of a variety of choices and was not totally confined to a German palate. Atelier was of mixed heritage which Nate thought might be Swiss, Arab and Spanish. He made a surprisingly successful living as a contractor for the U.S. military and many other countries for construction needs located outside their countries. To say he was not the normal construction contractor was a modest take on the guy. And unlike most construction contractors who'd developed an aggressive attitude from working with the trades, Atelier was almost effete in his personal behavior. They settled on a lovely private dining room called the Pfistermuhle. Nate thought, *sure, he picks a four-star place. Can't blame him. He knows the game. He gives me assistance no one else will and thinks an expensive meal is chickenfeed for payment.*

Once settled with drinks and a first course of some type or pork infused with orange liqueur and dotted with pistachios, Atelier asked, "Nate, you've gone way out of your way to locate this guy. The find either pays well or it's a big favor for someone. I'm curious. You see you've left a trail behind you. Not like you at all, I say. I figure you were so hungry for info, you deliberately didn't cover your tracks. You have my interest."

Pausing before answering, Nate said, "It's a big favor for someone who would return the favor in a heartbeat."

"Not the wife, Nate? Are you involved finally? If so, this is my wedding gift."

Atelier laughed and his laughter was deep and happy sounding. He said, "Your guy is dead. He was picked up by the North Koreans from a private yacht in the East China Sea. The excuse for stopping was drugs and apparently there were drugs on board. The Captain did not send signals out about the stop. Word got out later from the sailors onboard. The problem is this yacht was on its regular drug run. It's never been stopped before. The heads say the Captain told North Korea an American agent was on board. I don't know why your man would have taken this ship. He must have been in a corner. He was executed without a public trial two years later. We know from a hostage exchange five years ago."

"Why wouldn't the State Department tell his widow? And who paid her such a large amount of money?"

"He did good work and some in the government felt guilty. Joel should never have taken the job in the first place. He was one of those red, white, and blue Yanks who would do anything for his country. I knew him, you know. He was golden. This whole thing is shameful. We knew he was there but couldn't admit it, so we let him die."

"Atelier, how do I know this is the truth?"

"I've no evidence except for this. He gave it to the hostage who left. She smuggled it out. Don't know how, but she did it."

What he handed Nate was a partially mangled picture of a younger Beryl and two kids. With tears in his eyes, Nate said, "She'll believe this. He must have been crazy about her."

"Looks like she's got another one infected with love."

Jane Aubergine attempted to reach Mona Beauregard by phone before realizing Mona was teaching at the high school. Jane felt paralyzed by her fears for Laela expressing loudly at the quiet phone, "I have to talk to someone. This is getting out of hand."

Jane called Beryl who was enjoying a light lunch with Amore, her dog. Rather, Amore was enjoying some of Beryl's lunch. Tuna was the puppy's favorite sandwich. Beryl heard the tension in Jane's voice and said, "Has something gone wrong? How is your family? Is it that nutty member of the Library Board creating havoc again?"

Jane replied in the negative for all her questions. She said, "I think Laela's gone nuts. That concussion she got from her fall down the stairs has left her not thinking straight and I don't know what to do about it. Don't tell me I'm the nutty one. Laela repeated herself several times, to the point that I was almost nauseous."

Beryl laughed saying, "It can't be that bad. Laela is sensible. We did not see any adverse reaction other than a few stitches and black and blue from the fall. Tell me what she said that so disturbed you."

"Jad is so wonderful. She must have said it twelve times. He holds the door and my chair for me all the time. He never misses. He remembers all my likes and dislikes. When he gets me my coffee early in the mornings he seems to know when I would like espresso vs Americano. He takes a sip to make sure it's not too hot. Only once did he disagree with me over my purchase of Christmas presents for you all. He thought they were too tacky. He is quite morally straight-laced. Much more than Barry was. He is entertaining and willing to try anything. I'm telling you, Beryl, she's enamored with him. I want her home so she can calm her brain and, yes, I think her hormones. She should know better."

Beryl replied, "Jane, she is lonely. She's getting much needed attention while she deals with this great personal loss. Cut her some slack."

"Beryl, this is one time you're wrong. The guy got wacked out over a husband and wife dispute and said women get what they're looking for when they have affairs. I don't like any of this. Will you give her a call and knock some sense into her? Laela's at his lodge and who knows what's going on there. He could be feeding her drugs for all I know to keep her there."

Jane continued what Beryl thought was an ambush on Jad's character for another twenty minutes before Beryl could cut the conversation with, "I'll call her. Do not worry, Jane."

Laela lounged on a chaise by the enormous window in Jad's Berkshire home lolling under a warm L.L. Bean throw. The raindrops bouncing off the rails of the veranda outside were comforting to her. She thought, *I didn't want to come here and now I never want to leave. Imagine having someone so attentive to my needs. He is also a wonderful conversationalist. Jane thinks I'm crazy. She doesn't understand.*

Jad interrupted her meanderings and served from a silver carafe a cup of coffee. The aroma filled her nostrils making her sniff and laugh, saying, "Jad, thank you. I was just about to doze off, but I don't want to. Come sit and talk to me for a moment. Please!"

And they talked about nature, the beauty of the rain, his home, his allowing her to really rest. He discussed his view she needed several months to grieve over the loss of her husband, saying, "We are not all the same, Laela, but it took me quite a long time to get back to normal after my wife's death. Don't push it. I know what you need."

"I keep thinking about those dead women; the ones killed by the serial murderer. At least Barry didn't die that way. Imagine the struggle for their family's losses, mothers, fathers, sisters, brothers, children. What a horror show one person has created for society."

Jad cursed saying, "It's life, Laela. We don't have to live it. It's not healthy for you to obsess."

"I'm not obsessing."

And her cell phone rang. Laela greeted Beryl with laughter. "I'm so pleased to hear from you. Jad and I were having a moment looking at beautiful rain fall on the foliage. How are you?"

In an attempt to channel a soft connection to Laela, Beryl chatted in a light-hearted fashion. The conversation included questions about Laela's trip. Laela enthused about every detail and Jad. Jad, this. Jad, that. Beryl thought, *this is why Jane was concerned. Laela's acting like a lovestruck teenager. Could she be in love so soon after Barry's death? Does she realize there are questions Beauregard wants to ask her? Should I tell her and ruin her happiness? Jane thinks she's under Jad's Pygmalion spell. It's not that. There are no social differences. She thinks he's trying to take advantage of her grief to get her under his thumb.*

Laela continued with her saga and ended with her determination to stay a few more weeks with Jad at his wonderful home. This was way too much for Beryl who said, "Laela, you have enjoyed several months of relaxation. I think it was necessary for you. You were so overwhelmed, but you are needed here at home. I miss you. We all miss you. And the police need an additional interview with you. I'm surprised they haven't called you."

"Mona's husband's office did call. I didn't answer. Jad doesn't think it's healthy for me to discuss these matters. He thinks it's too early. Beryl, I didn't tell anyone but I think Delilah pushed me down the stairs. I'm afraid to confront her. She's still at my house. She called me and said she's going to stay with me for a year while I adjust to Barry's loss. I haven't told Jad. I'm telling you now because he is out of the room."

"Why would you not have told Rudy? You could have died from the fall."

"She's my sister and she's under great stress. I don't want to face her yet. I have to tell her to leave when I do get home. I'll be ready then."

Beryl quickly answered, "No, Laela, you need to come home now. This cannot be let go. Did you actually see Delilah push you?"

"Well no, but I heard the squish of her athletic shoes. They make this funny sound. And when she pushed me I heard her grunt. It was her. Beryl. I'm not telling the police. I'm not putting my sister in jail. I know she's got mental issues, but she is still my sister."

Beryl had a larger point to make. "Captain Beauregard wants to talk to you about Barry's death. He doesn't think his death was an accident. He's redoing interviews and looking into everyone's backgrounds."

"Delilah would not kill Barry. She hates me, not Barry. This is awful. I can't tell Rudy about her now. He'll railroad her into being a killer. She didn't mean to hurt me when she pushed me. I know it."

"Laela, please think straight. You don't know who killed Barry. Rudy doesn't know either, but he must follow all the evidence. Whether you like it or not, Delilah showed a violent side when she pushed you. You don't know if she pushed Barry. She certainly had motive. He was throwing her out of the house. Regardless of your tendency to protect your sister and the family's reputation, someone killed your husband. He was a good man. You must come home and sort this matter out. Now!"

Beryl was adamant in her tone and voice, which must have struck a chord with Laela who cried but finally agreed to return home by the weekend. Although successful in her quest, Beryl did not feel good about getting Laela to return to West Side. She thought, *I hope she won't end up in depression. She does sound fragile and her glowing description of Jad and their tour bordered on the irrational for a woman of her age. Oh, what do I know? Do I really know Laela or her past life? We have never had a conversation that got personal. She normally holds her experiences close to her chest. Now she's all gushy about this man, I don't like too much attention given by a man to a woman. It's like getting three dozen roses. That gift makes you think he's done something really wrong. I should be fair. I'd love attention to be given to me on a daily basis, but this is three months holed up with a guy who agrees to do whatever you want with no strings attached. Sounds like misogynistic foreplay to me. I've got to call Norbie Cull. I need legal advice. I don't think I can withhold Delilah's attack on Laela. Norbie will tell me and if he has to go to Rudy with the info, he'll get Rudy to understand the importance of Delilah to Laela.*

Attorney Norberto Cull was enjoying a typical weekday lunch at the 350 Grill in Springfield. The food was always good and the service was quick. He looked up from his lunch to find Beryl. "May I join you? I'm starving."

He rose while she sat. "How did you find me? I'll bet Sheila told you."

"Small chance for that, Norbie. She is the original 'I know nothin' girl. Have you forgotten I've had lunch with you, Rudy, and Nate here before? I figured from the way the staff treated you the last time, you were a regular."

Beryl ordered and while she waited for her lunch, she dumped her fears to Norbie's ears. He asked several questions, mostly about Beryl's interpretation to the veracity of Laela's account. He responded, "Thanks a lot, Beryl. You have now handed me a witness statement to an attempted murder. I am an officer of the court. You also have a duty not to interfere in a police investigation. What do you expect from me?"

She waited for a moment. "I'm uncertain as to how to answer you, Norbie. You've never questioned me like this. It's obviously good I've come to you. It is a legal problem and I guess it's a bigger issue for you now that I've told you. I didn't mean to put you in a difficult position. I just wanted your advice."

Norbie said, "Eventually Rudy will find out. Laela could never withstand scrutiny under an interrogation. I think you know that. You don't want to betray your friend so you tell me knowing I will inform Rudy. Sneaky, Beryl, and not like you."

"Norbie, I didn't think it out. I knew I had responsibility but I honestly did not intend to ensnare you. I promise. Please understand, I would never knowingly cause you a problem. I have such respect for you. Do not tell your wife, Norbie. Sheri and I are such good friends."

Norbie laughed and suggested dessert for them both.

The Desk Sergeant buzzed Beauregard. He said Attorney Norberto Cull was on his way up the stairs. Norbie must have taken the stairs two at a time because he entered Rudy's office before the Captain had time to shut his cell call. "It's four in the afternoon. Isn't this happy hour at some legal bar? What are you doing here? It's got to be to create havoc for me. You're not here to invite me for a game of golf, are you? Still some warm days left."

"Nope, I've some information for you, but I don't want you to run away with it. It'd be too easy to think this but, I can think how easy to use it as a solution. I don't think it is."

"Forget the legal slow down, Norbie, spit it out."

"Before I do, don't ask me how I know. Bargain?"

"Get on with it."

Norbie slowly shared that Laela thought Delilah shoved her down the stairs. He reinforced that Laela did not believe Delilah would have done that to Barry. She had several reasons including Delilah's fear of men. Laela would not tell Rudy this because she thinks he would misinterpret it. Norbie said a carefully constructed police interview would get the statement from Laela without her knowing the police already knew. Norbie said, "Please don't search for who gave me the info."

Beauregard had a smug grin on his face. "Beryl Kent is the only one who could have gotten that info. She's butting in again."

"It could have been Mona. That was Laela's first call, but she was in class. So, she called Beryl next."

Rudy said, "I get it. You think Laela's right about her sister, but you had to tell me what she thought to clear your conscience. Typical lawyer."

"Rudy, I've met Delilah and I agree she's a poor excuse for a sister. I don't think she would have even tried to push Barry. He was a big man. She'd be afraid to do that. Did she have motive and the answer is clear; as is the opportunity was available. I still don't think she did it. Call it gut, but there it is."

Beauregard went into a long tirade and ended with asking why should he reward the Kent woman or Norbie with polite discretion. "Rudy, don't be a stubborn cop. Beryl is never not going to be in your hair. First, to give her credit, she's everywhere and sees what you and I frankly don't see. You get uptight when info flows from other than the police. Myopic of you. Get over it. Mona would be the first to tell you about how sweetness gets more than vinegar."

"You idiot, that's not the saying. Okay, I'll give it a go. Now get out of here if you're not inviting me for golf."

"Gladly, I have only so much time for grumpy curmudgeons."

19

MOVEMENT

"Jad, I've told Beryl I'm coming home tomorrow. Now, please don't react. I am homesick and Captain Beauregard wants to question me again. If I don't come home, he'll send an officer here. I don't want to spoil this beautiful retreat with police business."

She continued to talk but was interrupted. "That's nonsense. Barry died from a fall. What's there to question? I don't want you to go. Laela, you just told me how well you were feeling. Let the Captain wait. You don't need a stressful interview now. Beryl should know better than to pressure you."

"Jad, Jane wanted me home. She must have called Beryl. I have to go. Please understand."

Jad left the room in a hurry startling Laela into yelling, "Don't be like that, Jad. Please. I have to take care of business. I can't have you so protective. I won't be able to face my life."

She heard his car peel off at a high speed. Now looking alert for the first time this day, Laela headed for the kitchen to make a snack. She had not been in the kitchen before and was surprised at the organization. Drawers, and there were many, were labelled with their contents in script writing. The cabinets were all lined with rubber mats perfectly fitted. Every item stored had its own place. She remembered her own kitchen which she thought was in pristine condition, but could not compare to this kitchen. The floor was in Italian tile with mosaic designs in some places. Laela mused, *he is OCD. So, what, everyone has a flaw. Knowing this is not a surprise when there was never a mistake on arrangements he made throughout our trip. Barry often botched in his planning. He'd forget to call ahead and confirm. I'm not certain I could live with this much perfection. I'd be afraid to make even small changes.*

Laela opened the fridge and found an appetizing looking salad ready make. It was too big for one person. She placed half on the English bone china plate, added a prepared citrus dressing which was one of her favorites and set it on the table while she got ice and seltzer and cut a piece of French bread. Normally, Laela would tear a piece of French bread, not slice it, but today, in this kitchen, she thought better of it. She settled down to eat her lunch when Jad entered and said, "Laela, let me get you a placemat and a cloth napkin. I'm pleased you appear to like my salad I made for us. I'd join you but I'm not hungry."

"The lunch is delicious and I was hungry. This is a lovely kitchen, but it's so perfectly kept, I was afraid I'd make a mess."

"Don't be silly. You don't know how to be messy."

"Yes, I do. I could never keep up to this level of perfection."

"I'd be quite forgiving of any level of mess you could make. Listen, I have a plan. I'll take you home today with the caveat we return this weekend for a week or two of calm. You'll need it after the Captain's interview, which will bring back all your old fears. What do you say?"

"I can do that. Thank you, Jad. I know you were unhappy with my going back."

"I don't think the stress right now will be helpful, but what must be done must be done."

The Westfield Police Station was cooking today. News about a dead girl found in a garbage bag over on Route 20 not only enraged residents about safety concerns but opened up gossip from those who knew about the serial murderer. The body's location and the closeness to his city of West Side drew Beauregard's immediate attention. The word was out everywhere in Hampden County. Before Rudy could call his counterpart in Westfield he received most of the facts on the murder site from his dear friend and Medical Examiner Gerald Simpson. He reviewed the conversation mentally, *Rudy, it's like the other ones. I talked with three guys in Westfield. This one is just strangled. I know you asked me about what I'd heard from my friends out and about. You were interested in aspects of the weapons used and DNA possibilities on six of the latest murders. I called on them all. This is the same, Rudy, the same perp. The perp understands a lot about investigations because the scenes are perfectly clean. There is, according to Westfield, a depression on this body's face. Looks like it's from a handprint; well mostly a palm print. Don't know how this helps. There's nothing on the perp to even try a match.* Rudy had answered rather cynically maybe the perp would make an error in the next ten murders. He regretted his sarcasm immediately.

The squad room buzzing stopped when the Captain entered. There was not a scheduled meeting and the Captain when he'd conference with one or all would normally announce he would be coming. Sergeant Border asked, "What's up, Captain? You heard about the woman in the garbage bag already?"

Beauregard said, "Yup. Sergeant, the whole world knows about it and you'll be getting calls. That road practically borders West Side. Do we have any data from cameras to intersecting roads going to West Side from West Springfield to Westfield?"

Lieutenant Aylewood-Locke questioned, "You don't think the perp is from here?"

"The center of the last six and now seven sites where bodies were found could be reasonably traced to here as a center of a circle. Call Lieutenant Lent from Traffic. He'll be able to get video from the cross streets and Route 20 in Westfield and West Springfield. It may not help now, but could in the future if we ever get a line on the vehicle he's using."

Border laughed. "He could be using ten different vehicles. Have Sergeant Lent check stolen car, trucks, and vans."

Nodded heads in a yes were everywhere. Lieutenant Ashton Lent, a former colleague in MCU, when elevated in grade, was required to serve in another area or shift based on need. That need at the time was in traffic. He continued to serve extraordinarily, often of great help to his former friends in MCU.

Beauregard explained the depression on the victim's face, asking their thoughts about how it got there. He said, "This guy has not ever made a mistake and now there is a handprint or at least a palm print on the face. Does he wear fine gloves and the print show lines on it or is it just black and blue from pressure? If it actually shows lines from a hand, he has been careless in taking off his gloves. And the question is, why would he be careless this time?"

Sergeant Tagliano answered, "Had to happen sometime. I had a strangulation on a prostitute case. We thought she was dead. She suddenly rose up like a ghost. It spooked us. The first thing my partner did was push her back down with his hand. Not hard but enough to prevent her from harming herself. She was shaking and unaware we were police. If that happened here, the perp would have pushed her hard and there should be something on the back of her hair. It might not have bled and if she had my bushy hair, you maybe would not catch it without an autopsy. I think we should inform the M.E. office in Westfield to look for a bruise on the back of the victim's head, Captain. It's farfetched but possible."

"Go with it, Sergeant. I want you to look over our other cases and see if the travel pattern info gathered from cameras have a pattern. Where does the guy come from? Call Bob Alcore. The FBI will need to share road footage on the other victims. We're looking in our area for a lead on where he comes from. We know he has a safe house somewhere. Maybe the direction he comes from will give us a clue."

An hour later, Lieutenant Lent entered the room. "I heard a call and just so you remember how brilliant I am, I've got results. Don't hold back on the praise, guys."

The detectives let out a groan. Not at all upset, Lent said, "Take a look at my computer. I'll tell you what. If this car is the perp's car, he knows West Side."

Lent followed all cars that passed the dump site. He calculated based on their speed the time taken between two cameras. One auto took fifteen minutes extra between the area measured. There was only a partial license plate caught. The cameras could not catch it all. The car was a 2010 grey or maybe beige Toyota and middle plate numbers were 89. He was certain of his data because between those two cameras there were no intersecting streets. Lieutenant Smith suggested the driver may be dropping off something at a home along the way. Lent said, "There are only four houses on that strip. You guys can question the residents. It was 12:30 a.m. at the time."

Beauregard asked Lieutenant Lent if he would try to locate all cars with the partial on the plate. MCU would follow up. And would he look for patterns from other traffic routes from other droppings of murdered women, saying, "You and Lieutenant Mason Smith are great at patterns. Please work with him when I get the files from the FBI."

Ashton Lent did not complain about his workload in traffic. He jumped at the opportunity, leaving Sergeant Tagliano to say, "Captain, when can we get him back here? He's good."

Beauregard replied, "When the Chief gets an available and good Lieutenant. Lieutenant Lent has been very helpful in a couple of our past cases while he served his time there. Let's just appreciate we have an important friend."

Nate Connaught waited impatiently for Beryl. She was in the kitchen opening a bottle of fine German wine he'd brought from his recent visit to Munich. He thought, *how do I tell her. She wants to know. She'll hate that secrets were kept from her, mainly to protect her from the knowledge the government couldn't or wouldn't bring him home. They did not even publicly recognize his extraordinary service. Maybe the picture will help.*

Two glasses with his expensive wine, bruschetta toast, brie with fig jam and rice crackers on a silver tray were enjoyed until she said, "I did miss you so, but I'm frightened. I know you have news. You don't fool me with your intimate night over wine business. And I know it's bad news."

He poured the wine into the glasses. His silence told her everything. She asked when did he die and was told years ago. Not quite the truth but he thought, *good enough*.

Beryl said, "Did Joel suffer?"

"Yes, he probably did, Beryl, but no one knows the specifics. He was imprisoned for a long time and then executed."

"Where did he die?"

"North Korea."

And she cried softly. The tears continued. He waited until they subsided and said, "There is more."

He fished out the damaged photo, now covered in a plastic case, and gave it to her. He said, "This was smuggled out by a woman prisoner when she was traded many years later. It is the only proof he was in North Korea. Joel gave it to her just before they took him for execution. I can give you her name but it won't help you. She died recently from an illness she picked up while imprisoned."

And she cried again. Beryl leaned on Nate's shoulder and said, "I already knew he was dead. Why does it hurt? And he thought of us until the end. Nate, he always thought of us. His personality was that of a loving caretaker, but also of an adventurer. He couldn't help being who he was. But why did he take such chances in life, and North Korea? Who would go near there and why?"

"You now have all the answers you will ever get, Beryl. But you know he loved his family. Imagine hiding that picture to the end. It's difficult to do while imprisoned. Frankly, I don't know how he could."

Beryl laughed. "We would play hide and seek with the kids. He was the best. I thank God for this picture. The children will love his memory of them."

Laela cried as they reached her home in West Side saying, "Jad, this home has always been my refuge. Barry and I did quite a bit of work on it when we first purchased it. Some of the work was fussy and only we could do it properly. Perhaps it was not quite the truth. We enjoyed doing it together."

"And I bet Barry had carpentry skills from serving in the Army."

"How did you know? Yes, and the level of skill he possessed was amazing."

"How did you know about his carpentry expertise? I know you said you met Barry, but I don't remember how you'd know that fact."

"Of course, we met. We both played golf at the country club and we played cards."

Laela said, "Barry stopped going. I mean to play cards. He said there was a guy there who made him feel uncomfortable. He couldn't remember why but was certain he met him in another life."

"Hmm, I wondered why he left."

Laela said, "In retrospect, I realize Barry was deeply suspicious about strangers, my working at the pantry and any friend of mine who looked out of my league. That's what he would say, 'out of your league, Babe.'"

He pulled into her driveway saying, "I'll help you get settled. We'll get some takeout. I don't want you alone. Don't argue. You can sit quietly by yourself while I watch television in the study. I don't want you alone for the first night."

"Jad, you simply can't stay over. What will folks think? It's bad enough we've been together. You staying the night would solidify their suspicions."

"Then call Jane or Beryl to stay, but I'm not going until you find yourself a companion for the night."

It took Laela two hours to unpack, load the washer, and change her clothes. When she entered the kitchen Jad had set the table with bowls of steaming tortellini in broth aside of veal in a cream sauce, salad, and roasted potatoes. The kitchen smelled Italian and she felt hungry. "Jad, you have quite restored my appetite. Thank you. I'll call Jane when we've finished."

He appeared pleased with her decision. They spent an hour over dinner chatting in the manner of dinners on the long trip. Laela thought, *this is lovely. Coming home has not been unbearable. There is life after Barry. But is this friendship or something more? Stop this nonsense. Call Jane.*

She was disappointed when Jane took the call, and said she was having what she called 'family night.' Laela was certain she would not stay over given her penchant for cleaning the kitchen immediately after company left. Jane suggested Beryl saying, "Call Beryl, Laela. If she's not out with that Colonel of hers, I'm certain she'd be pleased to stay over."

Beryl answered the call and said she'd be right over thinking, *it's just what I need so I don't focus on Joel dying in North Korea. And the picture, just imagine, in his pain, he held on to us. He always loved us. I must stop blaming him. He was who he was.*

Laela opened her door and practically fell into Beryl's arms. "Thank you, Beryl. I need someone for my first night home. It might be a late night with conversation and hot chocolate or wine. Whatever you prefer. I've made your room up."

"No problem. It's lovely to see you again. You were gone a long time and I missed you."

They settled comfortably on the couch while Laela went into her travels over the past three months. When Beryl asked where Delilah was, Laela scowled saying, "I texted her I was coming. When I got here I found a note. She's in New York City for a couple of days. She wrote basically I would need some time to settle in but she would be home in a couple of days. I had hoped she would have moved out by now."

Beryl was about to question her on her stairway fall when Jad entered the room. He appeared to be in a jolly mood with a happy greeting to Beryl. He quickly said, "I'll leave you ladies alone. No need to have a rooster at a hen party. Thanks, Beryl, for staying with her."

And he left causing Laela to say, "He's always the gentleman. He's offered to find a condominium for Delilah. I told him I want her out and I was willing to pay the mortgage. It'll be an investment. She has some money. She can handle the rest."

Beryl was pleased with the entre to talk about Delilah. She said, "I think it's best she doesn't live with you, don't you? I don't think she pushed Barry down the stairs, but the fact that she pushed you is very serious. I don't want you alone with her until she moves. Will she move out if you find her a home?"

"Now that I'm hurting and I take care of her settling, yes, Beryl, she'll move. Delilah does not like me. She is totally compromised by her jealousy and emotional harangues. When she's not in an environment that brings back old memories, she functions quite well. Moving out is important."

"Jane, Mona, and I can rotate nights for a couple of weeks and stay with you. After that, it will become more difficult for us. Do you think you can get her out by then?"

"I do. I have a connection. My neighbor next door Colin Phillips has a list of what's available. He would want to help me and he is good at residential real estate. I worked with his son when he got into trouble last year. He's a widower. He was most grateful. Who knew I'd be looking for a favor so soon."

Beryl worried that in Laela's adjustment she might forget to call Colin. She said, "Call him now, Laela. Every minute counts. Please."

The call took a good twenty minutes while Colin gave Laela a list of several condos in West Side that were immediately available. She questioned why so many since there was a shortage of available homes for sale since the COVID epidemic. He said these condos had been owned by older people. Some died and some moved permanently to South Carolina or Florida. He scheduled Laela for tours the next day, saying, "You'll have the pick of the litter. They're all empty. There hasn't been enough time on the market for a serious buy."

Both Laela and Beryl were thrilled.

SLOW DEVELOPMENTS

Murders unsolved weighed on the detectives' minds. Some reports were in. Mason reported for his and Ashton's review on traffic patterns. They'd carefully checked autos going in both directions of the dropped bodies. After twenty files reviewed, they thought there was enough information to draw conclusions. Mason said, "Many of them showed highways with few crossroads between cameras. Some files were excluded because there was a broken camera or because you could not see the video well enough. For those fifteen files accepted, it is interesting because in every place the auto passing that took extra time was coming from the direction of western Massachusetts. Two different vehicles were identified. Not one plate could be identified. Maybe one or two letters. We got a list from those states of vehicles showing the same letters. Not helpful now, but maybe later. You're going to like this, one of the two cars identified is a 2010 Toyota with one letter matching to the car. The other is a black Mercedes van. Can't tell the year. I have a call out to Patrolman Yang. He'll identify it. He knows every model of every car known to man."

Petra said, "Can we move Ashton back to MCU, Captain? He'd be a godsend."

She was pleased when he looked like he was thinking. To her it was a sure sign he was interested. He'd never jump on a yes. The Captain was not one to move fast. Sergeant Barr reported Laela's background search resulted in a mirror of the lady she and all her friends say she is. He mentioned two traffic tickets for going through a red light. He insisted she is a perfect lady; exactly what he said she would be. He got some guffaws for liking the lady too much. His answer was he knew a lady when he saw one. Bill Border jumped in, saying, "Well, our Delilah ain't no lady."

Lilly corrected with, "Sergeant, ain't is not correct grammatical usage and you are an MCU detective who's supposed to value the king's English."

"Ain't is archaic but not incorrect, Lilly. Back to non-grammatical matters, our Delilah is volatile. She's in and out of personal relationships constantly. Laela's details were a small part of the truth about Laela and her past. Broken hearts and empty wallets everywhere. Delilah is a heartbreaker who steals love and some money. She never gets into trouble because she disguises the borrowing as necessary rent or medical expenses and never steals too much. Most of her lovers were middle class, not extremely wealthy. The few police reports made were withdrawn. She must be a terrific actress. At least she doesn't murder them."

Lilly asked, "What about violence. You said she was volatile. Any record of volatility?"

"Lots of police reports relative to calls to whatever home she was living in at the time. Things like throwing clothes and computer equipment out on the curb, hitting the guy with a heavy iron pan, creating a disturbance at his workplace, damaging his car. You know, just the usual bull."

"What did the police say when the johns pulled back their complaints? Police don't like that happening regularly."

"One officer was particularly annoyed and dragged her in for a conference with an ADA known for her lack of sympathy. Delilah put a show on about being a brutalized woman. It worked. Her trail of romances led to four different police stations. Think about the ones we don't know about. Laela's story is a bit of a coverup."

The Captain replied, "Happens all the time. Our problem is determining whether Delilah has the motivation to murder. She hated Barry because he was throwing her out. What about her financial situation? Laela inferred she had some issues."

"That's another story. The lady Delilah is loaded. All with other people's money. She had a bunch of policies paying monthly out over thirty years after she reaches sixty. She'll live large. Right now, she's a bit strapped; I mean to the level she can't buy Gucci monthly. Funny thing though, I found no history on her being married or divorced."

Lilly asked, "How could she hide it from her sister?"

"Look, Sergeant, this lady had a lot of well-kept secrets. She's an evil marvel."

Discussion continued in the squad room. How could Laela think her sister was ever married or divorced? Did she attend a wedding? Could she document dates and places of marriage? Did she ever meet any of the supposed husbands? The Captain decided enough is enough and said so. Next on the agenda for research brought Lilly to say, "Jane Aubergine has the perfect American housewife's dream life. She donates twenty hours a week for charitable work for the Symphony, Museum, and Pantry. Jane was often absent from the pantry. She plays golf with hubby and her friends on weekends. She lives well within her means which are not skimpy. No arrests and no scandal. Her FB shows cute pictures of babies and uplifting remarks grabbed from someone else's post. If she's a murderer, I'm a Girl Scout."

Juan replied, "And you're no Girl Scout."

Beauregard groaned thinking, *why did I keep a married couple in my department.*

Petra explained the results of their investigation of Jad. "Jad is an interesting character. He lives a quiet life here in West Side. Owns his house free of mortgage. No debt we could find. He owns three cars. His house is worth a million five and is too large for a single man. It has a three-car garage. No other property is in his name. We tried looking in Richmond near Lee. No dice. He has a large revocable trust set up. The beneficiary is Laela Greer. If that's not enough, we also found no evidence of marriage. We looked in East Coast states and found nothing. His health insurance goes back only to the year 2014. Before that we found nothing. Only annual checkups and a couple of office visits showed up on his insurance. He files as self-employed and as a consultant. He did do three years in the Army. NADA! We think the guy has had another life somewhere. His tax return says he is fifty-three, but he's only filed for ten years. Captain, we tried to check him out all along the eastern seaboard, New York and New Jersey."

The Captain was interested. He asked, "Did you try RMV in those same states? Get a photo from Mass RMV and send it out. You can't go so long in this country without leaving a trail. Send his photo to Alcore. Have him run it for a match with drug suspects. Jad had to make this money somewhere. What about the military? Run his photo with them. Someone has to know him. Do you think he is just a hustler and takes older ladies? He could be after Laela. All the evidence points to a gigolo. When we interview Laela Greer, I want a question made to her about her being a beneficiary of the trust and how much intimacy she's had with him. They've been together for three months. Does she even know about the trust? What the hell! Is West Side loaded with folks having more than one identity? Three fake identities in three months is too much for me."

Beryl's stay with Laela lasted three nights. They lounged over coffee in the morning and went out to dinner in the evening. Beryl noticed Jad called three times a day. Laela put him off saying she needed more time before meeting with Captain Beauregard. That meeting was set for the early afternoon of Beryl's second day stay. For two days Laela cried off and on about poor Barry, balanced with raves about Jad's serious friendship with her and his good nature. Beryl had problems with Laela's inability to focus on Barry's fall and her fall. She now insisted she must have been mistaken about being pushed saying, "It's those damn five-inch heels. I should never have worn them."

Laela talked about her childhood. There was some sister rivalry by her younger sister. Laela was a good student and played by the rules of the day. What her mother wanted, she got from Laela. The reverse was true for Delilah. Delilah threw fits when she didn't get her own way. She did not do very well in school despite having a higher IQ than Laela. She created so much chaos when it came to college her parents did not care which college she attended so long as she boarded. Laela did not marry early, while Delilah had many romances and one elopement and divorce before she was in her thirties. Laela's marriage to Barry pleased her parents and that satisfaction seemed to ignite flare-ups in Delilah's behavior. When their parents died Delilah appeared to have a psychotic episode and was hospitalized for a month. A psychiatrist in charge told Laela her sister had a borderline personality. Laela told them her sister was simply spoiled. They agreed but informed her Delilah was ill. From that day on, Laela did what she could to appease her sister and to protect her from consequences stemming from her own actions. There were quiet times, mainly when Delilah was in a new relationship. It was Barry's daughter who had a sit down with Laela and told her she was not helping Delilah by bailing her out of her problems. Laela said, "It's not easy for me, Patricia. I have no other family than her and you. I have no children." Now she has Jad, who she says offers her calmness and logic and gentlemanly behavior. Beryl wondered, *what is he after?*

On her first evening with Laela, Beryl attempted to explore Laela's relationship with Jad. She started with kudos to Jad for the solace he provided. Moving on, she said, "Laela, I know of no man, even my Colonel, who would spend three months catering to my wishes and needs. Did you ever wonder if he had a thing for you?"

"A thing, you mean a sexual desire for me? No. Can't everyone understand he is just a nice man. He paid for his own expenses and at least two-thirds of our meals. I had to fight to pay for lunch or dinner. He arranged all tours and paid for them. And, Beryl, he never once made a move on me. He does make me feel warm and fuzzy. I do try not to get too comfortable. He has to be years younger than me."

Beryl answered, "I don't think he's much younger than you. I do think he must like you more than you're saying. His thoughtfulness is shown in extraordinary behavior. You must be prepared to ask yourself if there is more in his mind than warm and fuzzy."

"Beryl, I expect you to be worldly enough to allow also for the best and worst in people. If Jad means more then I will face that when necessary. At the right time, it wouldn't bother me at all if he cared more."

Moving forward, Beryl questioned, "Was Barry friendly with Jad? I mean did they golf together or play tennis or cards at the country club?"

"What are you inferring? You're not thinking he hurt Barry to get to me? If so, the inference is disgusting."

"No, Laela, I did not for a minute think that. I thought Barry may have confided in Jad about any worries he had or problems with people. The police think Barry was murdered and maybe Jad might know something."

"Oh. All right. It is a firm no. Barry stopped playing cards. Perhaps Jad can tell you who was the player Barry found distasteful. He continued golfing. Beryl, you are worse than Beauregard. I'm going to go through all these questions with him. Are you asking me these questions as preparation for my interview or to feed my answers to Rudy? Are you detecting or being my friend?"

Beryl said, "What do you think, really think? I'm your friend and because I'm your friend I want to protect you."

Beryl watched while Laela cried and begged Beryl to forgive her. On the third overnight with Laela, Beryl heard her rant and rave over her interview with Rudy. She appeared suspicious of the smallest and least invasive question.

Laela entered the police station accompanied by Jad. His interview was scheduled two hours later. The Desk Sergeant was adamant about allowing him entry upstairs, saying, "Mrs. Greer has an appointment.

Unless you are her attorney, I can't allow you to join her. You may wait in the lounge."

Jad's face showed his anger at the refusal to enter. Enough for Laela to comment, "Jad, be cool here. I must face Captain Beauregard alone. Please calm down. I don't want any drama here."

He appeared to instantly calm down. Laela was motioned to enter the stairway to the Captain's office. She thought, *he got angry so quickly. It must be because he thinks I'm at risk. For just a second, I thought he didn't like abiding by rules. Nonsense, I've never seen that before.*

Captain Beauregard and Sergeant Bobby Barr greeted her in the conference room. Laela noticed it was not an interrogation room and commented. The Captain answered, "I'm here not to interrogate you, Mrs. Greer. I'm here for the normal inquiry into a victim's life after a murder. You do know your husband was murdered?"

Laela answered, "How can that be? He had no enemies."

Instead of answering, the Captain explored Laela's knowledge of her husband's life before they married. She relayed a story about his wife dying from cancer leaving one daughter. Laela also reminded him she'd already told the police. When the Captain explained his wife had been murdered and was one of the victims of the so-called serial murderer of women whose bodies were left in garbage bags dumped on roadsides, her astonishment was evident. She answered, "What are you talking about? How could Barry hide this from me? And Patricia must be in on it. She's a nun. They're not supposed to lie. Am I such a wuss everyone protects me from the truth?"

Tears sprang and filled her eyes, but she did not cry. Instead, she regrouped. "Captain, this comes as a shock to me. I'm thinking about a question you asked me on my first interview about recent changes in Barry's behavior. There were, but before I answer you, do you have the autopsy back?"

"Why would that change what you were going to tell me, Laela?"

"Just please tell me if Barry had potential problems. I know he had knee problems, but he recently has had several doctors' appointments.

He wouldn't discuss them. He led me to think they were for preventive health reasons. I bought it. Tell me please."

Beauregard said, "He was headed for major coronary and vascular problems. His symptoms would have been shortness of breath, fatigue, and maybe some balance problems. His lung showed a small growth. The report shows a slow growing cancer. Was Barry a smoker? If he knew he was a walking timebomb, how do you think he would react?"

"He didn't tell me. That explains a lot. Barry kept his thoughts to himself. He never found fault with me. I assumed his life with me was perfect, but it is not about me. He must have had great angst keeping the truth of his past life from me. Oh, my darling Barry."

"What about other than health problems, Laela?"

"Barry was always well-liked. He was gregarious. The only change in recent months was his stopping his Thursday night card game. He used to enjoy playing cards. I think because he was often a winner. The stakes weren't high for the guys. Suddenly he stopped going. When I asked him why, initially I got nothing but a shoulder shrug. After a few weeks I insisted on knowing why. I told him I wasn't being nosey. I needed to know a good reason. I thought at the time it might be a health reason because he was going to the doctor more frequently. He said he didn't like one of the players. It was not like Barry to dislike someone or if he did, not to be so overwhelmed he'd leave an activity he clearly liked. I told him that. He said it was a flashback from another life."

"Did he ever mention the man's name?"

"He wouldn't tell me."

"Do you think the man was new to the club?"

"That is probable. Barry made quick decisions. One meeting would have been enough once he decided the man was a problem to him."

There were few remaining questions asked of Laela. Rudy did question her on whether she ever spoke with Barry about the homeless man who was subsequently killed at the pantry. Laela thought for a few seconds and said Barry had to pick her up one day about a month before he died. She'd had a slight auto accident a week before and was out of a car for a day. He had to come into the pantry and wait for her until she

SLOW DEVELOPMENTS

finished her routine. On the way home, he asked what she knew about the crowd who came in for lunch. She couldn't really say she knew a lot because it wasn't her job to sit with them. He asked about the younger men. Laela described the regulars under sixty. There were only nine men. Before the Captain could bring the conversation to a close, Laela insisted he tell her if she was being looked at as a person of interest. He told her no. It was clear by her demeanor she didn't believe him.

Sergeant Bill Border took a citizen's call. The voice identified himself as George Walker. He stated his address which hit the Sergeant with a vague recognition clarified by further conversation. The caller spoke very fast saying, "Sergeant, I live at 30 North Street in an apartment building. I've been in rehab for two months and in a halfway house. I didn't hear about my neighbor's murder until yesterday. He was a good guy. Before I was hospitalized, I saw abnormal activity around our building. I thought it was cops looking for me for drugs. I now think they were looking for Bud; that's Bud Hover. He was the nicest guy. He'd talk to me. He brought me to the hospital, which saved my life. My other neighbor just told me the car that was seen frequently driving around the building continued after I left. No one else in the building was into anything, just looking to survive with cheap rent. There are small families in the bigger apartments and assorted low-income residents in the rest of the units. That car's driver could only be looking for Bud. You see, I know Bud went to the pantry for lunch. That's where I met him and later was surprised to find him in my apartment building. I don't know what he was doing in both places, because, you see, he was smart. He talked like a college boy. He was military. I know because I was in the Army."

Border asked a few questions ending in, "Did you get the make of the car and a license plate?"

"It was a black Mercedes sedan and had Mass plate 140 A23. My other neighbor also said Bud got in the car at two in the morning one night. He couldn't sleep and looked out the window. He thought it was strange. I do too."

The Sergeant finished the call with a request that Mr. Walker come to the station and fill out a witness statement. He agreed to come the next morning.

Border in his baseball umpire voice said, "You guys recognize the street address 40 North Street?"

Once his audience paid full attention, he verbalized the telephone call. Lilly was the first to speak. "You've hit a pot of gold, Sergeant. Let me check the plate. I think I know it, but I have to be certain."

She checked the Registry for the number and while waiting she said, "It may be Barry Greer's car."

The car was identified as the same and the detectives' adrenaline spawned a garble of ideas floating in the squad room. Captain Beauregard entered the room thinking he was late for the afternoon meeting. No one noticed his entry. As he listened to their talking over each other he called a halt saying, "We have meeting."

Border explained the call and ID of the car. Beauregard said, "We now know Barry connected with Mel Laurent aka Bud Hover. They were both Army. I don't think Barry disliked Mel, and Mel's not the man who played cards at the country club. Bud may have been interested in the man who played cards, just as we are interested. I'll have a talk with our illustrious friend Attorney Norbert Cull. He is a member of the club. We don't have enough for a search warrant, leading me to think he will be able to discern who the guy might be and do it discreetly."

21

WHAT IS TRUE

Norbie Cull received his marching orders. Rudy hated asking Norbie for help, but, as he said, "I'm not a member. I golf when invited by a member. If I ask questions, it will be all over the club in minutes. Mona will know because she has lunch with her sister-in-law regularly."

Norbie considered, *I quit playing cards two years ago. If they let me sit in, I'll feel obligated to fill in when requested. I hate to be in the position of saying 'no' continually. Hell, it's Rudy and I want to know as well.*

He left his office for a supper at the club's bar. The food was good and met his wife Sheri's standards for nutrition. Tonight, was special for a fall dinner offering a king-sized lobster roll on a plate of salad and fries. The company at the bar was great and the bartender knew her business working at an accelerated pace in refilling drinks. He asked one of the regulars if poker was on for this night. It caused some discussion. There'd been some problems with the game recently. Several regulars, not sit-ins, had left the game. Only one player's excuse seemed reasonable to the men at the bar, saying, "His wife is bitchy. He played for a month as a regular and then said she wanted him home on Thursday nights to babysit."

The others gave weak excuses like too much work or the need to go to the gym. Norbie explored the idea that maybe those who left still played as sit-ins. The answer was a 'no.' He questioned the number of tables playing and did they fill up afterwards. Josh Speckler, a long-standing member of the club answered, "Norbie, many of the younger guys joining the club want to play. Losing four was a problem so the players let three of them join."

"Well, Barry Greer left, and he was very well liked, so they were using a sit-in until he thought better. He's dead now. They let another young guy in."

The diners at the bar went into a long discussion on Barry Greer's death. The rumors were rife about his death being caused by murder. Repeatedly said were accolades for Barry and the inability for anyone who would want to murder him let alone murder him by pushing him down his staircase in the middle of the night. Normally a wife would do something like that, but Laela wouldn't. Her taking off did seem suspicious to them. The suspect they were working on was Laela's sister. They had a number of stories about her from their wives who played golf with Laela. One guy insisted anyone named Delilah could not be trusted. Norbie was certain their conversation would continue for another hour unless he stopped it. "Let's go back to the poker game. Who were the guys who left? I could try to talk them back to the game."

Josh said, "What good would that do? The new guys have their reserved spot. Unless they're out at least four times in a row, they can't be replaced."

Nils Ludgren laughed. "I wrote the bylaws for the game. The four new players are there as temporaries for six months. Go ahead, Norbie. Talk to the ones who left."

Norbie took the four names from Nils.

Later that night he dropped the names off at Rudy's home. Mona was serving her homemade apple pie with ice cream and Norbie accepted her invitation to stay for dessert. Norbie said, "I am careful about what I eat but homemade desserts like yours insist I consume them."

Rudy received the names saying, "You've outdone yourself, Norbie, and you brought them here without trying to interview them first. And that is a first. If you could just teach our friend Beryl the difference between helping and interfering I'd be grateful."

"Rudy, when are you going to understand Beryl? She can't conform to police standards. She's not police. She is a dynamic moving body and mind who is the best partner in crime solving you could ever have."

"You and Mona singing the same song. Let's look at these four men. Barry's the first one, so we only have three. How do you know if the guy wasn't there longer? Why do you think he would have left the game after Barry departed as a regular? Why aren't we looking at one of the guys remaining?"

"I don't know the answers to these questions. When you get to interview the guys who are left, we'll have a history of all the players in the last six months."

Mason Smith made calls to the three. The meetings were scheduled two hours apart for the next day in the hopes the men wouldn't have time to contact each other. Lilly scoffed at Mason's plan saying, "They're a rat pack. Police calling one will set the alarm for all the members. Stop dreaming, Lieutenant."

A quick background check on the three men raised few red flags other than one DUI and a police arrest of one as a teenager demonstrating at University of Massachusetts. Rudy went over their histories deciding how to approach each one without raising suspicion.

Ronnie Samuels greeted the Desk Sergeant with a hearty grin and a big voice. He announced his appointment with the Captain with no effort at discretion. The Sergeant liked him and treated him with unusual courtesy, motioning him to the door to the stairs. Ronnie did not have to wait for the door to open. It buzzed before he got there. This was an unusual move by the Sergeant who was famous for waiting for visitors to ask twice. And his smooth arrival continued. He was greeted by Sergeant Tagliano. Ronnie thought, *never met a sergeant who looked as good.*

Directed to the largest conference room, Ronnie said, "You're not grilling me today. It's not closed in enough for a grilling."

Lilly laughed saying, "Do you have a lot of experience in police inquiries?"

"Some when I was young. My dad's lawyer got me out of justified consequences. I've been good ever since."

The Captain joined them. Lilly did the questioning. She asked him about his life at the country club, how long has he been a member, and if he was disgruntled by any of their practices. Surprised by the question, he answered enthusiastically about the club. Lilly countered, "Why did you suddenly stop playing cards? I heard you were a winner."

"Are you looking into our card games? We play for peanuts. Do I need a lawyer?"

"No, Ronnie, we're looking for verification of some alibis for a case. No worries for you as long as you give honest answers."

Ronnie said, "I'd only tell the truth, but I know you contacted two other guys. It's got to be about the club. Is the club hiding some bad folks? Is it drugs?"

Lilly explained the detectives were interested in the card game. Who plays cards? How long have they been in the game? Who left? Why did they leave? After each question, although Ronnie answered, he countered with a what are you looking for? We don't do drugs. Most of us are old and out of that scene. We drink scotch or bourbon with a couple of guys drinking fancy drinks. The repetition of this mantra by Ronnie prolonged the conversation. His final answers came with a sigh. "If that's all you want, I know one of us is a bad guy and it's not me. I left because I have another card game going at a different club and the stakes are better. I'm a gambler, not Las Vegas type, but I win. The club's game is penny ante. Gerry Shultz left because he had family problems. As to Rick Maron, he is a workaholic. He joined to relax. He doesn't know how to relax."

Sergeant Tagliano asked for the current members of the club. The list of regulars and substitutes came to eighteen. Two names stood out: Jad Morton and Norbie Cull. She asked how often Norbie played. His answer was not helpful. He said, "Norbie hasn't played in two years. We'd have loved it if he came back but he's too busy. He's a great player, doesn't have my gift, but plays smart. You know what I mean?"

"Let me get this straight, Mr. Cull hasn't played in two years, and he doesn't know who plays?"

"That's right. He's there for golf, functions, and connections. He has no interest in which members do what. He's a good guy. I don't play golf. I play tennis. I've played with his wife Sheri. She's also a tough competitor."

"Pricey membership if you only play tennis."

"I'm in business. Most of my clients have come from the club or have been referred by members. Cheapest public relations resource around."

"Who's this guy Jad Morton?"

"Jad is a very cool Manhattan type. Says he's in investments and it must be true. He gives advice to some of the members, and I heard the advice paid off. Playing cards with him is a challenge. He doesn't miss a trick. I think he memorizes the cards or has a photographic memory. I was never close to him. I did enjoy his stories."

"Did he ever talk about his wife who died?"

"I heard from someone else about his wife dying of cancer and that's the reason he's tightlipped about his personal life. Funny thing though, he certainly is the most eligible bachelor in the club, but the ladies don't hound him."

Lilly asked, "Why's that?"

"I don't know. I asked a friend of my wife who gets all the gossip. She said he's stand-offish when approached by any lady. She thought he'd been burnt by a woman or maybe had a low sex drive."

The Captain interrupted, saying, "Did he ever talk about any other area of the country? Maybe things like knowledge of vacation areas and suggestions given for where to stay?"

"Come to think of it, he was a veritable tour guide for Florida and Georgia. This area too. He is a nice enough guy."

Beauregard asked, "What about his stories you enjoyed?"

"He spoke about his Army service. The kind of tricks they used to play to get out of details. I'm telling you he looks like a golden boy, the type who beats the system. Other stories were about the South. He made you laugh when he told little reminders of the difference between a city slicker and a country bumkin. He always had the city slicker losing. I think he was laughing at himself. He had a good sense of humor."

Later, after Beauregard closed the session, he discussed the interview with Sergeant Tagliano. Her first response was, "I don't know, Captain, for sure. Jad could be one of two types. The first is a really nice, unassuming guy who is drop-dead good looking and kind, or a sociopath. I think we have to know what he's hiding. He is hiding something. That is one takeaway for sure. And we have missing data on him."

The Captain took a call and returned to his office. Lilly thought about the interview. She looked at the murder board noticing her notes from his interview and other info. He's paid taxes for ten years, widowed, wife died of cancer, used to live in Connecticut, was Army. She thought, *where did he go to college, if Army, get vitals. Mason's on background. No report yet. The Captain will have to speak with Laela, but from what I understand Laela thinks Jad is perfect. She may not tell everything she's learned about him. She won't want Jad to be a perp. I don't either. Petra and Juan did not come up with enough on their inquiry.*

Lilly checked the in-box and found the Army inquiry answered. Jad Morton was Army. He graduated from William and Mary in Virginia, served seven years and left as a Captain. His last three years served was in CID. There were no other notes in the file. She thought that was unusual. There was no trail of service. He was honorably discharged. She checked out the William and Mary College and noticed on the list of admin the name of an old friend, Cameron Circosta. She caught him on her first try. He did not know Jad Morton but he certainly could get his file. He was willing to speak with faculty who had known him once he knew the years of attendance. She gave him a hearty thank you. Lilly thought, *we know nothing about him. He had to be working to support*

WHAT IS TRUE

himself. Why no tax return for so many years? Was he on welfare? Should be some tax for the earlier seven years of service. Early ten years no return, middle years no return, last years' returns tell a missing story; is a conundrum.

Lilly walked into the Captain's office and announced in a few sentences her dilemma. "Captain, Jad is a show-stopper with plenty of money, no continual personal history based on Army records and IRS. His Army record is minimal at best with no reports on his progress. He is worth our deeper investigation. I'm waiting for his college records. But the man is an enigma."

"And I'm guessing, Sergeant, you want me to interview Laela about Jad."

"How did you know, Sir?"

"It's what I would have asked for. I'll wait until you hear from the college."

Beryl Kent spoke with Laela at 2:00 p.m. knowing Jad was in an interview. Laela cried, "He hid his past. Barry suffered so after the brutal murder of his wife. Why didn't he tell me? I would have understood. I could have shared his secret. Beryl, I think Rudy believes the serial murderer killed Barry. How could he get into our house and if he did once, will he come again? I'm so frightened."

"Stop it, Laela. Think about what you are saying. If Barry were killed by the serial murderer, it's because Barry knew about him. You don't know anything. You're safe. The question is, how did he get into your house? Who has keys? Did the police find any breakage in any of the doors? Was your alarm on?"

"The police never asked me. I had to shut it off when I knew the police and doctor were coming."

Beryl asked, "What about keys to the house and did you give the alarm code to anyone?"

"Everyone has the alarm code including my housekeeper, the gardener, the window cleaner, and some neighbors. As to the keys, I leave one set under the angel statue by the side door. No one I know would come into my home in the middle of the night, Beryl, if that's what you're thinking."

"Can you give me a complete list of persons having the code and or knowledge of the key placement under the angel?"

Beryl waited. The list was quite long with at least thirty names. She said her goodbyes and left for the station. It was a short trip. Rudy was leaving the building when she pulled up. He said he was heading home. Beryl told him to jump in, because she had something important to tell him. Annoyance crossed his brow, but he got into the car. Beryl reviewed her conversation with Laela and gave him the notepaper with the names listed. He broke into a smile saying, "I love a present, Beryl, and you give good presents sometimes. I don't think the alarm or door entry was evaluated by my guys. It looked to be an accident. Thank you. And best of all, you came right here without speaking to the Colonel or Cull first."

"Captain, this is evidence for the police. It is not just my meanderings. I've always known the difference."

She gave him, what her son Oliver would call a wicked smile, as he exited the car. She thought, *Barry's killer is Delilah, Laela, or someone with entry ability. This serial killer is local. It's someone who recognized Barry and was in turn recognized by him. This does narrow the field.* Beryl had taken a photo of Laela's list of names. *I must know more about Jad. Was he in the service? How many of these names were in the service?*

Rudy Beauregard nodded his head quietly talking to himself, "What's wrong with my cops and me? One of us should have done this. We thought it was an accident. Well, I wondered if it was a murder. That should have been enough for me to investigate. And thank you, Beryl. I never thought I'd say that. We know Barry drove by Mel Laurent's flat. I assume the two of them discussed the possibility of the perp being the guy at the country club. Could be, though that he didn't say the name, because he wasn't certain. The perp was on to Barry, or he wouldn't be murdered. The card player is our best shot."

WHAT IS TRUE

Nate Connault was meeting Beryl at a West Side Library event. Beryl was on the library board and was presenting changes expected in the coming year. Most importantly was the new library extension. Residents were eagerly awaiting its grand opening. She was to inform them it wouldn't be ready in the Spring but in late June. He was there for support, although he didn't think she would need it. The meeting took two and a half hours leaving Beryl and Nate quickly heading for the nearest open restaurant, a small Turkish place right over the Connecticut line. Once seated and having ordered, they discussed Beryl's conversation with a taxpayer who grumbled about the time delay costing more money. He was quite persistent, until the audience initiated a slow rumble of disagreement. Beryl said, "I think they wanted to go home. For whatever the reason, I'm grateful."

Beryl showed Nate the name list of those with either key or alarm access to Laela's home. He scanned the names, commenting, "Crazy. Why have security at all? Thirty names with some kind of access. Many have access to both alarm and key. Was the alarm on at the time of the murder, Beryl?"

"Laela said she had to shut the alarm off for the Coroner."

"Did Laela mention anything about damage to outside doors?"

"No."

Nate said, "If we go by this, Delilah, or Laela, or someone with the alarm code are key suspects. Let's look at those names. We think Barry's killer may be the serial killer. If so, service workers at the house won't be suspects. Don't you think we can exclude them?"

Beryl agreed. They reviewed the list. After deletion, there were only three names left. The three had the keys and the alarm code. Nate said, "Delilah, Jane Aubergine, and Laela herself."

Beryl said, "It's a dead end. None of them fit the profile of a serial killer. Unless one of them or one of the excluded names gave the code and key to someone."

Nate agreed. "That's the role of police. They have the manpower. You, however, can speak with Jane and find out who were the folks given the code and key. Also, did she leave the code on a slip of paper with the key."

"Right, I do that all the time when I've been given a code. I can't remember all those codes. Better yet, I'll visit and look around first before I ask. Did you know Jad was in the Army for seven years? That's what Laela told me."

"What's his full name?" Nate asked.

"I have Jad Morton."

"Maybe I can locate his social security number. I'll look into it, Beryl. Do you have reservations about him?"

"As I've said before, he is too good. He appears to be too good to be true and his care of Laela is overwhelming. His extreme attention makes me nervous."

"Laela did spend three months with him. It's a long time to spend with a sociopath and not have a few second thoughts. The only suggestion I give is she is outside the victims' age bracket profile. Did Laela give any suggestions of problems on her trip? Where did she go again on her trip? It was traveling all over New England as I recall."

The couple lounged a bit over coffee, having enjoyed great lamb shish-kebab and some kind of cheese filled pastries. Beryl asked Nate, "Am I just too close to this? I won't even look at Laela as a murderer. I know I should at least examine her background, but it doesn't make sense. Everything I know supports her as a wonderful woman. I think it's a waste of time to consider her. Am I wrong, Nate?"

"Probably not. Laela has shown incredible actions that could throw suspicion on her as a potential killer of just her husband. Number one culprit in murders is often the spouse, but from what I've heard, Laela has money independent of Barry."

Beryl asked, "Who told you that? I'd not heard that rumor."

"The police checked it out. It was the first question I asked. So other than financial gain, why do spouses murder other than for money? Mostly out of passion, envy, or anger. He was not a falling down drunk who embarrassed Laela. He's known as a gentleman. I've heard nothing about another woman. It's not in him. He's a faithful husband."

"You mean 'was.' I feel better now. I wanted to hear an objective view. It's funny to me, how you are clinical in all your interactions, but a total romantic with me."

"It is not strange, Beryl. I'm in love."

Mona poured a small portion of red wine into Rudy's glass. He moved his finger toward the ceiling motioning for a larger portion. He groaned when she gave him the fisheye of disapproval. Ignoring the glance, she served him pot roast which was one of his favorite dishes. Again, she got a look from him causing her to say, "Rudy, portion control is the most important action required in living a long life. And I want you to live long and well for selfish reasons. I need you."

He felt the guilt. He always felt the guilt, thinking, *why do I do this to her and myself. I know the rules. I know she's right. There I go kicking and screaming like a little kid when I don't get more despite knowing more would be bad for me. How does she put up with me? Her work with high school kids must teach patience.*

Rudy changed the subject saying, "Have you spoken with Beryl about Laela recently?"

Mona looked confused. "Rudy, you never want to know about my conversations with my friends. I am certain you're interested in Laela's husband's murder. Speak directly to me, Rudy, and I'll tell you what I know."

Rudy appeared annoyed but recovered quickly. "I want to know more about Laela and Jad."

"You mean the two together or individually?"

"I don't particularly care if they have a new blossoming romance after Barry died; I'm interested in a romance before he died."

"There was no outside romance before he died. I would have known. Jane Aubergine would be talking about it. I don't think there is a romance now. I know Laela well. She is not a cheater. She may currently be in need of comfort, but not an affair. She'd wait the year out. And as to Jad, I don't know much."

"You're telling me Laela dropped all her friends and went on a sojourn with a male neighbor she hardly knew, and she is supposedly a conservative. Hog wash."

"I'm telling you to take off your policing dark glasses and see people for what they are. Laela did not have a romance with Jad before Barry died and most probably not after he died to date. Is that specific enough?"

"And what do you hear about Jad, Miss Know-it-all?"

"All I've learned is from Laela and according to her he is perfect; actually, nauseatingly perfect. You'll have to look elsewhere for information."

"It's been my experience, Mona, people know more than what they originally share with the police in an interview. Might it be the case with you? Think about it."

"This is a police interview! My, my, I thought it was a marriage."

"What info did Laela share that hit a question mark in your head that you did not pursue?"

"Rudy, it's not what Laela shared, it's what I heard. Laela was planning to visit places she and Barry had never been. Two of the places she and Jad visited were destinations Barry and she had been to before. It's probably nothing. Another thought is, do you remember when your police were investigating the license plates of cars who traveled to where Patti was paid to take license plate numbers by our homeless man? Beryl and I did reverse plate numbers and investigated the locations of the person named on the registration's home address. There was a barn listed as an address on the good side of town. We couldn't see any signs of recent life. Why would it have a Toyota registered to it? I can't remember anything else."

"Thank you, Mona. Do you have a list where Laela and Jad visited, and the address of the barn?"

"Beryl had it. I'll get it for you. As to the barn, I can't remember the address, but I know I can find it. It's near that small variety store over by Overbrook. It's been there for years. I'll get the street and number."

22

A DARK PAST

The darkened house surprised him. Regina likes bright lights. He wouldn't dare complain about an electric bill. It's only 8:00. He'd been gone for three weeks on a sales trip. She hated his travel, but she loved the monetary results of his travel. He called earlier in the day as he did every day when he traveled. This time was to surprise her. He'd bought flowers. It was their anniversary. He'd been thinking about coming home for the last three days. His thoughts also focused on changing jobs. It would please Regina. She often said how difficult it was to plan when he was gone so often, and she was lonely without him. The question of children which he raised frequently was nixed every time he raised it. Her verbal comeback was practiced, and he could find no fault with it. After all, why should she play a role as a single mother when she had a husband.

He opened the door quietly, flicking on the small lamp on the side table, while thinking it would not startle her if she were sleeping. Looking around the living room to his right, his face showed confusion. On the coffee table, there was debris from what looked like a celebration: two champagne glasses half-full and a tray half-filled with canapes. Regina's famous cheeseball demolished on the neighboring plate. His face tightened. Removing his shoes, he climbed the stairs slowly and carefully to avoid the three stairs that creaked. His rage showed by the straightening of his body while his face grimaced. He moved toward the master bedroom. The door was open for all the world to see his beautiful wife lying in the arms of his next-door handsome neighbor. He whipped out the wire he always carried with him for safety and approached the man first. When it was done, his slowly awakening Reggie screamed, "Are you crazy? It is just a one nighter. He means nothing to me. You are the one I…." She did not get a chance to finish.

He said quietly, "You are like them all; just like my mother."

There really was not much of a reaction when Regina and her lover Stan disappeared. Stan's wife Lynette told the world Regina had been after her husband and she finally got him. Later she tried to recant when she realized the insurance company wouldn't pay off unless he was declared dead. There was no major investigation into their abrupt departure. Both his and her lover Stan's homes were searched. Nothing was found. No bodies were ever recovered. The police left it as an open case with two runaways. One big question related to the cars. Both cars were found in their respective garages. How did the two get away without a car?

He had cleaned up the mess he made. Regina had always been neurotic about cleanliness. Luckily, she had plastic covering under the bed sheets. Sleeping on plastic had always driven him crazy. He waited until two in the morning before taking the bodies over to the dump. At one end of the area, the continual fire sent flames up as two men threw in trash. He knew the men took a break at four and downed a few shots. He showed up one morning bringing some big stuff. He wanted it out of the house and had missed the collection. He paid them and spent some time talking about their job. Most people loved the attention he gave them. He knew how important it was to get some attention. Getting respect and love was far more important than giving it. He found it easy to give; less easy to get. Tonight, he waited until the men walked over to the shed by the road not noticing his car hidden behind a trailer used for stuff too good to trash. He waited. When the talking stopped, he drove over to the fire and dumped the bodies. The fire blazed. He waited. He added more stuff and fuel. He knew from before that the ashes would be buried with dirt the following morning. A new hole would be dug for a new fire the next day. This community did not invest in sophisticated rubbish disposal when they had acres and acres of land to use. He drove away satisfied with the burial. And he suffered. The whole town witnessed his suffering. He drank too much. He quit his job. And then the darkness.

His father came and visited him at the facility many times. He tried to console him. After all, hadn't he lived through the same thing? He'd survived. He had a second family. Life goes on. The facility psychiatrist showed deep sympathy for his trauma. As he said, "To go through this display of abandonment once is one thing, but twice makes for deep heartache."

He laughed at their limited thinking. He mumbled to himself, "Three not two." His father early on avoided knowing until that day of reckoning. That day was etched in his memory. It was when he knew no one could be trusted. His teacher told him it was their little secret. The next thing he knew, his dad was at his school. She told him about the welts on his back. She had said she wouldn't tell. Then he made a bigger error. He told his dad about the tall man who would wrestle with his mother in bed. She made him watch. What good did that do? They divorced and his dad got custody. He wasn't home much and when he met his new future wife, he was out all the time. His dad married when he was a senior in college. And that was the end of his home life. Dad was happy. He himself didn't let Regina live for him to be happy. Would he have been happier if he'd let it go? His mother lived through two other marriages. She never wanted him near her husbands. She said, "You told once. I can't trust you."

He thought what she was really thinking was that she couldn't continue to beat and humiliate him.

He had had enough. Mustn't there be one woman who would love him and be kind and faithful?

23

MORE OF THE SAME

They found Ronnie Samuels bludgeoned to death outside the Knights Hall. There'd been a game inside. He'd done well, winning over two thousand dollars. Detective Lilly Tagliano joined Patrolman Palmieri as the first on the scene. The gash on the back of Ronnie's head bled somewhat, but it was the bleeding from his mouth when he hit a large brick that spread a pool of blood. The winning purse was not on the body. The conclusion was obvious. It was a robbery. Who knew, in addition to the players and the waiter, who won the pot? It was a private game. Did some wannabes know about the weekly game and waited outside for the winner? Could be. There was a small window about five feet above the parking lot that gave an opportunity to see inside. It was early morning when the game let out. The waiter had gone home by now and the caretaker who was an old timer slept through the murder. He did not wake up until the police came. Ronnie's wife called his cell. He didn't answer. She drove to the club and found his body.

Rudy arrived later in the morning. He spoke with Gerard. The coroner quickly concluded it was a murder for the purse, saying, "It's quite common now to wait for the winner and grab the purse. This time Ronnie must have attempted to fight. Money's not worth it."

"No, it isn't, but look at the mouth. All his teeth are broken along with his nose. That's one hell of a push. The killer wanted him really dead. No wakey-up for Ronnie. I think he knew his killer. Ronnie was in as a witness earlier today. Could these events be connected?"

Gerard laughed and said, "I'll leave it to our illustrious crime solver. I do see your point."

Sergeant Tagliano was listening to their conversation. When Gerard left, she said, "I thought it was more complicated than a hit and grab. There is a lot of anger in that push. He must have enemies."

"Lilly, speak with his wife. I want to know what's been happening around him for the last few weeks. Take Mason with you to break the news."

Lilly and Mason were invited into the large garrison home. Miriam, Ronnie's wife, showed black circles under her eyes. They assumed it was from crying although she appeared in complete control. After she placed steaming cups of coffee at the dining room table, she said, "It's freshly brewed after grinding the best beans Ronnie could find and import from South America. I don't know the difference, but Ronnie did. He was not a drinker of alcohol but was addicted to coffee. I feel so lost. He was a dynamo. He was my inspiration to try different things and he cherished my work. He'd say, 'Meaningful work is the accelerant for good mental health.'"

Sergeant Tagliano questioned her about his work. Was there anyone there who disliked her husband. She answered, "My husband was liked by everyone, with the exception of losers from his gambling. Other gamblers would make inuendoes about his consistent winning, casting a question on whether he was cheating. He'd get riled up over that. Ronnie didn't have to cheat. He was gifted. Some said he counted cards. It could have been because he was totally aware of everything or one in a room. But he was never outlawed at Atlantic City or Las Vegas or Mohegan Sun."

When Lieutenant Smith asked about Ronnie's job versus amount from gambling, he was surprised to hear Ronnie made about two hundred thousand from his job and more than that gambling yearly. She said, "This investment in and running costs of this house and our Lake George home would not be covered by his job alone. I never angered over his gambling. It was lucrative and he never drank. To him gambling was a second job. He said several times his success at gambling was mostly due to his ability to read people."

Lieutenant Smith asked, "How was Ronnie's relationship with women?"

"You mean, was he a cheater? Absolutely not. He was a home guy. Anyone will tell you that. He adored our kids and turned off any other women with his golden phrase, 'I'm a married man and I like it that way.'"

Miriam continued, "Who would kill my Ronnie? I can only think a sore loser may. And he never bet large sums at local games for that precise reason."

"Miriam, you don't think two thousand dollars is a lot of money?"

She said, "Not at that club. To the players there, that was chickenfeed."

Sergeant Tagliano asked if Ronnie had ever commented on a player who left the country club card game. She didn't answer immediately. "Sergeant, Ronnie read people well. He was greatly disturbed when Barry Greer left the card game and for two good reasons: one was that Barry loved the game, the second was he knew Barry didn't want to leave the game.

"He knew it wasn't Laela who was behind it. We'd sat with the Greers on many a dinner at the club. He questioned him and got no answers. He thought about changes in the players and realized there'd been a couple of new players brought on. He wondered if one of them was bothering Ronnie because he threw in his cards a couple of times. He told me he wanted to see the player's reaction. He could tell a lot about someone when they win more than they lost. All losers react similarly but not all winners. I asked him who could make Barry leave and he said he thought he knew. He did not tell me."

Half an hour later, while enjoying lunch at the local tavern, Lilly and Mason argued over Miriam's interview. Both agreed she was telling the truth and was certainly not the perp in this case. Lilly said, "I am cynical. I know I am cynical, but this guy is a semi-professional winning gambler, holds down a full-time job, lives in a stately home, wins often, is not a heavy drinker, and has woman's intuition. Sounds too good to be true."

"Lilly, you're caught up in psychobabble. The guy was out-front about his gambling, and about every question we asked. He knew or had a suspicion about Barry."

The debate continued as the two detectives entered the station. Two men present had been told by the Desk Sergeant to wait for the detectives. The Desk Sergeant whispered to them, "It's about the Ronnie murder. They said they have information but would only talk to detectives on the case or the Captain. The Captain is at a conference with the Chief and the Mayor. Who knows when the long-winded will close. I'm glad you guys got back."

Lieutenant Smith met the two men and escorted them upstairs to a small conference room. Sergeant Tagliano brought in coffee. Alfred Joyner and Kevin Lassiter introduced themselves as workers at the West Side Department of Public Works. Alfred initiated the interview saying, "You know, we DPW workers see everything. We have our routines. You would think routines are boring. Sometimes they are, but anything outside our routine landscapes, we notice. Things, Lieutenant, most folks would never notice. We notice speeders and those who drive too slow. Most people who drive too slow are elderly. When they are not elderly, we notice them."

Kevin jumped in saying, "Yeah! There's this guy. He looks like an older lothario."

Before he could finish, Alfred quipped, "Big word for you, Kev."

Brushing the tease off, Kevin continued. "It's strange because the same guy is on our route driving like he's a hundred in three different vehicles. One's a Mercedes van, the second is a Toyota and the third is a small white truck. It took us awhile before we came here. We thought you'd think we were nuts, but we know Jim Locke who used to be a police detective. He's the best. He told us that's what good citizens do. They give info. Only the police know if it's relevant. He said to never withhold stuff. We're not withholding. Besides, my wife said if you don't tell the police what you suspect, you might be obstructing justice. She reads all these murder mysteries and knows a lot about the law."

Smith asked, "Is there anything else about this guy that is different?"

Alfred said, "He wears a Crocodile Dundee hat slouched down. That's why we know it's the same guy and he always waves like he's in the neighborhood. Neighbors always wave at us."

"Could you recognize him if you saw him again?"

"Not sure. Kevin, could you? You were real close one day?"

"He'd have to wear a hat like that. He has a brawny arm. Well-built, like he works out. Kind of lean muscles but no fat. Good looking with the hat on."

Lilly took all the particulars. The men left saying, "We saw him all around the area in West Side, near where that body was found."

Lilly put the new info up on the murder board. It required her to move attachments around. She had not kept up with Beauregard's methodology of reviewing data multiple times. Feeling slightly guilty, she did a quick review. A tingle went through her when she saw references to a black Mercedes, a truck, and a Toyota. It was time for her to connect with Lieutenant Lent from Traffic. Rush time, she thought, rush time.

Beryl and Nate were enjoying a dinner with Rudy and Mona and Sheri and Norbie at the country club. Naturally, in the midst of eating their entrees, Beryl, not Rudy, sandwiched a bit in the conversation about their most recent murder case. She asked Rudy, "A murder now in our own town and it's a product of our serial murderer. There has to be some evidence about him. Have you any leads?"

Rudy shook his head, looked at the others at the table and said, "Beryl, we're having dinner and murder is my business, not yours. Good citizen and good witness are your contributions, God help me!"

Rudy may have thought he was showing discretion in addressing the issue, but the ladies both had much to say. Mona defended Beryl's right to ask the question given Beryl's history of helping and cooperating with the police. Beryl insisted that as a neighbor in the area, she could follow any trail the police had on the perp a lot better than the police. Nate intervened as he watched the Captain's face shading red and maybe approaching an apoplectic attack. "Rudy, I don't think Beryl wants to interfere with your investigation. I heard through the DPW grapevine, workers may have seen the perp driving around. You tell Beryl about it, she'll drive the streets looking for the vehicle or a guy who matches their description."

"Nate, how the hell did you find out? If my guys let it out, they're dead meat."

"Nope, I had DPW digging outside my house for a new water main. I brought them coffee and one word led to another. That is all."

Rudy knew if he didn't explain the DPW workers' conversation, Beryl would run them down and extract maybe more. He said, "They saw a youngish man driving too slow for his age, multiple times. He was wearing a Crocodile Dundee hat which made a good description of his face difficult. They saw him in three different vehicles: one is a Mercedes van, the second is a Toyota and the third is a small white truck."

The info sparked conversation that ran the gamut from did you get a plate number to demand for a more complete description of the suspected perp. Beryl questioned, "Are Mercedes vans common?"

The answer from the two men was a 'yes.' Nate said, "Many of those Amazon and other delivery vehicles are Mercedes vans. They are rated the best in that category. One model is rated tops for sportsmen and families who use the van for camping."

Over dessert, Mona said, "I've been thinking. Why don't you look for one person owning all three types of vehicles?"

Her husband sighed saying, "Of course, already done. If this is the perp, and if he is at all smart, and we think he is, he'd use vehicles from different owners such as corporations or other peoples' vehicles."

Not to be put down, she pushed forward. "Well, corporations all have owners. Check any Mercedes owned by corporations and check their owners. As to those that seemed to be non-commercially owned and are registered to a West Side owner, interview them all."

Fortunately, the check came diverting Rudy's attention bringing out his guilt for never being able to pay a check at the club thinking, *I'm always a guest here.*

Nate drove Beryl home. He interrupted her free flow of discovering more information on the serial killer saying, "It's time we speak about the elephant in the room, Beryl."

She was confused and told him so. He softly said, "Wedding time is more important than solving mysteries. So, what do you say? I want to marry you soon."

Despite his serious note, she smiled and said, "You asked for my answer before you stated your desire. How can I marry a man who cannot propose in an orderly fashion?"

She laughed and sat quietly as he pulled into her drive. Turning to her he said, "A serious question requires a serious answer. Will you marry me soon?"

Beryl whispered, "Yes, but please don't die on me."

24

A SAD STORY

He changed his hat. He knew from before unique headgear would distract from identification. Those DPW men working in the area around his home and the seven parallel streets were a nosy bunch. He'd been careful about speeding. He hadn't realized their interest would be in drivers going below the speed limit. Why hadn't he thought about it? He'd made that mistake a long time ago. Why didn't he wise up? He thought the repetition of events made him careless. Perhaps he could stop the killing. Perhaps if he found a woman he could trust, he'd lose the desire to kill. Those crazy shrinks told him he was a sociopath. He'd googled it and many of the killings were done by sociopaths. When they killed without knowing the victim and had accomplished a few deaths, they called them psychopaths. He didn't believe he was a psychopath. He had his reasons. Those women he killed were just like the women in his life who continually reaped pain on him. It didn't matter what he did, they hurt him. These women out there were just like his women. They were hurting their significant other. Did he know this for sure? Of course, he did. A tart dressed to the nines out on the town with her supposed girlfriends but standing at the bar and letting men buy their drinks said it all. The poor guy is at home taking care of the kids. He'd been careful. He was certain he'd chosen well. When

A SAD STORY

the newsprint supported the details, he felt a surge of relief. After all, he was not a murderer. Didn't the Bible say something about separating the good seed from the bad. Same thing as he was doing. There are good women. He only knew a few. His aunt Evelyn was an angel. Why couldn't he have married a woman like her? His mother, such a bitch, told him he was too sensitive and clingy.

When he married, his wife said she would be the initiator of sex; it was a woman's prerogative. And it was great until she betrayed him. And later he met the perfect woman. She kept to herself, was modest, intelligent, and gentle. He thought she loved him. She was playing a role. He could not believe how she fooled him. Enough of the past for him to suffer just by remembering. If he could just not get stressed, he'd be all right. All he wanted was a good woman. That's not a lot to ask. He realized there were four women who hurt him. Why did he only remember three of them? The psychiatric social worker told him when a person is acting against his or her moral beliefs, they often forget their sins - stupid church woman.

His heart swelled at his new thoughts about this wonderful woman. She would not disappoint him. Her love would make him whole.

Lieutenant Petra Aylewood-Locke was playing house with her two-year-old daughter Carlotta while her husband Jim looked on. She asked why Carlotta was placing the daddy in the kitchen while having the mommy walk into the home from the car parked outside the doll house. Petra did not like the answer. Carlotta said, "Just like here at home, Mommy, the daddy is setting the table just as you come in from work. There's a TV show on showing stay-at-home daddies."

"Who let you watch that show?"

"Grandma. She thinks it's wonderful men are doing a lot of childcare these days. That's what Daddy does. He's home every day at 4:30. You're not. And he gets me ready for nursery school and drives me both ways."

Petra seethed, while Jim Locke rolled with laughter from his big, oversized chair. She said, "Cut it out, Jim. It's not fair. I can't help it if I work in policing while you lollygagged about in psychiatric counseling. I have to go when called even if it's the middle of the night."

"You explain it to Carlotta. I have nothing to explain."

And he laughed. Meanwhile, Carlotta put the mommy doll in the kitchen and the daddy doll in the living room saying, "See, Mommy. The home is now just like Judy's."

Petra quickly moved to the kitchen and pulled the quiche from the oven. She noticed the salads were on the set table along with two shrimp cocktails. Carlotta refused to eat what she called little dead fishies. She wouldn't forget to finish the chocolate cream pie her dad had brought from the bakery.

After Carlotta was settled in bed, Jim said, "You aren't still upset about Carlotta's truth telling, are you?"

"It's not fair that she'll remember me that way."

"Come on. We both know you were made to be a cop and if you weren't one you would be the worst wife and mother. I'm happy with the status quo. Admit it, you are too."

Wishing to change the subject, Petra opened up about chasing the details on Barry Greer and the homeless man. "Jim, tell me more about the two motives we talked about before. I mean why the violence on some and the clean killing on others?"

"Petra, I'm not sure the idea of clean killing is a concept I understand. You mean because some women were only strangled, that it's a clean killing. Strangling as a weapon means the killing is close and personal to the killer. At least, most psychologists think that way. Now your serial killer in his stabbing of victims, appears possibly to be killing out of lust; maybe to satisfy a sexual need. Many questions present themselves in those cases. Has he no other satisfying sexual outlet? Is he incredibly lonely? Is he on a mission to cure some aspect of society he sees as unacceptable such as rejection? Clearly, he's an organized killer. Possibly he had issues with his mother. Definitely he has issues with trust. He is a white male. He is well versed in general and appears to obey all straightforward rules of society. I say trust. He didn't trust his mother. Maybe she cheated on his dad. Maybe he was sexually abused. I'm quite certain he had a disappointment that completely wreaked havoc in him from an adult relationship such as marriage or rejection from a girlfriend after he'd been completely enamored by her."

"How do I out him?"

"You can't without more evidence. He must have a military connection, and also one with the country club. At least that's the direction you're headed. Find common ground between the country club and the military. I'm certain that's where Rudy is headed. And look for your most unlikely character. He appears to live well with no money problems. You said he has been seen in three different cars. Can't the police look for common ownership. I suppose they already have but if he's smart, his name won't be on registrations."

It was a sunny day in Western Mass. Laela returned to work at the Kitchen Pantry. Mona and Beryl's hopes were heightened by Laela's major effort to return to normalcy. She delved into her duties this day as server with kindness and friendliness to the pantry's guests. Beryl was delighted. She did tell Beryl at the morning opening that she would not bring garbage out to the back doors, saying, "I don't want to be anywhere near where that man died. I just can't. You do understand?"

Beryl told her it was quite understandable. The day went swiftly until Jad entered to pick Laela up twenty-five minutes early. Those last minutes at the pantry were always a bit chaotic. Generally, some guests don't want to leave and the last-minute cleaning was a job the workers all shared. Jad sat at the last table waiting and his face showed disgust at some of the clients still sitting. Beryl did not see compassion in his face. She shook her head thinking, *some people will never understand. Men and women sometimes have difficulty meeting the challenges in life. Divorce, early childhood trauma, substance abuse, mental health issues, they all existed in this group. How can you not understand, they need us?*

Jad motioned Laela to leave. She shook her head and said, "If you have an appointment, it's okay. Beryl will drive me home."

Laela noticed a stern look on Jad's face. He quickly replaced it with a small smile and told her he'd wait. When she told him there was no need, he turned and walked away without another word. She was about to call him back when Beryl asked for her help in moving a table. She thought Beryl had maybe seen her altercation with Jad and said, "Don't mind me, Beryl, Jad is just a little overprotective. He did not want me to come here today to work. He thought it was too soon."

Beryl replied, "Nonsense, you looked happy today. It's always a lift to help others."

Mona had watched the incident. She pulled Beryl aside and said, "I told you. He's big time controlling. I don't like it. We have to watch them. Jad wants to take the two of them away to his Richmond house. It's just more opportunity for him to isolate Laela. We have to stop it."

Mona rushed home from the pantry to make a special supper for Rudy. There was just enough time if she used her Insta-pot to make beef stew, a Rudy favorite. Later after dinner when she hoped his defenses would be down, Mona broached the subject of Jad's controlling behavior. Rudy at first attempted to slough it off. Mona said, "Three of us, Rudy, not just me, are concerned. Can you think of a way we can prevent Laela from going to Richmond? Maybe you need to question Jad and her more."

"Wait a moment here, Mona. You want me to use my office to prevent your friend from exercising her right to live her life the way she sees fit?"

"When you say it like that, it sounds wrong, but I'm telling you, she is at risk here."

"I could pay her a visit in Richmond. I'd like to take a look at his home. Laela raved about it in our interview. No reason why you can't go with me. I'll take a vacation day. But – but if I don't see him controlling Laela beyond the norm, that's it, Mona, nothing more."

A SAD STORY

A satisfied Mona made plans with Laela to visit Jad's gorgeous home. She was surprised to get an immediate response as Laela made no effort to ask for Jad's permission. Two days later Rudy and Mona traveled the turnpike to Lee and took the older route to Richmond. Mona raved about the beautiful countryside while Rudy questioned how far the house was located from the nearest grocery store. "Rudy, are you always thinking about your stomach?"

"Yup, someone has to, Mona. Look, there's a store that sells sandwiches." And without any kind of a check with Mona, he pulled into the drive. Inside, the passage of time seemed irrelevant as the two combed through the skinny, crowded with merchandise aisles. Mona fell in love with kitchen gadgets and selected a multi-size level bottle opener. She'd never seen one like it before. Rudy roamed the hardware aisle and decided Richmond had much to offer.

The two met again at the deli counter and ordered sandwiches and ice cream to eat outside on the deck. While waiting, Rudy caught sight of an array of candies in plain labeled containers: jellybeans, Good and Plenty, chocolate, various flavored cough drops and well just about every child's dream of a candy store. He was overwhelmed and put five different kinds of candy in his basket. When the sandwiches were prepared, he added some sparkling water, and paid the clerk. They sat outside on a deck and enjoyed two of the best pastrami and rye with cheese sandwiches, unparalleled in their gastronomic history. Rudy said, "Did you notice the clerk and her dress. They're Mennonite. This cheese was most likely made here and probably the pastrami. She doesn't have a rush bone in her body."

"What do you mean, Rudy, with the rush bone?"

"The life here allows you not to rush. All I do every day is rush, pushing myself in every way. These people don't. I'm not saying they don't have all the problems of running their farms and businesses. Just saying they appear to have no stress and I envy their calm demeanor."

Laughing, Mona said, "You've very little evidence to come to a conclusion like that."

After lunch they drove to Jad's home and were stunned not just by the home itself but also by the quiet beauty of the farmland surrounding it. As they approached the house, Laela came rushing out to greet them. Jad was nowhere in sight. Mona asked, "Where's Jad? I came to get to know him better. He has been so good to you."

"Mona, Jad thinks memories from West Side are disruptive to my healing. I told him he was foolish. I need friends. I need to talk to people who like me, know me, and wish me well. He thought it over and said he'd give me some alone time with you. See, he's not controlling."

Laela toured the home with them. Rudy was impressed with the absolute perfection of the home. He knew he could never live in it, while Mona said, "A clean house is my dream. The place is perfection not attainable with my Rudy and three boys. I guess I should say men now."

Laela laughed. "It takes some getting used to, Mona. I thought I was the best housekeeper. I'm not."

They laughed, had coffee, and talked about life when Rudy said, "Barry and Jad must have been good friends, Laela. They both belonged to the country club and played golf and cards. Did Jad join you for dinner out?"

"Oh no, Jad really didn't know Barry well at all. He was more my friend than Barry's."

Rudy answered, "I thought so. You trust Jad, and Mona has shown me men and women can have friendships. Did Jad come over for tea or coffee at all?"

"Never alone, he was always with Jane. We enjoyed each other. Jad offered to paint my upstairs hallway for nothing. I couldn't have that. Jane talked me into having him do it, but despite all our planning for it, Barry died before the job was to start. I'd forgotten that, Rudy. Maintenance details do not seem important to me now."

"Did Jad ever do small jobs for anyone else?"

"He painted Jane's closet and dressing room in this beautifully layered paint style she'd seen in a design magazine that no other painter she called was willing to do. It came out beautifully."

Mona said, "I didn't know he painted that. It's a wonderful job. Could I call him? I'd be happy to pay him."

"That's the rub, Mona. He won't accept pay. He says now his wife is dead, he likes doing a little work for ladies he likes."

Rudy thought, *over my dead body. There's something off here. The guy's loaded but wants to work for ladies for free if he likes them. Doesn't compute. I can see him wanting to get close to Laela and there is an intimacy when a painter is in a home alone with the woman of the house for days. Several of my cops did side jobs painting and electrical and two of them ended up sleeping with the lady and getting a divorce. Is this what's going on here? This guy has been approached by good looking ladies, but he likes them a little older. Big question mark like this warrants an in-depth review of his background. The murder victims are not in this lady's age range, and she is not out nights looking for trouble. Maybe that's the itch. He thinks he's found the perfect lady.*

Rudy asked, "Laela, how could you have your hallway painted when you're gone several days of the week?"

"Lots of workmen come and use the garage code to get in. Nothing would get done if I had to stay home for them."

Jad walked in with a boisterous, "You guys get enough alone time?"

Laela responded, "Never enough time with friends like these. They love the house but are most impressed with the hay fields and two barns. We didn't tour them yet."

Jad answered quickly, "Not today, I have some hay bales in there. Rats abound."

The four spent some time discussing the location of the home in Richmond, its true serenity, and its natural specialness. Rudy and Mona left kissing Laela who had tears in her eyes. She said, "I'll be home shortly. It's wonderful here but I also need home."

Driving home, Mona said, "Did you see the look Jad gave when Laela said she'd be home shortly? If looks could kill, his would have."

"Mona, I'm more interested in Laela's planning for the painting job. Did she give Jad the code to the garage and the house code or are they one and the same? Important I know these facts. I was afraid to push her. If she thinks I'm looking at Jad, she'd hold back on information.

Right now, she is totally fooled by him, and I don't think any normal man could keep his house that clean."

"Not to worry, Rudy, I agree. A house that clean, kept by a man, tells me he's way over on the OCD and controlling levels. But are you thinking he is involved in Barry's murder? That's a stretch even for you."

The next morning found Rudy speaking quietly with Petra. "Lieutenant, who are the regulars for lawn care and housecleaning in Laela's Greer's area? Don't ask why I can't get the info from Laela."

"Captain, I'm certain you have your reasons. I think you think if you ask her, she will ask them what you wanted. Am I right?"

"Yup, exactly the reason. See if you can get the vendors she uses. Visit them probably late in the day. Ask them how they have access to her house when Laela is gone. Do they know the garage and house codes for entry or have a key?"

"Captain, I have your info already. Before you were leaning toward a natural death, I interviewed all vendors. Laela was loose with access. The gardener had code access to the garage, the housekeeper, window washer, rug cleaner, and general maintenance guy had access to both the garage and house codes. Stands to reason Jad would also have access."

"There's my answer for opportunity," Rudy responded. "But that's not enough."

25

THE FEDS HELP

Agent Alcore walked into the Captain's office bypassing the Desk Sergeant on duty. Rudy said, "Is this osmosis. You now come in through the station walls. Don't you have any pretense for protocol? You might have caught me doing something illegal."

"No chance for that with the almighty honest serial murderer capturer. Oops, that sounds like a reality tv show."

And the conversation continued. Banter and real-life Q and Q and banter and so-on continued. Rudy, known as a terse conversationalist, grew tired of the word games and said, "Let's get to it, Bob. Why the visit?"

"I pulled all traffic for the areas around the various murders. Your guys had luck with timing the route for autos lagging, especially for road stretches with few cross streets. We got five and identified a Mercedes and a truck but no Toyota. We also got a lousy visual of a driver who was wearing a dirty hat with a big brim pulled down low. Not much else from cameras."

"You got a lot, Bob. We now know for certain the serial murderer is in our town. I think it's worth it to pull up all Mercedes vans registered in West Side and Richmond."

Rudy realized the moment he said Richmond he was giving unknown info to Bob Alcore. Alcore said, "Why Richmond? We know nothing about Richmond. It's a tiny town."

"Just a hunch on a guy doing maintenance who has a place up there. I doubt it will go anywhere."

"Your hunches are gold. I want to know more, Rudy, no holding back."

"I'm not. We've checked all the other maintenance people but haven't checked him out. This will help."

"Sounds squirrely to me. Maintenance men don't have houses in Richmond, which has probably the most millionaires per capita in the state of Massachusetts."

"I'm certain there are a lot of working people there. It's farm country with a beautiful view of the mountains and borders New York."

Bob insisted Rudy join him for lunch at which time he tried unsuccessfully to learn about advances in the investigation of Barry and the homeless man's deaths. Rudy reminded Bob, "You now know this guy is the same guy involved in all the murders and you know he is in West Side. You did not know him as the perp before. That's a hell of a piece of knowledge. We are not holding back."

Later in the day, Rudy and Petra viewed the man in the photo given by Bob Alcore. He also checked out the cameras on the roads related to the five murders identified by Bob. He asked Petra her thoughts. "Listen, Petra, put on your smart Boston cop street smarts. What kind of guy do you think we're looking for from this snapshot and the DPW guys' descriptions of the driver?"

"Captain, I can inform not from my street work. From personal experience, this guy's posture while driving and hoping not to be identified brings only two thoughts to me. He is used to being noticed, else why the pull-down hat which, by the way, looks like the 'Acubra' hat worn by Paul Hogan in the Dundee movie. Tells me he is good looking. See, he is slouching down preventing a good assessment of his height. They have him clocked in this picture at thirty miles an hour. That guy never kept to a speed limit. Of that I am certain."

"Meaning what, Lieutenant? Meaning what?"

"Meaning he is a cool dude. Think about the lack of evidence left at crime scenes. Meaning we know nothing about the ladies' struggles. Meaning I see him in a Mercedes but not in a Toyota or a truck. Meaning the guy's had rough experiences but they don't show. Meaning all the ladies appeared to have gone willingly into his vehicles."

"How do you know that? We have no evidence to support."

"He's still using all three vehicles. He wouldn't if the vehicle couldn't be completely cleaned. He'd dump the vehicle. I know he would, and he hasn't yet. He's probably had some experience in forensics and is OCD, but we've already guessed that."

The Captain smiled. "That's why you'll be Chief someday, Petra. I agree, keeping the cars is evidential. We have to find the cars. What if he has gotten rid of one of the cars maybe after a difficult lady victim argued with him? Can we look for a 2010 Toyota with a plate number of 89 for middle numbers or a Mercedes or truck? The plate number found on the Toyota by Lieutenant was only a good guess because the plate was covered with what looked like mud. Its state id was also not confirmed. Try Connecticut, Massachusetts, and Vermont."

"Maybe I should check recent purchases at the Registry and dumped cars and burned cars in the area from Insurers. Monster job and, Captain, it will take days."

"Do it."

Rudy fumed, thinking, *I've wasted time. I should have been on a full investigation from day one. The perp is here right under my nose. I know that. He's completed several murders since Barry Greer's and Mel Laurent. The country club and the cars are central to this. Could Laela's friend Jad be the perp? Nah, he's just a control freak, or maybe not.*

Later that evening, Mona told Rudy over dinner Laela was staying at Jad's home in the Berkshires for several more weeks. They discussed the wisdom of her decision with Rudy practically insisting Jad must be intimate with Laela. Mona insisted, "No, Rudy, Laela is looking for diversion. But not sexual diversion. Why she can't see she's embroiled in a troublesome relationship, I don't know. Jad will have built up some expectations and not unreasonably. He likes his own way with things. If it gets to the point he makes advances, she'll run home immediately. Therein lies the danger. What will he do when she says no?"

"You think he could be dangerous?"

"I don't know. I do know he is controlling and likes life to go along his way. He has two serious friendships with ladies, but no parties with guys at his house. He does play cards at the club. Do you know if he has men friends? I would feel better if I knew he had a robust social life."

Rudy laughed. "By robust, you mean out with the guys doing what? Most socialization by handsome single men who are not in deep depression has a focus on meeting ladies. Doesn't sound like that to me."

Rudy, as he often did, left the table to sit in his study to ruminate on the day's work. Mona's conversation at dinner ran through his mind like a repetitive refrain from an old song. He could not shut it down. So, he played his "what if?" What if Jad were the perp? How would that play out? He thought, *Jad has money. He could afford three vehicles. He has two homes, with one in West Side. The other home is out in no-man's land with two barns that could not be visited because they were filled with hay. He is in a relationship with the wife of a victim, and he hopes to control her. He has a trust in her name which she doesn't know about. At least I think she doesn't know. He could use it to help Laela see how much he loves her and it's not about money. Laela wouldn't quickly understand he could change the beneficiary in a heartbeat whenever he wants. He lied about his wife dying of cancer. We haven't found a wife. Why would he do that? Why is his tax history missing many years? He follows the law scrupulously. He must not have been working or working under the table. Is there a trust payable to him he's living off? Not important, there would still be evidence of income tax payments. I'll have to tell Bob Alcore about my suspicions if I can't get more info from his military history. My gut tells me this guy fits. He has opportunity. He's out two nights a week. Can we match those nights with murder nights? Probably not, because he's been away with Laela, and it would be difficult to match the two nights a week he was previously away with murders. He has in-depth knowledge of Georgia and Florida. We'll try.*

THE FEDS HELP

The Captain had a couple of problems to contend with in following leads about Jad. One was a lack of personnel. He expressed regret daily about his lack of detectives when in the midst of multiple investigations. He needed a detective to spend some time in Richmond. That alone presented problems. He'd have to notify local police of his detective's presence; or maybe not. What is in the barns is important. Mason has to pull info on Jad's military service. Lilly can try to match Jad's night excursions with a few murders and what's with the missing data on Jad's wife's death? He specifically was interested in the rape/murder in Rhode Island. Why the sudden violence? He thought, *I'll be spending resources on this hunch. But, what else do I have? Can it really be this guy? Why would he commit so many atrocities when he has everything in life. I don't even know how he got everything in life. The questions about him are too many not to investigate further.*

The next morning found the Captain in the murder room staring at the multiple boards. Slowly rising from his comfy chair, Rudy groaned saying out loud, "It's time to rock and roll. I'll be out for a bit. Need to talk to my civilian forces."

Petra immediately understood, leaving the other detectives scratching their heads. When the Captain left, she explained, "Now that he's focused on a specific target, he has no problem connecting with Beryl, Norbie, and the Colonel. He is wary of folks trying to push him in one direction or the other before he has seen the logic of the chase. That's just who he is."

Not one detective disagreed.

Rudy left the station and headed for Beryl Kent's home. Not surprisingly, he found the Colonel also visiting or maybe living there. He did wonder, *now that Oliver's gone, I wouldn't be surprised. Those two have been a couple for two years. Too long not to have a fire from the sparks. Still, Beryl has a history of losing her partners. She or Nate could be feeling some hesitation about entering a living together or marriage arrangement. We do get more cautious as we age.*

Back at the station, Sergeant Tagliano banged on her desk yelling, "Pay dirt!"

Three detectives responded with wise remarks. Sergeant Bill Border yelled the loudest, "Lilly, must you always scream at any modicum of success? You don't see us doing that. Men just accept they'll be successful whereas you find it as so rare, you must emote."

Her husband Juan laughed. "She yells when her pasta comes out perfectly. It's probably not important."

The remark resulted in a box of tape being thrown. Lilly said, "I'll have you all down for harassment including you, Juan. You have no idea what I've just learned."

And they waited until she explained the college history of Jad Morton at William and Mary. She said, "Cameron Circosta, a friend of mine, said Jad Morton graduated with highest honors. However, in talking to faculty who had Jad in class, Cameron said Jad left the college under a cloud. It seems he had a close relationship with a classmate. She was a beautiful woman. He thought they were to get married after graduation. Instead, she left the college and brought charges against him for stalking. Even over thirty years ago, stalking was not a good thing. The charges were dropped over lack of evidence. Word got out and two other coeds complained to the Dean. Seems our Jad can't take a 'no.' Two of the three took jobs in the international sector after graduation. The third, a victim of a car hit and run, was found dead by the roadside in Georgia nine months later. The crash was investigated but Jad's name never came up. Granted, the victim wasn't stabbed, but Jad hadn't finished his Army service yet. The victim was the gal he thought would marry him."

"Did you get names for the girls?"

"Is the Pope Catholic? I surely did. Caroline Birch is the accident victim and the one he was to marry. The other two are Lou Belliveau and Deanna Ward. The last two live in Virginia now. I think it's worth a visit. Will the Captain ok a trip to DC for me? These two live next door to each other in Alexandria, Virginia."

Sergeant Border replied, "You thinking you and Juan can catch a second honeymoon or something?"

Before Lilly could give an inappropriate reply, the Captain rejoined the group on his way out. He noticed the energy present in the room. Before he could ask his usual 'What's Up?' he was inundated with Jad's info and Lilly's request for a trip to DC. Without hesitation, he said, "Why don't you and Juan go. It will give you a break – two days only. Set meetings up in advance. Remember we can't convict someone on this info by itself, but he's looking better as a prospect."

Two minutes later, the detectives alone in the incident room showered Lilly and Juan. Border said, "I can't believe this. I'm getting my girl to join the force so we can vacay on city time. Is he out of his mind? And you, Lilly, are one pushy little cop."

Rudy thought about the news and wondered, *"Did I drop the ball on this one? Jad seemed like such a normal guy. So, he's disappointed in love, so what. I was disappointed in love. So, he's clingy. He doesn't like the word 'no.' Neither do I. Still, there's the geography on the locations and his knowledge about those areas, can I ignore their relevance? And what about his desire to control Laela and his surroundings? What about his cars and the barns on his Richmond property? What about his ability to insert himself so perfectly in Laela's life? What about his belonging to the card playing group just before Barry Greer left because Barry didn't like a member? Which member? What about Jad's checkered record in employment and tax paying? And his Army service, and, and... Yup, it's enough to warrant closing in on him. I find one piece of real evidence and I get search warrants.*

Lieutenant Mason Smith joined him while he was in reverie remarking, "You're doing that thing again, Boss. You know, going over a thousand pieces of evidence to keep you from jumping off the cliff. Go with your gut. You're always right."

"I wish I had your faith in me, Lieutenant. But don't worry, I'm getting there. I need one piece, one piece of hard evidence."

Without saying another word, the Captain left. Mason said to no one in particular, "The Captain's on a roll."

Driving slowly, Beauregard passed Jad's home in West Side. The stately house was quite big with perfectly manicured grounds. He thought, *doesn't look like a home. All the window shades were at the same level. He is one perfectionist. There's a three-car garage. I assumed there was only a two-car garage. Assuming is not evidence. He's in Richmond now. There are cameras. If I don't go to the front door, I'll be questioned later when the ring doorbell camera catches be at the side door next to the garage. I'll go to the front first. No one answers gives me a reason for checking the back. After all, I could be mistaken about the timing of their return to West Side.*

Rudy walked up the driveway which brought him up to the back-house door on the left and the first garage window on the right. He saw a car in the garage. The window was smoky glass and he had trouble identifying the auto. With a slight turn of his head, he realized the other garage windows had the same smoky glass. He continued to the back door, rang the bell, waited the appropriate time to pass, shook his head for the camera and walked away thinking, *not evidence, but a lead. He has a second vehicle. Maybe a third. I don't have enough for a warrant, but it's a lead. I need a little luck. He has at least two vehicles. They must be registered somewhere.*

The next day began with an admin headache. The District Attorney called for a meeting with West Side Police, the FBI and their prosecutors with no subject proposed. Rudy fumed and not quietly saying, "Alcore thinks we're close and he wants the FBI to be close. We have no evidence."

Lieutenant Aylewood-Locke said, "Captain, why don't you stall them? You can keep the wolves at bay. You've done it before. Tell them we have no evidence. It's true. They don't know we're on the verge of something. They'll just bring in Jad Morton and try to scare him. I don't think that will work. Besides, we have to build our budget for the reporting deadline next week. That should give us two to four weeks depending on your persuasiveness."

"That's why you'll be Chief someday, Petra."

The detectives all groaned with the exception of Lilly who said, "I can't wait for it. Petra will be awesome."

The Captain's look quieted the group. He asked for news on the Mercedes van. Sergeant Tagliano read from her report. "There are three black Mercedes vans registered to corporations in West Side and two registered in Richmond. No black Mercedes vans registered to individuals in either place. I'm going to visit them all starting after this meeting. I can't get anything out of the registrations. They are all LLC's or C Corps. Not one signer is Jad Morton."

Lieutenant Smith looked over the names saying, "No, not Jad Morton, but you have a Leonard Smith as a name. My surname is so common, folks use it as a make-believe name. Check him out first, Lilly. And this guy Brad Mourner had Brad for Jad and the last name begins with the first two letters of Jad's surname. Go after him next."

And Lilly left. While Lieutenant Smith continued the disrupted review of files from the Feds, he thought, *I should have finished this stuff a long time ago. Two waves of files were sent. The first contained summaries of their investigation. The second included evidence and traffic reports around the area with camera footage. It's kind of like a college course, the Prof offers a summary to study, but you have to read tons of stuff and figure out what he'll test. For me, I'd get lost in the detail I found interesting and forget the big picture about passing an exam. I got through. My wife said I was the one getting the most out of the courses.*

Two hours later a bleary-eyed Lieutenant rubbed his eyes. He pulled Lieutenant Lent's West Side traffic reports and DPW's reports. There was a film capture from a murder in New York: the Rivera Colon recent murder. It was on Route 202, a small road near I-87 in Brewster, New York. The street camera caught a photo of a greyish or beige Toyota

2010 with one letter (8) caught as a middle number and a man with a pulled down hat resembling a Crocodile Dundee hat. He yelled, "Gotcha!" to all, but there was no one to hear his gleeful remark. Only one thing to do, call the Captain.

Beauregard's response did not light his fire. The Captain said, "Great connection to have to our local guy. Great connection to more than one killing, but not evidence. The car's important. The driver with the hat is probably our guy, but we still don't know who the hell he is. Go through the rest of the stuff. I hope there's more. This is good police work, Lieutenant."

26

MOVING FASTER

Every 2010 light grey or beige Toyota registered in Massachusetts, Connecticut, New Hampshire, and Vermont was listed. Sergeant Bobby Barr reviewed the list thinking, *89 could start in second not just third place on the license plate.*

Barr loved this kind of stuff. He thought it was like his computer geography class where all he did was sort for towns and cities and their characteristics. It took him three hours to get a variety of sorts. He narrowed the possibilities to the western part of Massachusetts, southern New York, northern Connecticut, southern New Hampshire and Vermont. He now had two hundred names. He took the fifty in western Massachusetts because the West Side DPW workers thought it was a Mass plate. The plate was registered to a corporation named Computer Resources, LLC. He thought, *where have I heard that name? Bingo, it was on the murder board with a question mark.*

He found the name but felt disappointed. His find would not be evidentiary. "There is no connection to an event related to Jad Morton, just to a car in West Side. I'll check corporate records just in case."

Georgia Secretary of State showed a filing with the name Jonathan Myles as the corporate secretary and owner. The corporation's address was in West Side. Undaunted, Barr googled Jonathan Myles. He found nothing but an address in West Side, nothing in Richmond but a slew of names in Springfield, Holyoke, Boston and Worcester. He tried Atlanta. There were too many to explore. He next called the corporate phone number. It went to a woman's voice mail despite the call time being in the middle of the day. He decided the only action left was to visit the barn. He was surprised to see the barn was the only structure of its type amidst a group of luxury homes. His first thought was, *it doesn't appear to be connected to any related property. It's old but has been repaired.*

Leaving his car, he tried the large bay doors, but they were locked solid. There were two doors on the left side. The rear door showed a modern realtor's keypad. The windows were high but were also covered. In the back he found a generator. He thought, *most houses here don't have one. What's so important? Are the contents at risk in a power outage? It could be computer equipment or antique furniture or drugs. How do I get in there to see?*

The Sergeant walked around the back of the barn. He did not notice cameras but did see a hatchway. It surprised him. It meant there was a basement under the barn, not just a slab. The hatchway was locked. The lock was a standard padlock, one he could replace if need be. He thought, *I won't have to, I've picked this kind of lock before.*

Two minutes later, he was in the small basement. There was a stairway up and nothing else. He climbed the stairs and found a 2010 Toyota with 89 as the middle numbers on the plate. Other than the car, there was a workbench with tools all in perfect condition and a large metal table with drains. He was now left with the problem of his break-in. *How do I legitimately discover this? I can't. Someone else will have to do it. I can't be connected.*

Beauregard was irritated. On the one hand his Sergeant gave him info saying he thought he saw a 2010 Toyota pull into the barn. Bogus, he thought. He knew it was from the 'poisonous tree' and could not be used. He also knew and Sergeant Barr did not argue that another detective would have to do a watch detail. He did not have the wherewithal to watch for more than a week. He thought, *if it's our man, he'd probably use the Toyota at night. He was seen driving it during the day. I'll have Mason do a real estate search on the purchase of the barn. Sergeant Barr said the heat was on. He knew by touching the outside of the building. Bullsh**t.*

The Captain again scanned the murder boards. There were so many on his computer and around the room. So many murders and potential evidence or inquiries needed causing him to shudder. He exclaimed loudly, "The handprint on the Rhode Island victim's head."

Beauregard was on the move. He called Beryl. A call, a few years ago, he never would have made. Twenty minutes later he sat in her astonishing kitchen playing with her dog Amore and saying, "Beryl, we have a partial handprint from the Rhode Island killing. If we could match it, not even completely, it could be evidential."

Beryl laughed. She said, "And you think Laela can get a partial off Jad! She thinks he's an angel. She wouldn't do it. If he drank a Coke from a bottle, you wouldn't be able to capture the top of the hand."

Rudy answered, "Help me think of a way."

"Could you get an upper partial print?" she asked.

"How did you know it was an upper partial print? I didn't tell you."

A perplexed Beryl thought and thought. Rudy was patient. He didn't rush her. After a few very long silent moments, she said, "I can't remember, Rudy. You must have told me, but I've thought of a thousand ways to leave a print; but only one way in which the person has no idea he's being printed."

Beauregard nodded as a prod. She said, "He compulsively holds the door for ladies. Think how he can hold the door if he's following me or someone my height who opens the door, but the weight is too much for me. In that case the man behind me would take his left hand on the top of the door and pull it. It would leave a print. Do you have a left or a right print?"

"It wouldn't work, Beryl. He'd leave maybe half a palm print. How can you make him put his whole palm on the door?"

"Rudy, if I carry heavy bags and try to open a door, the person behind me will grab the door as before. If I also drop one of the bags, it stops the door from closing but doesn't leave a wide enough space for the man behind me to enter. He'll press the glass with his right hand to keep it open for entry while he'll pick up my bag."

Rudy said, "It has to be a glass storm door not a screen door. They're being put in as we speak. Are yours in yet?"

"Yes, and I know how we can get him back in West Side."

And she made the call.

Beryl worried about her decision, rather her two decisions. The first was to marry Colonel Nate Connaught, and the second to ask for help in planning the reception. She knew she would have no trouble planning a reception, but most others would get assistance with such an important occasion. She thought, *I told Rudy my thoughts and he promised to help. I'll get a committee at my house. I'll tell Oliver and Nate to be late. I'll buy stuff from Amazon and leave it on the front porch. I'll tell Jad and Laela to be here twenty-five minutes earlier to help me move boxes. I'll get you, Jad. I won't let Laela carry anything. After we're in the kitchen Lilly will be waiting with a print kit. She says it won't take but three minutes.*

Beryl made her calls, finding Jad almost refusing to come. He said, "I don't think Laela should be back in West Side right now. It's still too early."

Fortunately, his voice was negated by Laela who said, "Jad, I have to help Beryl. We are going. I'm excited you're taking this step, Beryl."

They said their good-byes and Beryl was left with a heavy sense of guilt in both her lie to Laela and Jad and her using her wonderful Nate and her marriage as an opportunity to find evidence. She remembered her conversation with Nate last evening. She'd told him she was ready to set a date. Excitedly he said, "Beryl, don't worry. I'm not going to die on you. I promise. When?"

"In two weeks if I can book Father McInerny."

"For a lady who's been dragging her feet, what triggered the speed, Beryl?"

She had been ready to lie to him. She knew he'd ask this question. She couldn't lie to him. She said, "I love you, Nate, but to be honest the rush to the altar is motivated by a need to get some evidence in the serial murders."

She waited for the uproar. It didn't come. Instead, Nate laughed and said, "Providence in the form of your persistence has worked in my direction. Not to worry. Darling, you would have dragged your feet for another six months without this push. Tell me the what and how of this evidence gathering."

Through tears she told him the story. He said, "Dear, Beryl, I could have gotten his palm print, but you won't need my help now. I want to be certain we'll be married in two weeks."

She thought, *I really have chosen well. He loves me. He understands me. He accepts who I am. Please, God, let him outlive me. I can't go through death of a husband again.*

Attorney Norbie Cull stopped by the club on his journey home after a particularly stressing day. He had two short criminal trials set on the same day. Since they were in different courts and he scheduled one without telling his Administrative Assistant Sheila, he had no one to blame. Sheila smirked in the morning as he was leaving. "I don't try your cases for you, why do you think you can schedule one? You can screw up any calendar. Let's just say it's not your forte."

Both cases were continued because the judges had other business. On top of that his lunch 'sucked,' a term his youngest son used frequently. He met with five new potential litigants. The two more serious cases took twenty-five minutes for the interview. The other three lighter cases each took an hour. He thought, *I not only can't schedule anything, I can't predict how long a client needs to talk. I'll have a nice bourbon on the rocks with an orange slice and talk to a few club members which hopefully will lower my stress.*

Just as Norbie sat at the club bar, Sheri called, "Honey, do you mind if I miss dinner tonight? Callista came into town, and I need some hen time."

With nothing better to do he ordered a hamburger with fries. Gene the golf pro asked if he could join him. "I saw you ordering. I figured you, like me, were off on your own."

Gene's order was similar, except for his drink which was a margarita. It did not go unnoticed. "Gene, I get a bourbon. I'm a lawyer and should be drinking trending drinks. You are the masculine mentor, and you drink girlie drinks."

"It's from my teaching golf to the ladies. They often buy me drinks and send over what they drink."

The conversation was at first typical of gossip about shenanigans by club members and about changes in staff, some of which were good and a few that were troublesome. Norbie realized he'd never asked Gene about Jad Morton. He felt certain Beauregard's detectives would have questioned him, but just in case, he said, "I've recently been in the company of Jad Morton. He's one of the card players. I stopped playing a few years ago. What's he like?"

Gene frowned before saying, "He's cool, a snappy dresser, drives a Mercedes, presents as a gregarious man around town, but divulges little about himself. He took special golf lessons from me and paid with a business check."

Cull interrupted, "What's the name of his company?"

"I don't remember. It had some boring title with I think the word computers in the name."

"Could you check your records for the name?"

"I will but, Norbie, first tell me what this is about."

"I really can't tell you. I think you know I wouldn't ask if it was not important."

Gene answered, "I'll get it for tomorrow. I don't think Jad is a criminal, but I can say he is a strange duck. There is absolutely no emotional depth visible. I gave him at least twelve classes and never once did he say anything to let me inside his psyche. You know, the kind of statement that lets you hear a story or point of view. He is a moderate Democrat. He never talks political issues or discusses the woke surge. He doesn't criticize anyone. That's unusual. He doesn't womanize or drink too much or drive too fast or create any kind of disruption. He's too perfect, Norbie."

Cull waited patiently for the next day but folded in mid-afternoon and sent a text to Gene. It was answered within five minutes and said, "Computers Advisory Associates, LLC." He asked Sheila to check the Secretary of State's records for several states for the name of the corporation and listed secretary and members. Shortly later Sheila sent a copy. The corporation was a Massachusetts corporation and had only one name as secretary and member. Its start date was January 1, 2018, and its secretary was Jonathan Myles with an address at 432 Congress Street, West Side. Norbie thought, I know that building. It's owned by Lionel Breen, a major holder of commercial real estate. There'd been great stress on Breen's business since COVID. Since he normally leased two-thousand square foot executive condos manned by up to four people, many of whom now worked from home, his business was down. The need for a glamorous business home base had now diminished in numbers. He called Lionel. They agreed to meet for a coffee at the new coffee bar at 432 Congress called 'The Congressional.' The six-foot six-inch tall Lionel, a former college star basketball player, gracefully tucked his height into the leather booth. The counter barista hurried over to take their orders. Norbie said, "I didn't know they had wait staff. I guess it helps to be the owner."

"Only part owner of 'The Congressional.' Who knew coffee was so lucrative? I thought it was chancy putting him in here. Nope, I was lucky."

It took a few minutes of discussion on rents, square footage, and burden, before Cull broached the subject of Jad Morton, saying, "Jad Morton, a member of the country club, has his office here. I can never figure out what he does. He golfs so often, I can't believe he's in business."

"He's what we call an 'ACE' (acting corporate executive). We have several of them. They are loaded, sometimes from the wife's money, and don't work. They bring friends up to their office, kick back with a cigar, and tell tales about their business. Although I haven't often, if ever, seen people visiting him. He looks the role of the top executive. He ought to be on television."

"Does he have admin assistance up there?"

"I think the only staff I've seen comes in two days a week. Cora is a dowdy fifty-year-old lady who arrives with multiple bags. We think she knits up there. Occasionally she leaves with a couple of envelopes to mail. She's there today, Norbie."

Breen excused himself, claiming a business appointment. Norbie thought, *time for his workout. Does he not know everyone knows where to find him at this time? Good timing for me, Breen has no additional information.*

After a particularly slow elevator ride that stopped at every floor before the sixth, Cull knocked at Jad's office. The door had privacy glass, but he could see a shadow of someone approaching the door. The woman opened the door saying, "It was open. Come on in. Are you looking for Mr. Morton? He's not in today."

Cull used his best manners, introduced himself and subsequently was invited to "have a cuppa."

"You're from England, aren't you?"

"Close but no cigar. I've lived there but I was born in Scotland, lived in Ireland and London. Tea or coffee?"

Cull saw intelligence in her eyes despite her demeanor. Her name given was Mrs. Ryan. She certainly didn't match either choice in victims. He asked her how long she'd worked for Mr. Morton. Her reply was ever since he moved to West Side. He said, "Mr. Morton appears to be a big city guy. Whatever brought him to our small city?"

"Ah, like all of us the twists of fate. He lived down South, but his wife died from cancer, and he really closed in on himself. He limits personal conversation. He appears social but is not. I see pain cross his eyes sometimes, but who am I to analyze someone else's journey. Now how can I help you?"

"Jad is a member of the country club as am I. I just found out about his computer business and need assistance with my office. Sheila, my main admin says I'm being ripped off by my current service. I thought Jad would give good advice."

"I suppose he could give you advice, but that company is not currently active. It's a vehicle for holding various investments. It was active when he was in Atlanta, so I'm told."

"When was that, Mrs. Ryan?"

"Well, I may be wrong about that corporation, but another one with a similar name was active."

"Did he sell it? Maybe I could get help from the new owners."

"I do have a contact. You said you are an attorney. I suppose Jad would be happy to help a golfing buddy."

And Mrs. Ryan gave him a corporate card with the name listed on the card as Jonathan Myles and a phone number but no address. It was time to share. Cull made his exit and headed over to the police station thinking, research like this is police work. He walked past the Desk Sergeant who just waved to him, took the stairs and found the Captain lording it over his detectives. He did not have to lure Rudy away. He immediately rose and moved towards his office. Norbie summarized his day's activities. The Captain said, "It's not your job to investigate for the police, but you did good. I'm glad you didn't call this Myles. It could be Jad himself. We'll check Georgia's corporate filings. If it indeed is a sale, we'll follow the money. But for us, Norbie, you have made the connection. We found a barn owned by this corporation. That's evidence. Now Mrs. Ryan said he sold this corporation. There has to be a trail. Why don't you run along, and we'll get to work. I have only one concern. Do you think Mrs. Ryan will tell Jad about your visit?"

"Absolutely."

"Watch yourself, Norbie, you may be at risk."

27

EVIDENCE, EVIDENCE

And there was lots of brouhaha in Beryl's wedding plans. Mona, Jane and Jocelyn stressed the cell towers with their constant checking details. Jocelyn said, "Mother, it must be perfect. This wedding, although small, must be a credit to Nate who has been very patient. I don't want you to let him go. He's a winner. He'll take good care of you, and I won't have to worry."

Beryl reacted, "So you just hand me over so your life will be simpler. I have Oliver."

"Na, Oliver is much too married, Mom. You can't expect him to jump at any investigative whim you have now. Besides, your wedding is a dress rehearsal for mine."

Since Jocelyn was still in New York City, Beryl could not check Jocelyn's left hand for a ring. Prompting her to say, "Are you engaged? When were you going to tell me?"

"Mom, I am an artist. We don't get engaged. One day we decide we can't live without each other. We're getting married in November on Thanksgiving at your home. Only ten of our friends, twelve of his family and our family are to be invited. My wedding ring will do for the engagement. I'm pregnant and I'm ready and he is the right one. Please be happy."

EVIDENCE, EVIDENCE

"We could move your wedding to mine."

"Nope, every bride deserves her own day."

And since neither Beryl nor Oliver typically won an argument with Jocelyn, Beryl oozed love and acceptance saying, "I'm to be a grandmother. Praise God, I didn't think it would ever happen."

Jocelyn laughed saying, "You'd better talk to Oliver. He may have some news for you."

Beryl could not reach Oliver, so she called Leeann's cell. She quickly answered, "Beryl, you know, don't you? We were coming over tonight to tell you. Imagine both your children are finally making you a 'grandma.' Are you pleased?"

Brought to tears, Beryl barely answered her yes with love and the two talked about the future. Later that day, Beryl recovered from motherly exaltation, and waited for Jad and Laela. They were assigned the task of bringing in the large box containing a beautiful seven-foot arbor to be decorated with flowers and placed in her living room. She hoped he would place his palm on the box but thought, *what if he decided to wear gloves. No, stop thinking negatively. We need that print. It has to be assembled. If I don't get it on the door or the box, I'll make him open my toolbox. One hand has to press the cover down in order to unsnap it.*

The bell rang. Beryl opened the door and found Laela holding the storm open while Jad held the box in both hands. He leaned towards the side of the door frame for balance. Hopefully Laela could not hold the door while Jad tried to get the large box inside, Beryl shooed Laela away and held one side of the box with her back holding the door, saying, "Tilt it towards me, Jad. It's too big for one person. Get your balance, your left hand on the box and the right hand on the door frame. Then walk towards me. I'm strong enough to hold it until you get inside."

Jad did what she said and thanked her. Once inside, he asked for her tool-box and a pry bar. She had them ready. The box was packed with two by ten-inch wood strips which required prying the strips off to open the box. She watched while Jad used his right hand on the pry bar and his left to tear the bow open. Beryl thought, *well the print better be on the side of the door frame.*

They all helped bring the pieces into the beautiful great room where the ceremony would be held. Father McInerny had made a request to the Bishop to allow the ceremony to be conducted in the private home. Beryl was hellbent on making the room majestic for the service and homey for the attendees. She chatted with Jad as he tried to open her toolbox asking, "What kind of lock is this, Beryl?"

She pointed out, "Think of it like a prescription bottle. Press down with your right hand and flip the lock with your left."

Jad automatically did as he was told. The arbor was assembled within twenty minutes and received a whole bunch of oohs and aahs. Beryl left the room to put the toolbox away. She opened the front door and handed it to the Sergeant hoping Jad would not need it again and was pleased with herself, *thinking, I have a print from the toolbox too.*

Beauregard and the detectives debated the corporation ownership of the barn with the secretary's name at Jonathan Myles. Sergeant Barr said, "This Myles has to be real. A social security number is required for all corporate secretaries. We need his to research."

Rudy told the Lieutenant, "I thought you would have already done that. We need info. Even if Morton's handprint matches the Rhode Island victim's forehead, because it's only a partial, it will not be a 99% match."

Shortly later Smith had the SS number and was putting it into a nationwide search. While waiting for the results, Beauregard asked, "How could Jad develop two identities? He has one for college and the Army and they're the same as he has today. He would have to have a different one for all his middle years. We have no evidence of social problems, with the exception of his girl disappointment in the Army."

Lieutenant Aylewood-Locke reminded the Captain of Jad's college lady problem. Before Rudy could respond, Lieutenant Smith returned. He announced, "It's weird, this social security number for Jonathan Myles shows a birth through a high school diploma, Georgia license, then a blank for some years after which Myles was institutionalized in the Darlington Mental Health Facility outside of Atlanta, Georgia, for a number of years. He left the facility a few years ago leaving no history other than in corporate filings we found."

Beauregard asked, "What have we? Are the two men the same? Does the timeline allow it? How could Jad get admitted to an institution with someone else's social? When was the last time we had Jad's social after the Army? Do we know yet?"

Beauregard answered his own question with a negative nod, saying "It's not a vacation. Call Juan and Lilly. I want them back."

Detective Torrington who had just walked into the room said, "They're on their way back, Captain. They said they have a story."

"I want evidence not a story. Get them in here the moment they hit town."

Lilly and Juan found the road trip back from DC tiring, leaving Lilly to say, "I hate long drives on highways. I like to coast along local roads and see little shops to peruse. This business travel is the worst."

"Stop complaining, Lilly. We've had three nights of dining with the best and an elaborate tea at Chez Deanna Ward plus good information. What more can you ask?"

Lilly went on about Deanna's condo, saying, "I've never heard of a nine-room condo before. Who'd want to live in the suburbs. Did you see the furniture. It's all high-end stuff and looks like a designer did the arrangement. And the artwork. I minored in art in college. I think some of the stuff are originals. What does she do?"

'She works for the Pentagon. That's all our search got. She's living large. She told me she's divorced when you were in the bathroom checking her drug cabinet. She's living large. Could be from the divorce. We didn't pick up her marriage on our search."

"We didn't check Vegas. Older couples often marry in Las Vegas, Juan. From what she and Lou said, I think they were both off of men for a long time. Even as a young man in college, Jad had a powerful effect on the ladies. They both believe he killed their friend. I was surprised when Lou said Jad was dating all three of them at the same time but offered Caroline a ring first. She was to keep it a secret until graduation and then tell her parents. Instead, she told him no. He went berserk. Whatever he did, it scared her. She went to the Dean and her parents. The news didn't get out on campus until Deanna and Lou got some of his controlling behavior and were frightened. Lou called Caroline when she heard a rumor about Caroline's going to the Dean about a sociopath boyfriend. She didn't know the boy was Jad. She just wanted advice. After her conversation with Caroline, Lou dumped Jad. Deanna lived across the hall in Lou's dorm. Lou caught sight of Jad from her window with Deanna holding his arm tightly. She later let Deanna know about Jad. Deanna stopped seeing him. Within a week both Deanna and Lou started getting harassed. They received porn type pictures with women looking like them doctored to be wearing some of their own clothes. Each remembered his taking pictures of them when on a date. They also got phone calls. Lou remembered the one phrase repeated often, "You play with men's lives. Don't feel safe. You're not.'"

Deanna was adamant saying, "I've never been so scared. He had such power over me. When I tried to stop seeing him, he was everywhere. It was a very long time before I could trust a man or to even understand most men are not like him. I was so stupid. Lou was on to his behavior first. When she called me, I was devastated. I broke it off and he threatened me, and it went on and on. Lou and I put up with a lot before we went to the Dean."

Lou said, "If Jad knew where we live today, I would be afraid. We both have positions that are classified. We have nothing on social media. But after Caroline's death only nine months later, we became entrenched in fear. We believe he killed her and would kill us."

Juan said, "I'll never get it, Lilly. Why would two such smart ladies let fear drive them?"

"Juan, the guy is a magician, a sociopath, handsome, wealthy, and domineering. He sucks his prey in and then controls them. I so distrust perfection in a boyfriend. It's never real, just a ruse. I see him now as a serial killer and I'm afraid for Laela. I wonder sometimes at women's position in our culture. My dad wanted to take care of me. I'm his little girl. He wouldn't let me take certain jobs that he'd let my brothers take. He hated my joining the force. I rebelled from what I thought was control when I now see the wisdom of caring. I want to protect Laela and other potential victims. If he makes advances and she turns him down, he won't take it lightly. He's OCD and possessive."

"You're getting ahead of yourself, Lilly."

On their return to work, the two travelers asked the Captain for a meeting. He put it off until later in the day. Loaded with work for an appearance before the Council, he was busy preparing positive statistics, saying, "Part of my job is to satisfy the citizenry of West Side which means reporting officially to the Mayor and the Council."

Not asking for a quick summary of their report before he put them off annoyed Sergeant Tagliano. Her spouse Sergeant Flores laughed at her. "You're taking things personally, Babe. You know better."

The MCU detectives met at two. Lilly passed out a summary of their trip and before it could be read, she described the demeanor of both interviewees so vividly. Lieutenant Smith said, "I know the type and I know their fear."

Juan was questioned by Sergeant Torrington. "Do you see these two as Lilly sees them?"

"There's no doubt Jad is a controlling SOB. They went into details, remembered whole conversations and the guy from my perspective can't take disappointment from any lady he has stalked. They both are still in fear despite one having had a marriage she says was okay, but her fear of men interfered. The spouse got sick of his having to 'babysit' her. Her words, not mine."

Beauregard said, "This is still not evidence. Do we have the investigative report on the Birch death?"

Mason had it and the detectives went over the details of the autopsy. Petra continued to review the photos of the body making Beauregard impatiently say, "Lieutenant, if you see something or have an idea, speak up."

"I don't know, Captain. The more I look at these photos, the more I think something's wrong. In the notes, it says deep abrasions with some dirt embedded on whole back of body, but her clothes were intact. Also, she had sex with some semen tested for DNA. Conclusion stated the semen donor was a non-secretor. I think two things. It was not an auto accident. She showed enough damage on the back of the head to support a previous head trauma. They did not do a lot of testing for ingestibles. If the perp in that case is a non-secretor, can we test Jad?"

A heady discussion ended with the Captain directing the Lieutenant to conference the doctor who did the autopsy. He also said, "I'm telling you all what I've said before. We go over details over and over. In this case we did just what the doctor down there did. It looked like Birch was run over, therefore she was killed by the car and she probably was. We thought Jad would have run over her. They thought it was an accident. We never examined it closely. What was her state before being hit by an auto? We did no better than them. Thank you, Lieutenant. As to testing Jad's blood, even if he shows up as a non-secretor, 20% of the population are non-secretors. Check his military file for health history. I suspect his blood type will be there, but do they do secretor status? I don't know."

Sergeant Barr said, "What about the barns on his Richmond property? We may find a truck there. We haven't searched the other barn owned by Myles who by happenstance has Jad's same initials."

"Sergeant, we will get there, but to check out Richmond requires Jad's presence in West Side and a viable connection. As to the local barn site let's not go there yet. We don't have one piece of evidence connecting him. We have a history of Jonathan Myles' social security number. I want a picture ID of this guy. You said he had a driver's license. Could be a match for Jad's. Check it out. They must have been a match."

Sergeant Tagliano said, "Captain, we've received a match on the palm print. It's not a hundred percent but over ninety. I think it's enough to get a search warrant."

Although Beauregard looked pleased, he said, "Not yet."

Dinner on the eve of Beryl and Nate's wedding included the bride, groom, and the bride's family along with all of MCU's detectives and spouses, and friends including Jad Morton. The only detective missing was Sergeant Bill Border who was home with the flu. The groom wondered, *I've worked to limit my professional investigative work and now on the eve of my wedding we're entertaining a suspected serial murderer. Only Beryl could have brought these circumstances to my life – only Beryl.*

Beryl's son Oliver and daughter Jocelyn, hosts for the sumptuous dinner catered at the Barney Estate in Springfield by Cece, treated the night as a roast of the couple with no mercy shown to their mother. As if in the know, the brother and sister steered away from inquiries into current and past investigations. Apparently, the bride and groom displayed enough noted personality quirks to bring the house down with laughter. Beryl took to the podium and said, "I know my darlings this was all said in jest, but I didn't realize you were watching me so closely and what memories you have. Poor Nate, you'll have to careful in the future. They probably have listening devices installed in our home."

Nate concentrated on only one term, "our home" and speaking loudly from his chair, "Jocelyn and Oliver, you get out of line, and I'll eject you from "our home."

Oliver said, "I expect Sunday dinner. That's what parents do when the youngsters leave the nest."

Beauregard couldn't help himself despite Mona telling him to shush, he said, "In today's world he's calling mid-thirties youngsters."

Norbie Cull found himself watching Jad Morton thinking, *he's cool as a cucumber and appears to be enjoying himself. He thinks because he's been invited nobody's on to him. Beryl's kids must be in on the game. In the whole roast nothing was said about Nate's career nor Beryl's favorite hobby. And he's practically stifling Laela's interaction beyond himself. It's weird he would fall for Laela who is about five years older than him. None of his victims are near her age. I wonder how Petra's husband Jim Locke would analyze this.*

The party broke up and Nate pulled Jim aside saying "I'll give you a call when you're driving home. OK?"

The call came five minutes later when Norbie and his wife Sheri had just settled in their car. With the car running but not moving Sheri realized for the hundredth time Norbie had some business. She sat back and listened as the call was on speaker. Norbie presented the age of all the victims in the serial murder and was stopped by Jim who said he knew most of the facts. Jim said, "Norbie, as I told Rudy I think the suggestion of two separate motives is viable. Now is there something else I should know?"

"You saw Jad and his total focus on Laela tonight. Can you build a psychological scenario that would fit with Laela's age close to fifty-eight years and Jad's at fifty-two. Is she in danger? All his other victims are much younger. We believe his mother was in the serial murderer's victims age range when he experienced a severe trauma."

"Norbie, I can quote Freud on his life and death motivation he assigned to these types of murderers. I can give you current history on the brain scans of noted captured serial murderers. I don't think it helps. What I think is important is early childhood. We can't know in advance brain scans unless medical records show the difference in a suspect's brain. To answer your question, I think this man had early and ongoing trauma that to him was opposite to his concept of right and wrong. His continual killing tells me he needs to kill. I don't know if he's trying to right a wrong. I do know he is intelligent and pays attention to details and he doesn't want to get caught. I know he's rushing his killings now. If he has targeted a relationship with Laela for himself and it goes wrong, I don't think age will make a difference. I think he wants perfection in a woman and no woman can give that. He has been dedicated at killing women who tarnish the reputation of all women. He didn't know those women. I wonder if in his past he murdered a woman he knew and he got away with it. I don't know Jad's past, but he fits my idea of a narcissist for sure and a controlling type of boyfriend. When did the killings get closer, you know, have less time between murders? I suspect they were more frequent after his trip with Laela up to today. I think Laela's in jeopardy. He needs to kill right now. Think of the love shown between Beryl and Nate. Think of all the intact relationships he saw tonight. That might goad him to move faster in his relationship with Laela and he does want one. I'd have her stay with the bride tonight."

They clicked off which was a good thing. Sheri heard enough to insist Norbie get a hold of Beryl. She said, "Tell Beryl I was supposed to stay with her tonight, but I have a headache, am going home and Laela is my replacement. Beryl won't need a program to understand. Call Laela and tell her to stay. She'll be pleased. Tell her you'll drive her over. Please. Norbie, call."

And he did.

Cull delivered Laela to Beryl's front door and stayed for a cup of tea. He had noticed Jad did not receive the news of her staying with the bride well. He thought, *this guy does not take adaptations well. He looked as if he were going to argue and then stopped himself. I wonder if these two are safe alone. I'll call Beauregard when I leave. I want a watch over.*

28

HAPPINESS DESPITE A CLOUD

And the wedding preparations began at five in the morning. Tents and tables and chairs had been delivered the day before and now the wedding planner with her designer was making magic in the home. Laela left at nine to go home and dress, which was a relief to Beryl who wanted to be alone for a bit before her daughter and son visited. She found herself nervous, a state she rarely felt. Beryl found it difficult to stay out of the party designer's way. She couldn't always visualize what the woman was planning. She thought, *if I just knew what she had in mind. She has created a wonder from what I've already seen, but, oh well, Jocelyn will fix things if they are awry when she arrives. It's good Nate and I are marrying today. All the fear around Laela reminded me of my loneliness. I need Nate, despite the dread I feel about marriage. I need him for help with the grandchildren.*

Later, after a small lunch was delivered by the wedding planner to Beryl's bedroom, Beryl emerged dressed for the early afternoon ceremony to greet Father McInerny who was astounded at the transformation on her home. He said, "Now not to worry, Beryl. You have had the fate of great joy and sorrow. Now you have the opportunity to have enormous joy in marrying Nate and expecting two grandchildren. Have faith. None can know their destination. Have hope life will go on. But most importantly give and accept love."

The ceremony was simple and beautiful. The couple matched the majesty of the music "All I ask of You" played magically by the four strings, horn, and bass instrument group. And the party started. Beauregard spent the day moving Mona to be near Laela and Jad. Mona finally nudged him saying, "I want to enjoy this day, Rudy. You're being obvious and I feel Jad doesn't like you. Mind you, that's okay. If he's a serial murderer, I don't want him liking you."

Rudy replied, "Thanks for turning your back to him. He may read lips. I wouldn't put it past him."

The bride approached the podium after the toasts by Oliver and Jocelyn and announced to all she was to be a grandmother to two babies in six months. Applause and foot stomping had to be stopped by the saxophonist who used his instrument as a wake-up call. The party continued until nine in the evening. When the guests left, the couple was alone. Nate said, "I have one caveat for tonight, no talk of murder or investigations or of Laela and Jad or of being a grandmother. Just talk about us."

Jad drove Laela to her home. He said on opening her front door for her, "You have a glow about you, Laela. You enjoyed the wedding."

Laela gave him what he thought was a brilliant smile and answered, "Happiness for my friend Beryl is an affirming present and possible prediction for the future. I am beginning to believe in the future, Jad."

As he in his gentlemanly style let her go before him, he was dumbfounded when she immediately turned saying, "I'll see you in the morning. I am going to bed with some tea and remember every aspect of this day. I feel happy."

He did not argue, but he did not smile. As he turned and left, Laela thought, *I know Jad is lonely, but I need this time for myself. It was such a lovely wedding. I remembered Barry, with all his secrets not showing, on our wedding day. We knew it was right for us. I thought of Barry all afternoon not with tears, but with wonderful memories. I know Jad will understand later.*

Meanwhile, as Jad walked down Laela's long front stairs, he noticed a West Side cruiser going slowly up the street and then stopping in front of Laela's. The officer yelled out, "Everything okay, Sir? You just leaving?"

Jad said, "Just brought Mrs. Greer home from a wedding, Officer."

The officer nodded and continued on his way. Jad thought, *Generally, they have two officers on this shift. Why only one officer? Is it a stakeout? Do they expect trouble in the neighborhood? And why did he ask if I was leaving? I don't think that's a normal question. I live a few doors away. If he were a regular, he'd know that.*

Jad entered his home, charging the protection system, and peeked out between the drapes to see the cruiser go slowly by his home. The cruiser now had two people in the car. He immediately checked his garage and basement wondering if there'd been an entry while he was gone for the day. He did not trust the police. He had reason not to trust them. *All higher authority wants control. Nobody's going to control me. I don't trust anyone who thinks they know what's best for me. Why would they be on to me. They're not. They can't be. I can't go out as long as they keep up this patrol. I'll get a coffee and watch.*

The cruiser was still patrolling every twenty minutes until four in the morning when Jad reluctantly closed his eyes.

Later at the station, Beauregard received the report on surveillance around Beryl and Laela and Jad's homes. All was quiet leading the Captain to think, *no eruption last night means the cost of the patrol may have been worth it. Or may be Jad is not guilty of anything. I watched him at the wedding. He looks to me ready to pounce on Laela. If society would not look askance at Laela being involved so soon after Barry's death, he'd have Laela to the altar and at risk. I know it's him. My gut tells me so.*

Beryl and Nate looked the very happy married couple they were. Sipping much needed café au laits and a breakfast of five cheese souffles cooked by Nate, Beryl said, "I could get used to this married life, Nate. The food is great, and I didn't cook it. I hope you don't think I'll give up my kitchen that easily. I didn't get my name Chef Beryl for nothing."

He laughed and quickly remarked, "If you're starting a quarrel so quickly after the vows, we better talk about crime."

And the conversation flowed freely. She was thrilled to discover Nate and Rudy had a conversation about protecting Laela last night. She said, "In the glory of the day I forgot about her safety. You didn't forget. I love you for that and thank you."

The two opened their wedding gifts throwing wrapping and tissue paper everywhere. There were expensive unique gifts and some gifts commemorating their romantic journey. One well framed doctored photo caught the two of them in Sherlock Holmes hats and plaid coats following a shadow on the ground. Another painting given by Jocelyn was an image of Nate with a lascivious look gazing at an old image of Beryl in a skimpy bathing suit. Beryl laughed. "Nate, I did look good then. I was in my thirties."

She took his hand and returned to his earlier remark. "How are we going to help Laela while we get enough evidence on Jad? He'll want her to go back to his house in Richmond. I am afraid for her."

"Laela is lonely, Beryl, but she's not stupid. I saw her really enjoying herself yesterday. My guess is it'll take him at least a week to get her to return to Richmond. Let's have a cocktail party on Thursday. She'll stay for that, and I'd love to show my bride to the world."

Beryl said, "The world already knows me."

"Ah, that's true, but not as Mrs. Nathaniel Connault."

Captain Beauregard was interrupted by Sergeant Tagliano. He said, "This better show some evidence, Sergeant, I'm busy right now."

"I can't be certain, Captain. I'm afraid of wishful thinking but these photos are about an eighty percent match."

They examined the photos. Jad's photo showed a clean-cut guy with an air of entitlement. Jonathan's photo showed a young hippie with a Cochise bandanna around his forehead and a sneer. Beauregard said, "They look similar but they're not the same guy. It's not just the outfits and the haircut. They could pass for each other if they're actors, but they're not the same. The timeline makes me wonder. Did Jad get into some trouble requiring him to not be himself? If Jonathan is still alive, we must find him. If not, we need a date of death. What did Jad's father do for a living? Was he politically connected?"

"I'll get on it, Captain."

The Captain called Attorney Cull for lunch. He was available.

An hour later, over toasted BLTs and iced tea, Rudy made his offer. He gave no drama, just the gist of his thoughts with a copy of the two photos. Cull said, "You want me to go to The Darlington Mental Health Facility under what guise? He's not a client. What story do you have for me? A police inquiry would get further."

Rudy said, "Do I have to create a scenario for you? If I were a paying client, you'd think up something great."

"Like I'm settling an estate for a client and we're trying to locate him?"

Rudy answered, "Just like that, I knew you'd come up with something."

"If I get into trouble, Rudy, I'm going to rely on you to back me up."

"Of course."

The Captain took the long route home passing the Aubergine, Morton and Greer homes and Beryl's house. There were multiple cars and trucks parked nearby. Mona had called and told him about a celebration party at Beryl and Nate's home. He knew the party was meant to keep Laela in town. He thought, *all this effort to protect Laela from herself. I need more evidence. How much? Well, if we caught him in the murderous act, that would work. What do I have? There's the palmprint match but not enough. That would connect him to multiple murders. No, the match is a weak circumstantial connection at most. Jad's psychological history is supportive at best. Jad's military training shows his connection to the murder weapon along with thousands of others. His stalking of three women on their college campus is supportive of motive but not strong enough to stand alone as evidence. His missing personal tax and other background leaves major questions. His corporation, bank accounts, autos, and other history to ownership by a man who has a resemblance to him is just an inquiry now. And the autos may be important if I can search them. May be, maybe is not* enough. His playing cards with Barry and Barry's leaving the card group he loved is inference at best. Jad's available access to the Greer's home is shadowed by the many others who had access. He's the man but I can't prove it yet. Where's my murder board? I bet I've omitted other details. The 89 numbers on the Toyota connected to Myles by itself is not enough.

The Captain drove above the speed limit to return to his office to document his thoughts and match them to the murder board. He brought Lieutenant Petra Aylewood-Locke into his office and after a few minutes of small talk said, "Lieutenant, I need information on this. I want you to take a trip. Bring Jim. This guy Myles has to have a history. Is he dead? Did he have trouble with mental health issues. Talk to what's left of his family. How could Jad insert himself into a timeline fitting with Myles? Did they know each other? Atlanta area is pricey. Don't go wild."

Rudy viewed his murder boards sliding one over the other thinking, *have I missed something? It feels like I missed something. Petra and her husband Jim won't be back until Friday. Laela is safe until Friday morning. I've got to have a plan. Jad is going to act soon. I feel it. I don't want another woman dead. Can he psychologically last until Friday? If not, he'll kill near here? After Friday, he'll kill near Richmond. Or he'll kill Laela when she refuses him. I know it's him. I'll have a detail following his movements until Friday. After that, I hope I have enough evidence to arrest. I could bring him in as a person of interest if Petra brings something I can hang my hat on. I think I'll call the FBI on Friday if I have nothing new. I can't hold out any longer.*

The next few days brought a most disagreeable Captain to work, and at home. The detectives in charge of a 24-hour watch on Laela used area uniforms and cruisers during the day. At night, the detectives rotated for the eleven to seven shift. They ignored Beauregard's temperament after Lieutenant Smith said, "He gets like this when he can't close a case and he knows who should be arrested. I've seen it before. He's strategizing. Don't be surprised if he comes up with something novel."

Rudy's wife Mona was not so forgiving, saying, "You chose being a detective, Rudy. Your choice, not mine, should not bring deep darkness to our home. Go in your study and stop grumping."

And listening to Mona, the Captain decided action was needed. He called Lieutenant Smith and directed an inclusion in the watch for the barn owned by Computer Resources, Inc. He called Detective Bill Border. Border had worked up in the Richmond area during summers when he was a student. He asked, "Do you have any connections with the police in Lee or Richmond?"

A quick study, he answered, "You want in on Jad's barns, don't you? I used to drink with a guy up there. He's not on the force but it's a small community in Richmond. He knows all the cops, farmers, and merchants. He is a quiet guy and works for public works up there. He'll get what's there to get."

"You know we can't go in the barn up there without a warrant. But, Sergeant, can you work all your contacts about what vehicles going in and out of there without the police getting involved. Your people can't know you're looking."

"Captain, every townie in that area knows everything. I'll find those cars if they're there. That and the Toyota I know Barr found together would give us a warrant."

"You know I can't connect that Toyota until I see we pull it over on the street despite it being owned by a corporation with Jonathan Myles' name connected. We may later get in there once we have Jad as a person of interest."

"Okay, I'm on it. Gives me some interest in the case until Beryl's Gala on Thursday. I won't being doing my night watch. Thanks, Captain."

And the clock for Beauregard moved too slowly. He visited Beryl and Nate for lunch on Tuesday. Beryl and her puppy Amore were happily preparing a luncheon feast while he and Nate talked about the murders. They settled with homemade crunchy beef tacos supreme loaded with sour cream, cheese and salsa. The tacos were accompanied by tortilla soup and Crème Brule. Rudy became much more animated causing Nate to say, "Tell Mona to feed you. It's your cure for depression."

"Who says I'm depressed? Mona?"

"Nope, not Mona, but everyone else. You don't like a waiting game, Rudy."

Beryl pitched in, "Rudy, neither do I. Sitting by idly without an action plan stresses me. I call Laela three times a day attempting to discover Jad's plans for the day. She has felt the need to stay home. Jad brings in lunch and wants to go out for dinner. She's been holding her own on that score limiting it to once a week dining out and the rest take-out. Laela explained she's a recent widow and can't be seen out regularly with a man. She's getting stronger which I think could let loose the monster."

It surprised Beryl and Nate when Rudy shared some of his plans. Nate thought his detectives, if successful, may be able to turn the tide. He said, "I think you have quite a bit of circumstantial evidence now for interviewing him as a person of interest. He's uptight now. He could break."

Both Rudy and Beryl disagreed. Beryl said, "Nate, Jad is smart, devious, and apparently experienced enough not to fall for any accusatory police interview. There are just not enough connections. I think with the pressure that's on him with Laela not being as acquiescent as he would like, he will act out. That's how you'll get him. And even then, what will you get; assault and battery? Arresting him now would not allow connection to forty plus serial murders. We have to wait."

Thursday arrived. Beryl and Nate's party was in full swing. The early October evening presented all the trimmings of cool crisp air, pumpkins, a beer fest, and German/Polish polkas, and romantic melodies. Laela and Jad and most of their guests were enjoying the beer garden. Mona came alone. Also missing were The Flores' and Locke's. Beryl whispered to Mona, "Rudy's coming, isn't he?"

"He's met with Petra and Jim. They should be here shortly. Do you think he'll arrest Jad here at your party?"

Beryl laughed. "No, outside my door maybe, but Rudy is not a showman, Mona."

Two hours late, a frazzled Captain joined the revelry with Mona and his detectives seated at a long table. Within minutes he set down a plate filled with Weiner-schnitzel, potato pancakes, apple sauce, sour cream, and red cabbage along with a pint of beer. One could say he dove into his long-awaited dinner.

Norbie and Sheri Cull joining the group startled Beauregard. "You back already, Cull, or you haven't gone? Which one is it?"

"Sheri just picked me up from the airport."

Beauregard said nothing further. They enjoyed the party until later when the Captain pulled Cull aside. "What gives, Norbie? I can't wait any longer."

Norbie detailed his trip to Atlanta and the mental health facility saying, "Getting information directly from the facility would not be at all easy. I decided to do some checking first. I have an Army buddy, a therapist who did some work at Darlington. He's retired now, but he knows the system there and has many contacts. He knew Jonathan Myles on his first trip to the facility before he escaped. Jonathan was in the locked unit for drug induced psychotic episodes. He spent committed for three years or until healthy enough to rejoin society. The picture you have of the scraggly Myles was the one he most remembered. The family was quite involved in his recovery and there were few problems until after the first three months when Jonathan escaped for no apparent reason. It was a good long time, maybe ten years before he showed up again committed by his dad. That's when I met the family."

An impatient Rudy said, "Did you show him the photo of Jad?"

"I did and he recognized him. He thought they may be the same man. He insisted a guy on hallucinogenic drugs could explain away the differences in the photos until I pointed out the Jad did not have a mole on his neck and Jonathan did. He said moles are often removed in the neck area when shirt collars rubbed them causing infection. He could not be persuaded. He thought the two photos were the same man. I asked him about Jonathan's parents. He said the parents were divorced and the father had a second family. His mother was a sexual nutcase and abusive to him. Further, his father had gone to court for guardianship for his care and the court ordered a commitment. The commitment incident was based on a threat to his mother's life. The therapist had read the file but was not his therapist. He was asked in as a consult. He remembered the dad who was an attorney. He also remembered the dad was an attorney on the previous admission which he thought supported the idea the two men were the same man."

Rudy asked Norbie, "And so you firmly agree they're the same man?"

"No, I don't. I got connected to several long-term employees at the hospital. Two were security, and one was a nursing carer, not a nurse. I discovered there is a difference. Only one of the security had been there when both men were there. He was about to retire and it's good I found him. He said the first admission showed an absolutely crazy. It took four guards to hold Jonathan down when he was admitted. He was not on duty for the second admission. The security officer had observed Jad or Jonathan in the game room later. This Jonathan was always immaculately dressed and understood quickly rules to be obeyed. The psychiatrists spent a great deal of time with him, but from this officer overhearing conversations, the shrinks thought he was a creative liar, and they didn't think they were getting anywhere. When his parents died, there was no push to keep him there. Jonathan got an attorney who filed for his separation from the institution. Jonathan was released never to be seen again. Remember, Rudy, Darlington is mostly private pay and is quite expensive. I think this alone may play a role in his separation."

Rudy said, "You spoke to Jonathan's attorney."

"Yes. He contacted me. He said it was an easy case. The hospital records were not required by the court, just the current psychiatric opinion which stated there were no signs of his previous instability. He was happy to help. I asked him if he knew the parents' family attorney who filed the previous involuntary commitment. He did. That attorney was retired from practice. He called him and he was happy to meet with me over drinks."

"And...?"

"It gets deeper. Apparently, Jonathan's father was an attorney who was this attorney, Hector Godwin's good friend. Jonathan was a druggie and went absolutely berserk, which required a commitment. The father was lost. He blamed Jonathan's high school friend Jad for Jonathan's descent into hell. He said the two boys grew up together and were close, but Jad moved away to be with his father. He was unhappy there and would often return to be at Jonathan's home. Jonathan was spoiled and much loved but his dad had also said he was easily influenced and he blamed Jad for introducing him to drugs. It all ended sadly when Jonathan died at twenty-two from an overdose."

Rudy asked, "Jonathan's dead at twenty-two. How could he be re-hospitalized at a later age?"

"He couldn't. The relationship explains the substitution possibility. The boys knew each other but went to different high schools after Jad moved out from his mother's home. Jonathan's parents both died within six months of each other about eight years after his death. He was an only child and born late in life. They couldn't deal with their loss. And now really good news, Attorney Godwin handled Jonathan's dad's estate and Jad's father's estate. He had access to Jonathan's social security number, birth and school records. Remember, Godwin handled both estates."

Rudy answered, "I love this realistic possibility, but Attorney Godwin took a hell of a chance at being disbarred. Both kids went to grade school together. Someone who knew them both could blow the whistle. Why would he take this chance when Jad was not his kid?"

Norbie said, "Not that big of a chance. After high school, they were separated except for a few back-home visits from Jad to Jonathan's home. Also, Godwin was Jad's uncle, a brother of Mr. Morton's second wife. The bluster of the guy was when he helped the dad put Jad in the same hospital as Jonathan. That was chancy, but unless they fingerprinted him, the hospital would never know. I checked the website for Darlington and they do not fingerprint patients. You might want to get one of your detectives to do further research. My guess is the hospital had a turnover in personnel and Godwin knew. The change could have been from new ownership of the facility or some new requirement of a state agency's audit findings. It makes some sense, Rudy. Jad was brilliant in school.

A psychiatric hospitalization would ruin Jad's chances at public success or future jobs. They were trying to protect the boy's future."

Typical of Rudy where good work was never enough, he said, "Thank you, Norbie, but I don't have an answer as to why Jad was committed, do I? And how big an estate are we talking about?"

"Big, I think. No, Rudy. No more work. Pulling the estate is police work and I don't do policing. I also don't want to be a witness in court. Further, as you have informed me many times, I am not police."

Rudy answered, "I've been watching Jad with Laela. He's acting antsy to me."

Cull said, "From what I feel now, someone's going to die soon to feed his psychopathic needs. I am concerned about the mental health profession. Darlington had Jad under the name of Jonathan for quite a few years and they made no progress. How did he sustain his need during that time? The hospital's employees I met never saw him act out."

Rudy smiled as he remembered some earlier conversation with his detectives. He did not fill Cull in on what he heard from Petra. Petra and Jim were a winning team. Jim, his former detective, was the best at eliciting info from folks who did not want to share. And it worked. The report answered a bunch of questions. First, what happened to Mr. Morton's children from his second wife? The two boys drowned in a boating accident during the time Jad (Jonathan) was at Darlington the second time. Mrs. Morton died a few years later of heart disease. Mr. Morton was inconsolable and often visited his son Jad afterward. Jad's mother had already passed. Friends did not believe Jad was ever in Darlington. They said he had graduated from William and Mary and was in the Army. Neighbors who still lived near his old home said Mr. Morton was the nicest man. They thought Jad was dead. The estate Attorney Godwin visited them looking for other family. They only knew of a cousin who came to the funeral.

Jim had asked the neighbors what happened to his first wife. They were told she was a horrible woman and had drug problems. She died before Mr. Morton. Petra researched the mother. She was alive when Jad entered Darlington, but no one remembers her. No one in her old neighborhood remembered except one old lady who told Petra she was a whore and would not say why. She said the new owner was holier than God. She figured he knew about what was going on there before he bought it.

The police overdose record on file listed a brother as next of kin. He now lived in her house. Petra met him. He was uptight about his sister, saying his nephew was screwed up by her. Jad had a bad marriage. He married a beautiful girl. This uncle thought at the wedding Jad was marrying a revision of his mother. She ran out on him. He hadn't seen Jad since Jad's father had him committed. Later, Jad left the hospital never to be seen again. Petra said, "I couldn't find out why he was committed other than his threatening his mother. It must have been serious. We should use the address on file on the commitment date to get a police report on the disappearance of Jad's wife. Also, the uncle remembered the name of the church in which they were married as Saint John's Episcopal in Ohio. That's why we didn't know he was married. There was no life insurance involved. We can get more info if needed."

Rudy replied, "Great work. Fills in some gaps in Jad's life. Get all the dates on his wedding, commitment, mother's death, etc. I'll have Mason get the police report and look at newsprint on the missing woman. Probably dead in the woods somewhere."

The Captain smiled and rejoined the party.

DIFFICULT CLOSURE

At almost the close of the Gala when all Beryl and Nate's guests appeared quite partied out, Laela lay her head on the table. Rudy saw the action first and hurried over. He heard Jad say, "Come on, Laela, I'll bring you home to sleep. It's all been too much for you."

She motioned him away leaving an opening for Rudy to whisper in Laela's ear,

Let me carry you over to the kitchen. Mona and I are staying late. We'll take you home when you feel better."

Laela responded, "Oh, thank you, Rudy. I think I've had too much prosecco. Jad, you don't need to worry about me getting home. I'm staying here, maybe for the night."

She gave him a brilliant smile. Rudy thought, *I never realized how beautiful Laela is.*

Jad said he was willing to wait, but with another of her brilliant smiles she said, "No need, Jad. I'd be embarrassed staggering out on your arm."

Beryl and Nate joined them and when asked assisted Laela holding her between them. There was no invitation to Jad, and he noticed. The expression on his face was rather snarky, but with Rudy present he seemed in control saying, "I didn't realize how much Laela drank. It's not like her. I apologize."

Rudy laughed. "No need, Jad, the ladies sometime go overboard on a lovely evening."

Jad waited a few minutes for the hosts to rejoin the party, but they didn't. He finally left, not aware of the watch detail monitoring his movements. Rudy joined the hosts and Laela in the kitchen and asked, "How you doing, Laela. You okay?"

Rudy got a glimpse of Laela crying. He was not always the best with crying women or men. Children could cry. He made no judgment there. He said, "Laela, why the tears. We've just had the best party."

"I know. I'm just a brat. Everyone is so good to me. I've gotten to know you. You are kind. And knowing Jad and traveling with him took my mind off my grief when I wasn't strong enough to bear it. I loved Barry. He's always been the only man for me. Now I think Jad has thoughts about a relationship with me. He is a wonderful man, but I don't want a relationship with him. I want him as a friend."

And she continued her sniffling. When he tried to say something, she stopped him. "I've been drinking. I rarely drink more than a couple. All I thought of tonight was Barry and our wedding. Now that was when I was being happy. Was he perfect? No, just perfect for me. I know he lied about his past life and even Patricia lied for him. He'd suffered such a loss. He was looking for his wife's killer. I understand that. I miss him."

Beryl saved the moment, setting a hot chocolate with whipped cream in front of Laela. Before Laela could refuse or say thank you, Beryl said, "Shh, drink up. Of course, tonight and all its festivities would make you think of Barry. He loved life and at times was larger than life. What would he want from you, Laela? I'll tell you. He relied on you. He'd want you to continue the life you built together doing good for others and yourself. Jad must accept the friendship status. Going back up to Richmond with him is not helpful to you or him. Stay here and settle in your recovery. You haven't been to Yoga in a long time.

What about your membership in the chess club? And we have missed you. Stay here."

Laela nodded and drank the hot chocolate. "This is good, better than coffee. I think I agree, but I find it difficult to turn Jad down. I don't want to go to Richmond. He is such a perfectionist, I'm afraid to move. And I've never eaten three meals a day. Mostly, I just eat breakfast and nosh my way to dinner. I eat small dinners. I rarely drink unless I'm out with friends. I can't be what he wants."

Rudy asked, "Are you afraid of Jad? Do you worry about his reaction if you to tell him you want to be just friends?"

She nodded. "He wants more. I don't want to hurt him."

Rudy said, "Don't tell him now. Just say what you've been saying. You need to be in your own home much of the time to accept Barry's loss. He may not like it, but he's smart enough to know it'd be no good to push you right now. Tell him Sister Patricia wants to visit. Could she visit you given restrictions at her convent? Give him time to figure out he is not everything to you."

Laela said, "It's not just a binary choice of yes or no. There is a third choice of maybe, but I don't mean maybe, Rudy. I mean no."

"Maybe is a lead into no and could be easier for him."

She said, "I think you're right. It is a choice for now until I'm more comfortable with myself. It is selfish of me, kind of stringing him along. I'll call Sister Patricia. She told me she'd come back if I needed her."

There was a rhythm to the tailing Jad Morton over the next few weeks. Daily twenty-four-hour reports were generally boring. At least three times in the early mornings at three a.m. Jad would leave his home and drive around West Side. On one evening he drove by an after-hours joint noted for ladies of the night hanging out. He never stopped. The detectives said he did not know he was being followed. For added security, the detectives used unmarked cars from the police auto bank. Today's report from the night before included a drive through Westfield and Springfield, initiating at one in the morning. The Captain called Sergeant Barr who was at home after a long night for his insights. Barr said, "He was on the prowl, Captain. It's the first time he left town. On every night he went out, he had not been at the Greer house. I checked the dailies. He's gone by that barn we're looking at every time he drove around West Side. Who gets up in the middle of the night and drives nowhere?"

Beauregard continued the order for surveillance. And Mason was directed to find every Episcopal Church in Ohio named St. Peter's for the marriage record of Jad Morton. He thought, *I have to call the FBI. Hell, I have to call the District Attorney. Jad's the killer. Not yet. I'll call tomorrow.*

Sergeant Barr entered Beauregard's office without knocking. The Captain smiled. "No knock means you have something. I hope it doesn't mean just a blatant disregard for protocol."

"Don't you worry, Captain, you're going to like what I have to say. My people in Richmond have a present for you."

Three hours later, Richmond police Captain Ronald Jones entered the barns on Morton's property in Richmond with a warrant issued by a friendly Pittsfield judge. There was no effort made to inform the owner of their visit. Detectives Aylewood-Locke and Flores were present. A Mercedes van and a small white truck were found, one in each barn.

Beauregard called an immediate staff meeting. Despite it being later in the day his detectives were all in the building. Beauregard shushed the low buzz emanating from his detectives. "No time for guesswork anymore."

Before he could say one more word, Lieutenant Smith intervened. "Captain, we've been in contact with one of Jad Morton's half-brothers, Simon Morton."

The Captain asked for an oral report. Simon had last seen Jad when Jad brought his bride home to meet the family. It was a nice occasion, but he heard his father (Joseph) and Jad's stepmother discussing Jad. They were concerned for his mental health. Jad had discussed his own mother with his dad, and it left Joseph with grave concerns about the relationship. The other stepbrother had already passed. Simon only heard about Jad at a later date when Jad had been put into Darlington Hospital. He wanted to see him, but Joseph forbade it. He knew Jad's mother died but no one went to the funeral. He said Jad had the worst luck when his pretty bride disappeared a few years after their wedding, running off with a neighbor. They lived in Morgantown, West Virginia. He didn't know the address, but Simon's mom thought Jad may have been very difficult to live with given his perfectionism."

Beauregard started to speak when his cell rang, and he took the call. Seconds later he said, "Jad's on the run or out hunting. He's picked up the Toyota from the barn. Sergeant Tagliano, find Laela and baby sit her. Sergeants Border and Barr, take separate cars and follow him. Don't lose the tail. Once you're on him, cancel the regular detail."

Lilly Tagliano's instinct was to call Beryl first. She thought maybe Beryl would be out of town on her honeymoon although no one at the wedding mentioned travel plans. She made the call and was in luck. Laela was working at the open Pantry with Beryl.

Beryl acted surprised at Lilly's visit. When Laela who was cleaning tables caught sight of Lilly, she said, "Want a coffee, Sergeant? I just made a pot for us."

Lilly said, "I've had a hell of a day, Laela. Can you sit with me for a few minutes. I need some counseling."

Laela said, "You need counseling? What's happening? Is Juan okay?"

"No, Laela, it's about balancing my home life with a small baby. Beryl thinks you are the best at understanding people. I've the afternoon off, but my mom is today's caretaker. I just don't feel like going home. Mom will tell me everywhere I've fallen short at housekeeping and baby care. Best of all this Irish/Italian veteran thinks my Mexican husband walks on water."

Laela noticed Lilly tearing up. Laela hugged her as Lilly went on a long story of life and the difficulties faced when our parents aren't on the same wavelength as we. The conversation continued until it was time to close the Pantry. Beryl, who had overheard most of their conversation, suggested they both join her and Nate for supper saying, "Of course Juan is invited too."

Lilly was adamant. "Tonight, I need sisterhood."

Beryl called Beauregard. "Laela's with us until at least nine tonight. Call us if we should not let her go home."

She also called Nate and asked him to disappear for the evening. He replied, "Beryl, there better be a good reason. It is our honeymoon."

Her story calmed him as she detailed Lilly's wonderful one-act play. "No problem, I'll call Beauregard. See if I can help."

Detective Border caught up with Jad as he left West Side headed to I-91 interstate. Border texted Detective Barr. "I'll follow him. He could be just taking his route through Springfield, but he may have gotten word of the search of his barns in Richmond. Go near the Pike just in case he goes that way. I'll let you know."

Barr answered, "How could he not know. He's got surveillance up there."

Border said, "Apparently there is an electrical and cell tower problem up there today. Thank you, IT gods in the department."

Meanwhile, Beauregard made a call to FBI Agent Bob Alcore, Assistant Attorney General Meredith Malcolm, Assistant District Attorney Cameron Mace, the Richmond Chief of Police. His message was short just sharing their closing in on a person of interest. He was not surprised when all were available to come to the station. What did surprise him was Nate Connault's sudden visit. "What the hell are you doing here? Did Alcore call you?"

"Nope, try again? I'm not psychic. I thought you might need some help handling the riff raff coming."

Beauregard smiled. "Any help you can give me. They'll try to nail me for calling them at such a late time."

Beauregard shared the connections made in Richmond and Jad's now known history. They both thought it was enough for an arrest.

Although, Nate said, "The judge who allowed the warrant based on surveillance of two vehicles with no plates known took a chance. You did connect it to Jad's ownership of the identified vehicle in the other barn through a dead man? It's circumstantial at best but maybe will hold up."

Beauregard did not reply. The invitees were brought to the conference room along with several more FBI agents, three state police, and police attachés to the DA's office. The Captain used the multiple sliding murder boards to make connections. Most were familiar with the serial murders and Greer and particularly Mel Laurent's murders. The timeline of discovery of connections brought a few loud questions. Nate asked Rudy if he could take over and the yes answer surprised them both. Nate said, "The Captain and his team have used local knowledge of West Side citizens in a way we as outsiders never could. If the person of interest, in my mind the perp, got a whiff of knowledge about this investigation, we'd have another forty murders. Morton is smart and I fear dangerously psychotic. Let's see if any of you have a thought of how our West Side Detectives can safely make an arrest. It's quite possible he's on the prowl for a victim. He has been severely frustrated and has not been able to fill his murdering needs. Or he may just be checking his property, but it's time for an arrest."

The Lieutenant pulled down the map of the area west of West Side from the computer. His app of the two police cars was added. Thus, he created close to real time for the detectives' movements. Over the next hour and a half Jad drove within the speed limit on a circuitous ride through Springfield, Chicopee, Holyoke, West Springfield onto interstate I-90 west. Detective Barr drove ahead of Jad while Detective Border followed. Morton did not go where expected. Instead, he headed to Lee and stopped at the Red Lion Inn in Stockbridge. It was now getting darker. Detective Barr doubled back. Donning glasses which he never wore and an Irish Donegal Tweed Cap, he asked for a table for one in the dining room. He had checked first to see if Jad was in the bar. Bobby ordered coffee and looked around. Jad sat at a table at the other end of the dining room. Bobby could see him ordering. He figured Jad was having a nice dinner for himself.

Bobby ordered a couple of appetizers and asked for the bill telling the waiter he was waiting for his wife to call and could possibly be leaving quickly. He noticed Jad appeared to be quite relaxed. Two hours later, Bobby was on his third coffee and a dessert when he noticed Jad motioning the waiter for his bill. Bobby thought, *if this guy is going hunting for a lady to murder, he's not going on an empty stomach. I don't get it. He's as relaxed as can be. Has to have nerves of steel.*

Jad moved towards the men's room which was not far from the kitchen and where Bobby presumed there was a back door. He texted Barr to watch for him.

Barr was lucky enough to share a couch on the front porch. Normally seats there were at a premium. Five minutes later, Jad headed for his car which was parked five spaces away. Barr followed. Jad drove around apparently familiar with the area. Barr thought, *tailing this guy is not easy. I'm having trouble figuring a destination. Could be he is wandering and doesn't know where he's going. There's no walking traffic where we are now and no bars for a pickup.*

Meanwhile at the station Beauregard said, "He's in Lenox now. There's a wine bar there, craft beers too. It calls for the twenty-five to thirty bar crowd." He messaged the detectives about it.

Barr went ahead and messaged back, "There's a stand-out crowd. Quite a few walkers and they are women."

Jad parked his truck near the bar and waited. For what, they didn't know. One gal dressed in jeans with so many holes in them, nothing was hidden. Barr noticed she was not wearing really high heels. He had a nice view of her ample breasts. She looked like she could walk ten miles. Her pace was faster than normal although she swayed some. He didn't think she was sashaying. He thought she had too much to drink. The Captain texted, "That's the kind of lady who inspires his interest."

The lady was tiring. She stopped and took off her shoes and appeared to walk faster. By this time, she was out of sight of the bar and there was no walking traffic. Jad pulled over and appeared to offer her a ride. She spoke with him for a few minutes. Detective Barr thought, *don't take too long, lady. If walkers come, he'll pull away.*

But walkers did not come, and the lady got in the truck. Barr texted Border and Beauregard. "It's a pretty quiet road. I have to be careful. Tell Border about any side roads he can come out on to give me some cover. Eventually he'll head to Route 20 or to his house in Richmond if he's on the prowl to murder."

And the wait started. Jad appeared to know his way around the side roads making it more difficult for Barr to follow. Beauregard assisted Border on advance routes to be taken when Barr needed to slow down in his tail. And in slowing down Barr lost his mark.

Beauregard enlarged his map for more detail and saw a small parking area in the woods he thought was there for hunters. Barr turned around and within minutes he found the entrance. He shut off his lights and pulled in. Jad's truck had parked in a tree canopy and was not facing his car. The lot had space for about ten cars. He took his night binoculars and hoping there was enough light from the full moon he focused on the truck. He saw what looked like rapid movement. He couldn't wait. He made a decision, and turned on his car's bright lights, got out and started towards the truck. Jad turned his truck around as the woman rolled the window down and tried to shimmy out. As the truck flew by him, Barr pulled her from the window and they both fell to the ground. The lady's leg and arm were gouged and bleeding with blood also dripping from her neck. Barr saw a wire hanging loosely from her neck. He cradled the lady who was having trouble talking. Within minutes Lee's police and an ambulance were at the scene.

Meanwhile, Border was on the road and Beauregard at the station. Working as a team, they were attempting to follow Jad. Beauregard said, "He is our killer for sure. We can't lose him. His adrenaline is pumping. He'll have to kill again."

There was only one problem. The elusive killer frustrated the detectives. He appeared to know every side street connecting to a connection. Beauregard requested outside help. There were cops at all I-90 exits and entrances in Massachusetts and lower New York. Coverage for Route 20 with all its local bypasses was more difficult. When they were not successful for the first twenty minutes, they concluded he was already on a portion of Route 20. Gauging the incremental time changes and his car's probable velocity, Lieutenant Smith pointed to the map where a treed cul-de-sac was located. "Captain, it's a perfect spot to hide if he knows about it. I think he knows this whole area. Have Westfield police check it out."

The Westfield police found evidence on the gravel road of the truck having left digs in the road. They made an emergency call to forensics for imprints to identify the tracks.

And Beauregard waited impatiently circling the large open room. Local West Side Detective Flores, having come back already from Richmond and out circling West Side spotted the Toyota pulling into the barn. Beauregard told him not to apprehend Jad. The watch continued. The Captain said, "He's trying to clean up himself and his act. It's time for the taskforce to make the arrest. He's a desperate man. He is dangerous."

Minutes before the team arrived, Flores saw a lone man in farmer's jeans wearing an old hat walk out from the back of the barn lot. Flores could not be certain he exited the barn but still followed him. He thought, *he could be Jad, but has a little limp and is hunched over. Could be an old farmer who came down the back road behind the barn. If Jad's still in the barn, Lilly will catch up to him. I'll follow this guy, but it's going to be difficult. He's already out of sight. There're no streetlights up where he is. I'll move a bit. He's emerging from a bunch of trees. Dear God, a driver making a wide turn from the street opposite the grove of trees doesn't see him.*

Beauregard heard the crash. "What the hell happened, Juan? Are you all right?"

Within minutes every cop in West Side was on the sight. A seriously injured Jad was brought to the hospital. The car's driver was sobbing miserably. She said, "He came out of nowhere. I wasn't speeding. The poor man looks like a local farmer. My dad was a farmer. Oh my God, how will I live with him. Please save him."

And she dissolved into tears.

30

A MESS IN CRIME SOLVING

The press was on it. Every television station, social media, and other media were stalking the police for info. A bedraggled Beauregard, who loved his eight hours of sleep, was a happy man despite the complexities of the arrest. He and Sergeant Aylewood-Locke visited ICU. Petra said, "He's going to die, Captain, before we get a confession. Imagine an innocent driver takes out a serial murderer. He's killed so many women. She should get a medal."

"None of that, Lieutenant. Here's the doctor. I hope Jad's alert enough to speak."

The doctor said Jad had suffered grievous injuries and he did not think Jad would recover. "He has crushed two femurs, four ribs, has three breaks in his left arm and a severe head wound as well. He's awake but despite his extensive injuries is receiving morphine for pain."

Given the circumstances he said Beauregard and Lilly could visit for no more than twenty minutes. A nurse would ask them to leave if the patient became too agitated.

Both detectives believed Jad would be agitated the minute he saw them. But it didn't happen that way. Jad although struggling said quietly, "How'd you catch on?"

Beauregard answered, "Slowly. I need your help."

Lilly thought, *fat chance, this guy's not into helping anyone. Why is Beauregard treating Jad with kid gloves? He's a psychopathic murderer.*

Jad said, "Do you think I'm stupid? You wouldn't have found me if you didn't know everything."

And Jad groaned in discomfort. Rudy thought the pain was being controlled. His intuition pushed the conversation forward. "What about Laela, Jad? What about her? If she thinks you're contrite, that the murders were based on your childhood and life experiences with women, she'll forgive. I'm certain of that. What she won't forgive is if you don't make some amends to the murdered women's families. That means telling us you did that. You don't have long either way. I need your help."

Crying, Jad said, "Leala is perfect. She's who I needed. Honest and open and moral and I can't keep her. It doesn't matter, Rudy if I live or die, either way she won't be in my life. Get your people in here."

Rudy said, "It means coughing up on Barry Greer's death."

"I know she'll never forgive me for that. They'll tell her, no way around that."

West Side's Police Station's front steps were crowded with officials from every governmental policing level. The illustrious MCU Captain Rudy Beauregard confirmed an arrest of the accused serial murderer of over forty murders of women and the murders of three local West Side men. He added, "This is not a day for celebration. The victims have all died, all left loved ones, and the fear and anguish caused has rippled throughout the east side of the Atlantic and here at home. Our West Side detectives and uniforms along with the guidance given by the FBI, our Hampden County District Attorney's Office, other city policing, the Sheriff, Attorney Norberto Cull, and Mr. and Mrs. Connault were invaluable in stopping these crimes. Thank You."

Each other speaker gave up a bit of extra information, adding to satisfy the press' need to know. One question asked as to the murderer's identity was answered. The District Attorney went through the

A MESS IN CRIME SOLVING

multi policing following Jad after he was attempting another murder unsuccessfully. This tale brought out a reaction from the more than one hundred attendees. Finally, the real question asked was, "Do you have a confession for all these murders?"

A yes answer brought an outpouring of approval. Finally, a question as to when a trial would be scheduled was answered not by the District Attorney but by Captain Beauregard. "Jad Morton is in the hospital suffering from probable fatal injuries from an auto accident."

Beauregard left the step platform. The crowd clamored for more info.

A local historian asked for an appointment with Captain Beauregard. He wished to write a true crimes series on the Jad Morton murders. He was related to one of the victims in Georgia and had been an FBI agent. Agent Bob Alcore insisted Rudy speak with him. "Rudy, you're a specialist in finding bits of pieces and putting them together. You work well with the public. Help him out."

His answer was, "Too soon. Jad is still alive. His early life was a disaster. Maybe in a year, I will have the time and energy to give to him."

Beauregard gave his detectives instructions for getting the case ready for trial with the help of the ADAs assigned to it. Sergeant Flores asked, "He's going to die, why do all this work. Can't we just do a summary, Captain?"

"No, Jad may live. In fact, I bet on it. Do you want your policing under a magnifying glass because all the evidence wasn't documented properly? Later, when a reporter decides to do an expose on our solution and one will, you won't remember everything. Do it right. Do it once and for all."

Beryl had called Laela early in the morning after Jad's arrest. Beryl knew Laela had not heard the news. She asked, "Could you please come over for breakfast. It's important."

Laela did not press for more information. Instead, she said she was already dressed. Jad and she were to go for lunch later.

Beryl was pleased that Laela would be with her when she learned the news, but thought, *how do I tell her? How do I say you've been traveling with a murderer, a psychopathic con man, a controlling ongoing evil man? Is there a good way to tell her? She'll have to take questions from Rudy. She will be made famous for her own husband's murder. There is no way around negative publicity for her. There would be less if Jad died. Am I hoping for his death?*

Beryl heard the doorbell ring and let a crying Laela in. She didn't know quite what to say so Laela just hugged her. A sniffling Laela said, "I'm so glad you called. I was going to do it today, but I really do need your support in what to say."

"About what, Laela? Of course, I'll help in any way, but I have something to tell you. You go first."

Laela went into a long spiel about Jad. She said she couldn't see him again. He was too controlling although she admitted she loved the attention. She felt he wanted to wrap her up in a cocoon. Whenever her opinion differed from his, he did not want to explore or develop the ideas behind her analysis. She said, "I feel overwhelmed by him as if I don't really know him. I never knew Barry's back story. I never asked. I can't go on with this friendship. I feel out of my depth. I lose any approach to a debate with him. Do you think I'm ungrateful, Beryl? He's been so good to me."

Beryl took her hand and said, "I have to tell you about Jad."

Laela said, "Oh no, is he the pedestrian hit by a car in West Side?"

"Yes, I hoped you hadn't heard. But I have more to say."

Laela said, "Will he be all right? I can't leave him now when he needs me."

Beryl said in a firm tone, "Yes you can, Laela. He is not the man you think you know. He murdered Barry and the homeless man, and over forty women. He is a serial murderer. He is a psychopath. He fooled all of us. Rudy didn't initially recognize Jad as mentally ill."

Laela stopped crying. Instead, she started laughing, uncontrollably. Knowing this may be a reaction to the shocking news, Beryl continued to squeeze her hand and waited.

Laela said, "Mentally ill, no, he must be pure evil to destroy my dream and so many others. How could I be so stupid. I actually compared him favorably to my Barry because he could dance and would endlessly shop with me. My Barry, he couldn't hold a candle to him. How could he kill Barry with me sleeping in our bedroom? How could we not know it was him?"

"Many people had the key to your house. Many also had the security code. Jad somehow knew Barry's schedule of getting up in the middle of the night for a snack. He took advantage of the knowledge."

"But Delilah was there. She could have walked in on him pushing Barry. Why kill Barry? That serial killer kills women not men?"

"Barry was on to him. Barry was in fact working with the homeless man who was undercover. That's why Barry left the card game. He knew Jad may be a problem. He knew of him and some of his background."

Beryl saw the horror in Laela's eyes be replaced by anger. She listened to the expletives spewing from Laela and waited. It took an hour of Laela's questioning and receiving answers before she quieted. Laela said, "Barry said I was an innocent. I wouldn't know evil if it sat on my lap. That's what he said. And he was right. I could have been the next lady killed."

Beryl's doorbell rang. She let Rudy in along with two other detectives, Sergeants Flores and Barr. The work was just beginning. Nate joined them in the kitchen and made coffee. Questions and answers kept the room from overshadowed grief. And then Sergeant Flores took a call.

Jad Morton had died.

CARE TO REVIEW MY BOOKS?
(OR "HONEST REVIEWS DON'T KILL")

Now that you've read the story to the end, I'd like to know what you think of it – and read your honest review about the book on Amazon, Goodreads or other major online book retailers where it is featured.

https:/kbpellegrino.com/review-a psychopaths-pause

Review some of my other books:

https://kbpellegrino.com/review-sunnyside-road
https://kbpellegrino.com/review-mary-lou
https://kbpellegrino.com/review-brothers-from-another-mother
https://kbpellegrino.com/review-him-me-paulie
https://kbpellegrino.com/review-a-predatory-cabal
https://kbpellegrino.com/review-killing-the-venerable
https://kbpellegrino.com/review-beryl-kent-bleeding-man
https://kbpellegrino.com/review-beryl-kent-and-mixed-motives

Thank You for your interest in my books!
Kathleen

MORE BOOKS BY K. B. PELLEGRINO

Evil Exists in West Side Trilogy:
–Sunnyside Road: Paradise Dissembling
(Livres-Ici Publishing) 2021, (Liferich Publishing) 2018
–Mary Lou: Oh! What Did She Do?
(Livres-Ici Publishing) 2021, (Liferich Publishing) 2018
–Brothers of Another Mother: All for one! Always?
(Livres-Ici Publishing) 2021, (Liferich Publishing) 2019

Other Books in the Captain Beauregard Mystery Series
–Him, Me and Paulie: Drugs, Murder and Undercover
(Livres-Ici Publishing) 2019
–A Predatory Cabal: Worm in the Apple
(livres-Ici Publishing) 2020
–Killing the Venerable: It's Their Time!
(Livres-Ici Publishing) 2020

Books with Beryl Kent

–Beryl Kent and the Bleeding Man
(Livres-Ici Publishing) 2021
–Beryl Kent and Mixed Motives
(Livres-Ici Publishing) 2022

You Can find K. B. Pellegrino's books on all major online Book Stores, such as Amazon, Barnes & Noble, kobo, and iBooks.

FOLLOW K. B. PELLEGRINO

On her website:
www.kbpellegrino.com

On GoodReads:
https://www.goodreads.com/author/K.B.Pellegrino

On Facebook:
https://www.facebook.com/kbpellegrino

On Instagram:
https://www.instagram.com/kbpellegrino_author/

On Twitter:
https://twitter.com/kbpellegrino

JOIN MY PRIVATE EMAIL LIST

To receive updates about books, new releases, upcoming events, or to simply keep in touch with me, join my private email list. We do not release your information to any other vendors.

www.kbpellegrino.com/join-list

Milton Keynes UK
Ingram Content Group UK Ltd.
UKHW032003230824
447235UK00001B/95